I0732539

The Lost Warrior

Book Three of the Sevordine Chronicles

by

Shawn P. B. Robinson

BrainSwell Publishing
Ingersoll, Ontario

ISBN 978-1-989296-61-5

Cover design and artwork copyright © Shawn Robinson
Interior Page Dividers designed from images downloaded from Freepick.com.

BrainSwell Publishing
Ingersoll, ON

Dedication and Thanks

To my wife who puts up with not only my strange stories, but also my holey socks. And this, to the average person, may not seem like a big deal, but I sit on a couch in our living room (that's where I do most of my writing), and I put my feet up. So… like… she has to look at it. And I know she wants to come over and rip those socks right off my feet, but she doesn't. Instead, she just holds the anger inside. Which is really cool, because you know that's not only a sign of true love, but it's also the healthiest way to deal with anger. Just… bottle it. So, to Juanita, you da best!

This book is a work of fiction.
Characters and places and such are fictional. Now, the previous sentence is actually just a way of repeating what I just said in the first sentence. So, to sum up, the book is fiction, but also, all of its components (characters and places and such) are also fictional. Which makes sense. Because, if all the components were not fictional, then the entire book would, more or less, be considered non-fiction. But since the components of the story are fiction, then the book is considered fiction. That makes sense, right? Someone check my logic! Assuming, however, that I am correct, what I am ultimately trying to communicate is two things. First, the book is fiction… it's made up. Second, I'm trying to communicate my growing disdain for the idea of declaring that a fictional book is fiction. It's like saying, "Whoa, you see that airplane that flies in the air? Let me tell you that it flies in the air."
Perhaps ultimately, this is a sign of where we are at as a society. We need reminders for things like, "Yo, a book with teenagers using enchanted items is fiction… not real. I mean, the not-real version of fiction."
Enjoy!

Preface

Now, book three of this series is kind of my favourite (notice my fantastic Canadian spelling there, although that doesn't show itself much in my books). I love book 3 because it shifts gears and lets us walk this road through the eyes of another person. And… I think this young lady is fantastic! She's far, far more than books one and two reveal.

Enjoy!

Shawn P. B. Robinson

CHECK OUT THESE BOOKS BY
Shawn P. B. Robinson

Adult Fiction (Sci-fi & Fantasy)

The Ridge Series (3 books)
ADA: An Anthology of Short Stories

YA Fiction (Fantasy)

The Sevordine Chronicles (5 Books)

Books for Younger Readers

Annalynn the Canadian Spy Series (6 Books)
Jerry the Squirrel (4 Books)
Arestana Series (3 Books)
Activity Books (2 Books)

www.shawnpbrobinson.com/books

Table of Contents

1

The Lord and Lady

I follow three soldiers, doing my best not to look terrified. I wish I had Ellcia's confidence. A quick look to my right tells me she just looks annoyed.

I glance to the other side of Ellcia. Caric looks like he's ready to take charge. I love that about him. He's the strongest of all of us. In a way, he's stronger than even Rulf. Rulf has muscle, but Caric has heart.

I look to my left and relax. Hemot's there. I feel a lot better when he's around. I love his smile. It's like he's telling me all the time that something else is going on—that he's just having fun no matter what.

As we walk, the one guard explains, "We're going to need to interview each of you separately."

He doesn't sound upset. He doesn't sound like we're in trouble. He just sounds like it's… routine.

I stumble on the uneven floor, and Hemot grabs my arm.

"You okay, Marleet?"

I smile back at him, and I think my face just blushed. I'm glad it's dark in here. "I'm okay, Hemot. Thanks. I just can't see the floor very well."

The soldier stops in a small room, or whatever you call these areas in the mountain. Three caves head off in different directions, all of them quite tiny. I'm not sure what to make of it. In addition to the three guards we've been following, another six stand in this room.

"All right, here we are."

The man turns around, and I get my first glimpse of his face. It's dark here in the mountain, but from what I can see, it looks like his face has been burned—terribly. He's kind of scary looking, actually, like he's going to attack me. But, his eyes are serious and focused. Nothing he's said has sounded mean in any way.

"You are going to have to leave your armor and weapons here. They will be searched while you are in your interviews, but nothing will be taken unless it is deemed suspicious. You'll all enter separate rooms where you'll give your names and prove your identity." The guard points to an area on the floor. "Please leave your weapons, packs, and armor in that area, and I'll show you where to go next."

We all set to work on taking off our packs, armor, and weapons. When I'm done, I feel a little exposed. I'm wearing my traveling clothes, and they are quite modest—in fact they're anything but attractive—but I've been so used to wearing that armor that when I take it off, I feel like I'm naked.

The others seem fine, so I just pretend I don't feel any different. Again, I wish I had Ellcia's confidence.

"I can't leave my sword here, unless I get your word that it won't be examined."

I turn to Caric. He always talks like he's really in charge. I can't help but think the soldier should salute him. He is the General's nephew, after all. Maybe that makes him some kind of leader or officer. I never paid attention to that kind of thing before.

"I'm sorry, Your Majesty. I recognize that you are likely a loyal Prince and as such have my own loyalty, but I cannot allow anything past this point without a full inspection."

A wave of irritation comes over me. I don't think he should mock Caric by calling him, "Your Majesty." Caric is just trying to do the right thing.

But what the soldier says about the inspection makes sense to me. Caric should maybe just accept it. I know he wants to hide the enchantment, but he probably can't have what he wants here.

Caric steps forward but raises his hands as if to say he's not going to try anything. I can just make out his words as he starts to whisper. "I don't mean to be disrespectful, Captain, but it is vitally important that my sword not be inspected. I can't explain why, but it is necessary."

The Captain frowns. Well, he does something with his face, and I can tell he's not happy. He opens his mouth to say something, but a man runs up at that point. He hands a note to the Captain who reads it carefully.

He nods back at the man. "Tell the General I have received his orders and will obey."

He turns back to Caric. "That's good timing. The General has actually informed me that none of your weapons or armor are to be inspected—especially yours, Your Majesty."

I expect the Captain to be angry about this. My only experience with a Captain has been Captain Tilbur. He would have been enraged if someone stopped him from doing what he wanted.

This Captain, however, seems fine.

"May I ask each of you to move your armor and weapons off to the side? None of it will be inspected or touched." He turns to two of the soldiers. "Ensure only the armor and weapons are moved to the side. Nothing else is to be moved. Only their packs and cloaks are to be inspected."

He doesn't trust us. I thought maybe he did, but he's just being polite. I guess he has to be thorough, but I don't like it when people don't trust me. I don't lie or do bad stuff.

We move our armor and weapons to the side, and Ellcia and I follow two soldiers down one of the caves. After a few steps, it splits into two more caves, and Ellcia goes down one, I go down the other. A moment later, I'm in a small room. I hate to leave the others, but I don't think I have a choice.

Two people stand in the room—a man and a woman. She points at a chair on the far side of a table, and I take a seat. They sit across from me.

The woman pulls out some papers and sets them on the table. "We have some questions for you."

"Okay." I feel like I should say more, but I'm actually feeling scared.

"First, your name?"

"Marleet."

"Who are your parents?"

I shake my head. "I don't know. They were killed in the rebellion."

"How old are you?"

"Seventeen."

"You're small for your age."

I stare at her for a moment. I'm not sure what I'm supposed to say to that. I always liked being small. It made me feel special and different. "Thank you."

She furrows her brow, and I realize that was not the right answer. I almost apologize for my size, but then I can't see how that's my fault.

I glance at the man. He's staring at me in a way that makes me uncomfortable. I don't think he has any mean thoughts, he's just looking at me in an intense way.

I can't hear much from the other rooms, but I do hear one thing. "Send for the Captain. Quick!"

A soldier rushes by the entrance to my cave, and the two people interviewing me turn around. A moment later, the Captain with the strange face runs by. I can just make out his words.

"Ellcia?"

He's crying. I don't know why. But there's something there. I can tell he's happy to see her, but I can't imagine he knows her. If he did, I would think he'd have recognized her.

My two interviewers turn back to me with smiles on their faces.

"What's that about?"

The woman shakes her head, but her smile remains. "I'm sorry, Marleet. We can't talk about what's going on outside this room. We are here to talk about you."

I nod. I hear a lot of excited voices in the other room. I hope Ellcia's okay. It sounds like happy noises.

The woman is about to speak again, but the man leans in and whispers in her ear. He doesn't take his eyes off me the entire time. I can't make out what he's saying because he's cupping his hand over his mouth.

As he whispers, the woman's eyebrows shoot up, and she stares at me as intensely as the man does. When he's done telling her whatever it is, they both examine me closely. It's like they're studying my face.

The woman doesn't take her eyes off me as she asks the man, "How do we know for sure?"

He shakes his head, eyes firmly on me. "I have no idea. Maybe we should start with memories before the King's murder."

She nods slowly. "That sounds good."

"Can you tell us anything you remember from before the rebellion?"

"I don't remember much. I was the daughter of servants in the castle, and the Regent rescued us."

The woman's face turns to a deep frown for a moment, before compassion covers her face. I know what I just said was wrong; it just came out. It's what I've believed for so long.

"Well, maybe I wasn't the daughter of servants. Rulf told me that we were all either royalty or children of Nobles." I smile at the thought. "So, maybe I'm a Princess."

The woman shakes her head. "No, not a true Princess."

I frown at her. I don't know what's wrong with me that I wouldn't be a true Princess.

The woman closes her eyes for a moment. "There were no Princesses in the royal family, aside from those much older than you. The King had only a son, and Prince Geran and Lady Tallia had only one son, but then you know both of them."

I decide not to respond at all to that one. I know Mic—or Prince Roran as we've come to find out, but I have no idea who this Prince Geran and Lady Tallia are, let alone their son.

"So, does that mean I'm the daughter of a Noble?"

"Well, this is part of what we're trying to figure out, Marleet. There was a Marleet in the castle who was the daughter of Nobles, but we simply don't have enough information about you. Can you tell us anything? Anything you remember?"

"I remember my dad a bit, I think. He was tall and had a big nose."

They both nod, and the man pushes back his chair and stands. "That's good enough for me. I'll go get him. Maybe they'll recognize her."

"Who? Who might recognize me?"

They don't answer me. Instead, the man rushes out the door, and the woman smiles. "Tell me about your time in the castle and your journey here."

I'm just getting to the part of my story when we entered the caves when the man comes back. He doesn't say much, just, "They're on their way."

The woman smiles, and I finish my story. She wants all the details, even up to the point where we walked into the large cavern with the General.

As soon as I finish, a man rushes into the room. He takes two steps in, then stops, his eyes on me.

He has a large nose. I don't mean to be rude with it or anything, his nose is just… long. It's not wide or anything, just far longer than any nose I've ever seen before. His eyes are small and beady, and he moves like he's slinking wherever he goes. His hair is thin and hangs all over the place in weird directions. And his head… his face… it juts forward… like a turtle.

I think I saw him briefly when we moved through the caves, but I didn't give him much thought. There were so many people I didn't know, and I didn't know what was going on.

As I look at the man, there are two things that immediately come to mind.

The first is that this is the strangest looking man I've ever seen in my entire life. I think that will be true until the day I die. I can't imagine ever seeing a more oddly put together man.

The second thing is that I know I love him. I don't know why, but I think everyone everywhere will love this man. He's clearly lovable in every way.

His face moves even farther forward as if his neck is stretchy and can reach anywhere in the room. When it appears to have extended to its limit, his eyes twist into the saddest expression I have ever seen. His mouth then drops into a closed-mouth frown, and his nose rises. I'm not sure how that's possible, but I see it happening right before my eyes.

He then lets out the strangest, oddest, moan I have ever heard. It's like he's mourning the greatest loss in the world.

I want to either run into his arms and comfort him or laugh at the absurdity of what's happening before me. Instead, I just sit there.

A moment later, a woman rushes into the room.

She is, by far, the most beautiful woman I have ever seen in my entire life—even more than Ellcia. Her face is perfect. I think she's somewhere around forty years old, but I also think there isn't a man in all the lands—young or old— who wouldn't think she was perfect in every way.

Her face drops into sadness, and even in sadness, she is stunning. Her shaking hands come up to her face and cover her mouth. A moment later, she steps close to the strange turtle-man, and they each put one arm around each other.

I wouldn't have thought a strange-looking man like that would end up with a woman of such beauty, but then again, I can see he's very lovable.

My thoughts are pushed to the side when I realize both of them are not only weeping, but they can't take their eyes off me. I glance at the two people who were interviewing me. I hadn't noticed it before, but when the new man and woman entered the room, the two interviewers stepped off to the side. The way they stand, these two new people are either royalty or Nobles.

I stand and step out from behind the table. I give my best attempt at a curtsy. As a servant, I've curtsied many times, but I feel awkward this time. "My Lord. My Lady."

When I say this, they both break down in tears. I think to myself that I won't say or do anything else until someone lets me know what's going on.

But then again, I do know what's going on. I've known from the moment the Nobleman entered the room. I just couldn't admit it. If I'm wrong… it's… it's too painful.

Because I know who these people are.

My eyes fill with tears, and I can't hold it in anymore. "Mama? Papa?"

The two rush forward and grab hold of me. I wrap my arms around them and sob, unable to hold it back.

I remember.

I remember them.

I remember our life together.

I remember everything.

2

The Arrest

One week later...

"Yessss… Marleeeeteeee."

I try again, and this time I master it. I still struggle to believe I can do this. I flip over, land on both feet, run up the side of the wall, jump, pushing off the rock and flip over my dad's head.

"Yessss… Marleeeeteeee. You are certainly doing wellll."

I love the way my dad talks. Everyone loves him. He's the kindest, funniest, most interesting person I've ever met.

He comes over and wraps his arms around me. Every time he does that, my mind rushes back to when I was little. He used to pick me up and slowly swing me around while he hugged me. I feel just like I did back then: safe.

"Weeee must talk, Marleeeeteeee."

"Sure, Papa." I try to act like a Noblewoman as he and mama are teaching me. I stand straight, give a proper smile, and ask in a formal voice, "Where would you like to speak, Father? Here, or is there somewhere else?"

"Verrrry good, Marleeeeteeee. You are learning wellll."

My papa, Lord Yune, is one of the most influential and powerful men in the kingdom. Even though he has spent all these years in hiding with those who are called the Rebel Army, he's still powerful. The Regent would not dare move against him as he is close friends with nearly every Nobleman in the kingdom.

"Weeee will speak in my officccce."

I give a short curtsy, and he smiles at me. He smiles a lot. He's such a happy man.

Over the last week, I've learned more than I can imagine ever learning in such a short period of time. I've learned that I am their only surviving child—as far as we know. Although, they didn't actually know I was still alive until a week ago. I used to have two older brothers and a younger sister. All of them were killed, we believe, in the rebellion over ten years ago.

I think I remember them, although the memories are faint. My brothers used to tease me a lot, but they were still nice, and they were loyal. My younger sister, my parents tell me, was a lot like me. She was smart and fun to be around. I don't know if I'm all that smart and fun to be around, but I like the idea.

I've also learned that I'm the heiress of a huge financial empire. My dad has business deals everywhere. In fact, he owns most of the land around here and all the farmland that provides food for the Army is his.

And I've learned lots about the others as well. I've learned that Caric is not actually Caric. He's actually Prince Draydon, second in line for the throne. That explains why he's such a great leader.

It also turns out that the Captain with the burnt face is Ellcia's older brother. He's extremely loyal, and General Lirnal expects he'll have a successful career as an officer. Ellcia is the daughter of Nobles and will inherit, along with her brother, their estate.

And I've learned that Hemot is the son of a Duke. I was quite excited for him when I heard that. I know he always wanted to be a Duke. But it turns out that in Sevord, you have to earn the title of Duke. It's not inherited.

But still, Hemot will at least get to inherit their estate. Although, for some reason, he's not a Lord. So, while I'm "Lady Marleet," he's just "Hemot." I expect that annoys him somewhat, but he always manages to find the best in everything. He'll be okay.

I've also learned how to fight with my sword. It turns out it's enchanted. As long as I'm confident, I can do just about anything with it. I just have to be careful that I don't get arrogant. It's a hard balance to hold, but I'm getting the hang of it.

Finally, I've learned that my parents are both wise. I mean, they're REALLY wise. They're super smart and super wise. They know just about everything they can, and they know how to use it to do good stuff.

My dad is a Duke and one of Prince Roran's advisers. He was an adviser to King Hartor years ago, and now he's giving great advice to the King-to-be. My mom tells me that I need to trust my dad. He always has it figured out, no matter what.

We walk through the hallway toward his office. It's not far from my training room. This whole area belongs to my family. Everyone else who walks these caves are either our servants or soldiers who are seeking advice or bringing messages.

A man walks toward us. He stops just before we reach him, and steps to the side. I remember doing the same thing countless times when Nobles walked by me.

My dad stops and faces the man. The man smiles back, but I can see he's uncomfortable. "Alllldrinnnn, what is wroooong?"

"Nothing, my Lord."

My dad slowly shakes his head. "Noooo, that's not true, Alllldrinnnn."

The man takes a deep breath. "It's my wife, sir. She's sick. She's having trouble breathing again."

"I knoooow."

The man nods. He's not surprised. Neither am I. My dad knows everything.

"Why are you herrrre?"

"I have to work, My Lord. The medicine is expensive."

"I already sent it to your hommmme, Alllldrinnnn."

"You did, my Lord?"

"Of course, Alllldrinnnn. You know I've always taken care of you and Sallllah." My papa leans in and does that thing where his head moves forward as if his neck is extended. "Go home, Alllldrinnnn. Be with your wife while she recoverssss."

The man bows and smiles. "Yes, my Lord." He turns to leave.

"Waaaait. Youuuuu are forgetting somethingggg."

The man smiles again and comes in and gives my dad a hug before running off down the hallway.

When someone first gave my papa a hug, I thought my dad would order the man's arrest. No one treats a Nobleman in such a manner. But my papa is a very huggy person. I've seen him hug just about everyone.

Even General Lirnal, who did not… appreciate it.

We continue through the caves until we reach his office. My mama is already there, and she smiles sweetly at me. She is beautiful.

"It's time for our lesson, my dear."

She pulls out some papers and prepares to teach me. My papa always stays for it, but he talks far too slowly to be a good teacher. Now and then he adds a comment and explains some details that my mama doesn't know, but for the most part, he just sits there and smiles at me and my mama.

Before she can get started, however, a soldier comes to the door. He gives a quick bow and then hands a note to my papa.

My papa reads it quickly—he may speak slowly, but he's a fast reader—and then thanks the soldier before adding, "Tellll the Captainnnn that I will commmme to the cellll."

The soldier bows again and rushes out the door.

My dad hands the note to my mother, then turns to me. "Marleeeeteeee, tell me about your friennnnd, Prince Draydonnnn, or as you call himmmm, Caric."

I'm confused about that. My dad has asked me a lot about my friends already, but something else is going on. "Well, he's a great guy. He's a good leader, he's really nice… um… I'm not sure what else to say."

"Issss he loyallll?"

My mouth drops open at that question. "Loyal? Caric?" I blink a few times in my surprise. "There's no one more loyal than Caric. He will face a dozen Talic wolves before he lets a friend down."

"I meannnn, is he loyallll to the thronnnne?"

I frown. That's a strange question. He's a Prince! "Papa, what's this about? Caric is loyal to the throne. He believes the same thing I do, that Prince Roran must be King."

"Would Cariiiic like to sit on the throooone?"

I laugh before I can catch myself. "Papa, Caric would be a King if he had to be, but he would never choose such a thing. Don't you remember when he stepped forward in the cavern? He did that because he thought he was Prince Roran, but he didn't want to. Ellcia had to push him forward. I can promise you, he was relieved when Mic turned out to be the Prince."

"Did he tellll you all thissss?"

"No, I just know Caric, and I can see it in his eyes. He doesn't want to be the King. And Ellcia doesn't want to be the Queen."

"What doessss the Lady Ellciaaaa have to do withhhh it?"

I can tell he already knows, but he's asking me anyway. "Caric loves Ellcia, and Ellcia wants to marry Caric. She's never told him that, but she's told me a few times. She would be Queen if she had to be, but she doesn't want it either." I laugh. "In fact, she would hate to be Queen."

"Thank youuuu, Marleeeeteeee."

"What is this about?"

My papa takes a slow, deep breath, then says, "I am glaaaad you pay attentionnnn to other peoplllle, Marleeeeteeee. Your friennnnd, Prince Draydonnnn, has just been arresssssted for trying to kidnnnnnap and kill the Princcccce."

I gasp. "No, he would never do that! They're… they're liars!"

"Marleeeeteeee, I am going to seeeee him now. I will find out what I cannnn."

"I want to go with you!" I shout, far louder than I should.

"Noooo."

I pause. I expect an explanation, but it looks like there's not one coming. Instead, my papa appears deep in thought.

Before he leaves, he says to my mama, "Prepare herrrr, just in casssse."

"I can't give her up again!" my mama blurts out.

My papa's face fills with grief. "I knooow, Aldora, my lovvvve, but it maaaay be the right thingggg to doooo."

My mama nods, and my papa leaves.

I've heard him say that kind of thing before. "It's the right thing to do." It seems that when he sees the right thing to do, he does it, no matter the cost.

My mama jumps up and runs into my sleeping quarters. A moment later, she comes out with my pack.

"What's going on? What do you have to prepare me for?"

My mama doesn't stop. Instead, she calls to me to follow her.

We rush into the kitchen area where Mildren is hard at work. She's preparing what she calls, "Cave Cakes". They're tough, but they fill you up and last for days in the cave without going moldy.

"Mildren, we need some traveling food for up to four people."

"Yes, my Lady."

We run into the sitting room, my mama still holding my pack. Before I can ask again, she summons an older man named Rint. Rint has been with my family since he was an infant, and he's married to Mildren. His parents served my grandparents and my great-grandparents.

"Rint, I need you to sit down and listen."

"Yes, my Lady."

Rint has a seat, and my mama motions me toward another seat. When she speaks, she addresses me, not Rint.

"Marleet. Listen closely." At this point, my mama begins to tear up a bit, but she catches herself. "Not everyone among the Free Armies of Sevord is loyal to the throne. There are some who are traitors. When we identify them, we remove them, but there are always more. An attempt has been made on Prince Roran's life and your friend, Caric, has been accused of the crime."

She lets that settle in for a moment. I have a thousand words to say and nothing to say. I just… can't put anything together. Instead, my mouth hangs open.

"I don't know what your father will find, Marleet, but it's possible that Caric will need to be broken out of his cell in order to save his life." My mama takes a deep breath. I see she's trying to control herself. "If that's the case, then you, Ellcia, and Hemot are the best ones to get him out. You will have to…"

My mama breaks down in tears at this point. I move to her side and so does Rint. The man is like family. He's loyal beyond question and loves my parents.

When my mama calms down, she says, "If that's the case you will have to leave with your friends. Your father knows his connections well, but I suspect that he will send you to Haner to an inn named the Horse and the Bow, although the locals call it the 'orse and the 'ow. Once there, the innkeeper, a man named Phil… he's a wonderful man. Loyal, committed, brave. But he doesn't speak clearly. It's not a problem with his tongue, he's just…" She pauses as if she's struggling to find the right words.

Rint jumps in. "He's lazy, my Lady."

She nods and says to me, "He can speak clearly when he wants to, he just can't be bothered to form the words. But aside from that, my dear, you can trust him completely. He will allow you to stay in his inn until we can send for you."

My mama turns to Rint, and he nods. "My Lady, I will see to it." He bows and rushes out of the room.

"What is Rint seeing to?"

My mama closes her eyes for a moment. When she opens them, she stares at me for a moment before saying, "Listen, my dear. You might have to run with Prince Draydon—or Caric. There is likely something else going on. It is interesting how Prince Roran, the King-to-be, and the second in line for the throne, Caric, have both been targeted within a matter of hours. That means we need to increase the Prince's security—there is no doubt this has been done, and your father will confirm that—but we also need to protect Caric."

"And Rint?"

He will find your friends, Ellcia and Hemot, and bring them here, along with their traveling clothes and packs. We will then make sure that the three of you are ready in case you need to run.

I slump back in my seat and cover my face with my hands. I don't want to run again. I just want to be safe. I thought I was safe. I thought we'd just have to travel back to the palace and then I could just be… safe.

But… Caric would do this for me.

"I have kept your pack ready to go in case there was ever a need," my mama explains. "Your clothes and traveling gear are already in here, along with enough money for you to make your way across Sevord a few times, even staying at inns at every chance you get. You'll have plenty of money. I've hidden it in various places."

My mama then begins to show me where the money is. I won't remember it all, but I try to focus. She's hidden money in strange places. If we're robbed, I guess that'll mean they likely won't get it all.

Just then, Mildren comes in with a large sack of food. My mama and Mildren set to work on squeezing as much traveling food as they can into my pack, and my mom orders me to go change.

I rush into my chambers and stop. The last week I've been able to wear beautiful dresses again. I have missed that. I don't really want to go back to traveling clothes. They're comfortable, but they're far from pretty. In fact, they're ugly.

My traveling clothes have already been set out. They've been cleaned and mended. I change into them quickly, and once I have, I actually feel better. It reminds me of the adventure I've had. When I settled into the caves and got myself cleaned up, I was pleased that I had a lot more muscle from my time crossing Sevord. I think this journey will be easier than the last one.

I strap on my sword and armor. It actually feels good to be suited up again. I pull out my sword and go through some of the moves. Since learning of the sword's enchantment, my skills not only with this sword, but also with any sword, have improved a lot.

I head back into the other room to find my mom with her face in her hands.

"Mama? What's wrong?"

She quickly wipes away the tears. "I just can't stand the thought of losing you again, but your father is right. You and your friends are the ones to rescue him—if there is need."

She stands up and comes to me. "I'm so proud of the woman you've grown into, Marleet. So is your father. I wish we had been able to..." She pauses for a moment. "One day, I hope this will all be over. One day, I hope we can be back in Sevord and live as we once did. But for now, we need to get some food in you, so you are ready to go if needed."

We go into our dining room, one of the many caves which are part of our living quarters, and I find Mildren has already laid out a meal for my mama and me, along with two others.

Before we finish eating, Rint comes back with Ellcia and Hemot. Both are dressed in their armor with their packs on their backs and worried looks on their faces. Not only that, their eyes are bloodshot, and I remember how late it is. I suspect it's sometime in the middle of the night.

I squeal with joy and run into Hemot's arms, then into Ellcia's. We're all happy to be back together again, but they're worried. I take each of them by the hand. "Come, we have some food. We can talk over dinner."

Over our meal, we talk through a little of what's happened over the last week, and I fill them in on what I know of the situation with Caric. I'm just about to tell them where we're to go when we get out of the mountain—if it's necessary for us to escape—when my papa comes in.

Ellcia and Hemot rise in his presence, and I'm reminded again of how important my papa is. He just seems so nice that it's easy for me to forget.

"Pleeeease, sit down, my friennnnds."

He sits in one of the seats and starts to lay out what he's learned. He explains it slowly, but clearly. It turns out, Caric has been arrested, he's being kept for questioning, and the trial is set for early in the morning.

At first, I think maybe that's a good idea. A judge might consider the evidence and clear Caric, but before I can suggest that, my papa explains that this is all suspicious.

"It is unnnnlikely that heeee will come out of the triallll as anything but guilllllty. Thinggggs are in motion that I cannnnot stop. The only optionnnn for your friennnnd is to get him out of the mounnnntainnnn."

"Lord Yune," Ellcia says very respectfully, "my brother is a Captain and quite influential. He might be able to hold the trial until Caric's uncle returns."

"I am sorryyyy, my dear Ladyyyy Ellciaaaa." My dad shakes his head slowly, and I see the sadness in his eyes. "Captainnnn Granellll is a good man, but he cannot hooooold off the triallll. He is able, howeverrrr, to help us release the young mannnn before the trial takes placccce." He then pauses for far too long before adding, "Howeverrrr, you will all have to leeeeave with your friend, if he issss to survive."

"Where do we go?" Hemot asks.

"Youngggg man…" My papa leans forward and asks without hesitation, "Do youuuu have your eye onnnn my daughterrrr?"

Hemot's face drains of color, and I look at my mama in shock. She just smiles back at me and gives me a look as if to say, "Just let your father do his thing."

"I… uh… I…. uh… um… what do you mean, Sir?"

"Iiiiiii am not a Sirrrr, youngggg man. Iiiiii am also not a soldierrrr. You do not need to call meeee Sir. I am a Nobllllle. Specifically, I am a Duuuuuke. There were only twoooo Duuuuukes at the time of the rebelllllion. Officially, you maaaay call me Your Gracccce, but I prefer My Lorrrrd."

"Uhh… okay, My Your Grace Lord."

My papa smiles at Hemot and says, "Youuuuu are just like your fatherrrr. He was a gooood friend of minnnne."

"You knew my father? Can you tell me about him?"

"You havennnn't answered my questionnnn, young mannnn. Are you going to tell meeee if you have your eye onnnn my daughterrrr?"

"I… uh… well… at the moment, I'm not looking at her."

My papa smiles at Hemot and then says, "Thennnn, in the worrrrds of a very wise mannnn… Neither will I answer youuuu."

Hemot's face turns an even brighter red.

My papa turns to my mama and asks, "My Ladyyyy, have youuuu given Marleeeeteeee instructions on where to goooo?"

"Yes, My Your Grace Lord."

I love the way they talk to each other. They often use formal titles, but their smiles say they're only joking around. This time, using Hemot's messed-up title is even cuter.

"Thennnn, the four of you musssst resssst. In four hourrrrs, you will have to leeeeave."

Ellcia and I move off toward my chambers. I glance back to see my dad whispering to Hemot. I don't know what he's saying, but I think it has something to do with Hemot having his eye on me. My dad doesn't have to worry. Hemot only sees me as a friend.

3

The Touch

A little over three hours later, we're moving down a hallway. Hemot seems to know these caves well, so he's leading Ellcia and me. He moves quickly, and it's hard to keep up with him, but I'm managing. I'm a lot stronger now than I was when we left Sevord.

The plan is simple. We get Caric and get out of the caves. We head to Haner and meet my parent's friend at the Horse and Bow. I haven't had a chance to tell the others some of the details, but if we don't get out of the caves, none of that matters.

We weave our way through a lot of dark tunnels. Very few people walk the caves at this hour. We pass the occasional soldier, but each one just nods at us. My dad gave us a route to take that would lead us by soldiers whose loyalty was without question.

Finally, we reach our destination. It's an area of the caves I haven't seen before. It smells like rotting... something... and human urine. I don't really want to be here. I hope Caric isn't stuck somewhere in this area.

Two soldiers stand sentry, and they wave us over. "You should have been here ten minutes ago!"

"I'm sorry," Ellcia says. When Caric's not around, she's in charge. She does it well, although she hates it.

"All right," the one soldier says. He's whispering. I guess we have to keep things quiet. "You're going to have to hit us hard enough that it leaves a mark, otherwise we'll be brought up on charges."

"Hit you?" Ellcia looks back at me. "I didn't know we had to hit them."

Hemot steps forward. "It's okay. I've got this."

Ellcia moves off to the side, and the men turn around. One of them says, "You should hit us from behind. That will be easier to explain."

Hemot reaches back and punches each man in the back of the head.

"Ow!" the soldiers each say. They turn around and glare at Hemot. "We didn't say punch us. You have to leave a mark! Not too much, just enough to suggest that we were knocked out."

"Okay, sorry," Hemot says. "I got this now. Turn around."

The men turn around, and Hemot pulls out his dagger. At first, I think he's going to stab them, but instead he brings the butt of the knife down on each of their heads.

Both men drop to the ground. After a moment, they look up at Hemot, and I fear they're about to turn on him. Blood trickles down their faces.

The one man growls, "It's all or nothing with you, isn't it?"

Hemot nods. "I've been told that many times in the few years I've walked this earth."

The soldier shakes his head, but then I see that he regrets it. I gather he has quite a headache. He hands the keys to Hemot and tells him to move quickly.

Hemot steps to the door and starts to fumble with the lock. There are only four keys, and within seconds, he's tried all four. None of them work. He tries them again, but still nothing.

One of the guards stands up and pulls the keys out of Hemot's hands. "Just give it to me!"

The first key he tries works right away. He drops the keys on the ground and whispers, just leave them there.

Ellcia pushes forward and swings open the door. I can't see Caric, but there's no response at first. Then again, Ellcia has her face covered with her cloak. She pulls it back, and I hear a happy sound come from inside the cell.

The soldier who opened the door shakes his head and lies down on the ground. He and the other soldier lay perfectly still, and with the blood trickling down, they look either dead or at the very least, knocked out.

Ellcia whispers into the cell, "Come on! We have to move."

Caric comes out and the four of us immediately turn to run back the way we've come. We stop short as one of the soldiers hisses, "No! The other way!"

We turn and run past the soldiers. As we do, one of them grumbles, "It's like they didn't even plan this out!"

We move a short distance and pull into a side cave where Caric's pack and weapons are. Without a word, Caric pulls on his armor and weapons, securing his cloak and pack in place. I want to ask how he is and to check his cuts and bruises, of which he has many, but I don't dare take the time now. When he's done, we wait while some men walk by. I think those are the men we're trying to avoid.

When they're past, we rush out and through the caves. Ellcia leads this time while Hemot gives her directions. I don't know why Caric isn't leading again, but maybe it's best we just leave it as it is until we get out of the caves.

We round another corner and come face to face with my parents and Captain Granel. The Captain is a strange-looking man, but he's quite nice.

Now that we're safe, I wrap my arms around Caric. I can't believe what they did to him. He looks like he's been kicked in the face by a horse about six times.

"Are you okay, Caric?" I check each of his cuts. I want to cry. I don't know why Ellcia isn't doing this, but if she won't, I'll take care of it. I pull out some ointment that I brought for the journey.

He tells me he's fine, but I can't imagine that's true. He's not a liar, but he always downplays his injuries.

Ellcia pulls me away. "We don't have time to do this now. We have to leave."

We say our goodbyes and then rush on. It's not long before we're at the exit we've been looking for, and we're all bundled up. I'm surprised at how cold it is on the mountain. My mom explained to me that it would be this way, but I thought it would just be a little chilly.

As we make our way along the side of the mountain, I'm not sure if it's because we're all back together again or what, but I know we're doing the right thing. Somehow, I know this is exactly where we're supposed to be. And somehow, I know this is exactly what I'm supposed to be doing right at this moment.

The more we walk, the better I feel. The others seem cold, but I just feel energized.

We continue for hours, working our way across and down the mountain. I'm not too keen on that. I think being on the mountain is a better place to be, but I don't say anything.

We come to a giant waterfall. It's as beautiful as the rest of the mountain. I've never seen a waterfall up close before, let alone a frozen one. It's hard to believe how it could freeze like that.

I'm shocked when my friends try to turn left. That would take us down the mountain! That's certainly not where we want to go. I would have thought my papa would have explained that to them.

"Get down!"

I drop low. I've learned that when someone I trust says "get down" or "run" or "hide" that I'm supposed to just do it without question. There's usually no time to waste.

I watch Caric. He's the one who saw the danger. I'm not sure what he sees. I look down the mountain but can't quite see anything or anyone. However, the good news is whatever he saw is making him head in the opposite direction. We rush up the side of the mountain. With each step, I want to cheer for joy! I know this is exactly where we're supposed to go. It's like someone is calling to me. I bet it's my mama and papa.

We run farther up the side of the mountain. I see the perfect place for us to hide, but Caric points it out first. That's okay. I don't want to be a bother, but I know that's where we should be.

I push on and pass by Caric and Ellcia and Hemot and make it into the cave first. Already I feel better.

I glance back to see soldiers step into the entrance to the cave, and I'm not surprised when snow drops down on them, blocking the entrance.

The others mumble about something, but I just don't care. They sound upset, but it's not likely because we're in the cave. They probably just want some light. I understand. It's hard to see without light.

My head feels funny. I'm in a bit of a fog, but it's a good fog. It's exactly where I'm supposed to be. I just know it.

Ellcia's voice catches me off guard. "We have to find our way out of here."

I can't believe her attitude. She doesn't understand how important it is that we be here. I think all of them want to leave!

"I don't like this." I think if they just know that I'm not happy with what they're suggesting, then maybe they can calm down and see what's really important.

They mumble back and forth about something or other. I don't really care. I just want to go deeper into the cave. I can't see where I'm going, though. Maybe someone has an idea.

I hear Hemot trying to light a fire. That will help us head in the right direction!

"You're so smart, Hemot." That's one more reason I love him so much. They're talking about something, but all I can think of is how much I love Hemot.

The torch lights up. The cave is beautiful. With the snow behind us and the rock walls, it's almost as beautiful as the view of the mountain. I want to go deeper into the cave and see what we find.

We move in and with each step I grow happier. Caric seems a little worried, but we all let him know it's okay. This is part of the plan, I think. Yes, it must be.

We enter a well-lit room, and I hold Hemot tight. Our good friend is here. Caric seems a little worried, but sometimes he's like that.

Caric grabs me and holds me tight. That's fine. I don't mind a hug from Caric, but it's frustrating because my new good friend wants me to go to him.

Hemot helps me out. He's so wonderful. Caric lets go, and I stand in front of our friend. He puts his hand on my forehead, and I feel warm all over. I then walk toward the wall, and I feel my body jump.

Captain Frindor smiles at me. "Welcome, Lady Marleet."

I smile. He's so nice. I trust him. He's not like that sneaky Captain Granel. That man's wicked. I don't know how Ellcia can trust him. He's a liar and a traitor.

"Do you have a request for me, my Lady?"

I nod slowly. I do have a request. I just don't know what it is. My mouth opens, and I find myself saying, "I must speak privately with the Prince."

"Wonderful. I will take you directly there, my Lady."

I follow him. There are other soldiers with us. I don't know them, but if Captain Frindor trusts them, so do I.

We weave our way through the caves. I think I feel dizzy, but happy. I still feel that fog, but it's okay. The closer I get to the Prince, the better. I have a message for him. It's important.

We reach an area with a lot of soldiers, and the Captain orders me to stay put.

Frindor heads through a doorway, leaving me with the other soldiers. I don't like that. I should be with the Prince. But I know Captain Frindor will do the right thing.

He comes back a moment later and leads me on. I reach an area with a curtain across the doorway and six men stand guard outside. We're just about to enter when I stop. "Wait." I'm not sure what I'm about to say, but I'm worried. My voice comes out in a whisper. "Rulf. Is he in there? I can't go in if Rulf is in there."

Captain Frindor smiles. "Rulfor? No, he's not here. I assigned him elsewhere for the afternoon, and I just checked. It's just the Prince right now, along with two servants."

I step through the curtains. The Prince sits up in bed, looking a little dazed.

"Marleet!"

"Hello, Your Majesty."

He laughs. "I keep telling you, Marleet. Call me Roran. Or you can call me Mic if you prefer. I'm more used to that name."

He swings his legs over the side of the bed, and a man steps close, offering support. Roran waves him away and pulls himself to his feet.

"I told them Caric had nothing to do with it. He's been cleared of charges."

I nod. "I have a message for you."

He frowns. "Do you? Since when are you a messenger?" He laughs again and starts for a chair. He's unsteady on his feet.

I move toward him and reach him before he makes it to his seat. "I must give you the message right now."

"Before I sit?" He smiles at me. I think we've spent a lot of time together in the last few days. It's been easier to get to know him now that he's no longer pretending to be Mic.

"Yes, before you sit."

"What is it, my Lady?"

I don't know what the message is, but my hand comes up slowly and gently. I rest it against his cheek, and something in his eyes change. I'm happy for the change. It's a good change.

His eyes focus on me, and he whispers, "Thank you, Marleet."

I pull my hand down and step back, blinking. I don't know how I got here. I look around. I'm in the Prince's chambers. We were here just yesterday with my papa, but I don't remember coming here today. I thought I was leaving with Hemot.

I turn around a few times. Captain Frindor's here. My papa warned me to be careful around him. There's a lot of suspicion around the man, but no evidence.

I turn back to Roran. He's looking at me in a strange way. I glance at the servants, and they look concerned. No, not concerned.

Horrified.

"What… what happened?"

One of the servants whispers something to the other, and that man makes for the doorway. Captain Frindor puts up his hand and shakes his head. "You'll remain here until the Prince relieves you."

Roran addresses them in a very authoritative voice. "You will not speak of the events in this room to anyone. If word of this gets out to anyone, you will be charged with treason. Is that understood?"

Both men bow to the Prince, and the man who had nearly left returns to his place.

I want to go back to my mama and papa. They'll help me remember why I'm here.

I turn to the Prince but step back. Roran's looking at me in a way I don't like. He looks… like he wants me. Like he can't take his eyes off me. Like… he's hungry.

I step back a little farther and turn toward a side door. I hear a commotion outside the room. The curtain parts, and Rulf comes in.

"Rulfor!" Captain Frindor hollers. "You were assigned to guard duty on the western entrance for this afternoon!"

Rulf growls his response. "They didn't need me. I…" He stops and turns toward Roran. He studies him for a moment and then rage fills his eyes.

I don't think Rulf will hurt me, but I also don't think he'll notice if I get hurt in the process. Whatever he's about to do, it doesn't look good.

"I don't care if you think you…"

Rulf interrupts the Captain simply by raising his finger. Rulf is not one to mess with. I think if he decided to attack the soldiers, he might kill half the army before he tired even a little.

The entire time, he hasn't taken his eyes off Roran. I glance at the Prince. He's not looking at Rulf. He has his eyes on me. He's still looking at me in that weird way. I don't like it.

"You're enchanted."

I turn back to Rulf. "What did you say?"

Rulf glances at me, and I think this is the first time he's noticed me in the room. "I said, the Prince is enchanted."

Roran laughs. "No, Rulf, I'm not. I'm fine. In fact, I feel better than fine. I am ready to give the order to leave the mountain. It's time to reclaim the throne."

Rulf takes a step forward. "Draw your sword."

Roran shakes his head. "Rulf, you don't have the authority to order me around."

"You have to, if you're told to."

"The law states that a Nobleborn can order the King to draw his sword. You are not Noble-born, Rulf."

Rulf turns to me. "Order him to draw his sword."

"What? His sword?" I look back at Roran. He's smiling at me like it's all just a joke.

"Order him!"

Rulf doesn't do well with using lots of words. He rarely explains anything well. But… Rulf is acting normal. Roran is not.

I turn back to Roran. "Draw your sword."

Roran smiles at me. "Thank you, Lady Marleet. But I cannot."

Rulf steps a little closer. He looks like he's ready to attack. "It's the law, Mic. If you do not, you are immediately put under suspicion."

Roran places his hand over his heart and shakes his head. "I will not. The law applies to the King, not the Prince. On my honor, I will not draw the King's sword until I take the throne in Sevord. It will be my sacrifice in my integrity." His expression then grows serious, and he adds, "From now on, Rulfor, you will refer to me as Prince Roran or Your Majesty, not Mic."

I don't know what any of that about the sword really means, but I think I want to get out of here.

I hear a familiar voice. "Step asiiiide."

The curtains part, and my papa walks in. He looks a little surprised to see me, but covers it up well. Bowing his head to the Prince, he says, "Your Majestyyyy."

"Lord Yune," Rulf says. "The Prince is enchanted. I have ordered him to draw his sword. He refuses on his honor."

My papa nods. He examines the Prince for a moment, then me, then Rulf. Finally, he turns back to the Prince and smiles. "It is gooood to see youuuu back on your feeeet, Your Majestyyyy. My Ladyyyy and Iiii have been quite worriiiied for youuuu."

"Thank you, Your Grace." Roran moves to his chair and sits down. "I am ready to leave the mountain and return to Sevord. I hereby give the order."

My papa bows and says, "Yessss, my Princcccce. I will seeee to it immediatelyyyy. Weeee have been prepaaaaring in anticipation for your orderrrr for the last five daaaays. We will be ready to leeeeave withinnnn four dayyyys." He turns to me and says, "My Lady Marleeeeteeee, will you join meeee?"

I nearly run to his side, but Roran stops me. "I would like to keep the Lady Marleet by my side for the time being."

I don't want to be here, but I think I can't refuse a Prince's request. I turn back to my papa and see he's relaxed and has a large smile on his face.

"Ahh, yessss," my papa begins. "She is a beautyyyy, and a joy to allll who spend time in her presencccce. I can see why youuuu would want to keep her heeeere."

My heart sinks. He was my only hope. The Prince is not himself. I want out of here.

"I musssst, howeverrrr, take my dear daughterrrr away from your presencccce, Your Majestyyyy. I hope you can forgive meeee of this terrible injusticccce to my future Kingggg."

I turn back to Roran. He seems unimpressed, but there's something there that I don't understand. After a moment, he smiles and bows to my papa. "Yes, Lord Yune. I understand. I will honor your request." Roran turns to me and takes my hand. He raises it to his lips, and I nearly vomit.

"Ahhhh, my Princcccce," my papa interrupts. "You must not kissss the Lady's hannnnd. It is my desirrrre as the fatherrrr that her hand remains unkissssed at this timmmme."

Roran's face fills with confusion as if he's never heard of such a thing but nods his head. He lets go of my hand and gives me a respectful bow. I curtsy in return and quickly join my papa.

He offers me his arm, and we leave Prince Roran's chambers.

We pass the guards who all bow respectfully to my papa. Two soldiers stand waiting a short distance down the hallway. When we reach them, they trail behind us. They are two of my family's personal guards, and my parents only employ those we can trust.

When we are far enough from Prince Roran's chambers, my papa asks me, "Do youuuu rememberrrr how you got herrrre?"

"No, papa."

"Did youuuu touch the Princcccce?"

"I think so, papa. On his face."

He nods. "Are youuuu confuuuuused?"

"Yes, papa."

He walks in silence for a moment before he begins to explain. It turns out that Rulf is probably right. Giants are able to sense enchantments on people—it's like they can smell it. Occasionally they can sense them on objects as well, but it's not as easy. He explains that the way Roran acted toward me was also an indication.

"What way? What was Roran doing that made it clear he was enchanted?"

"Hmmmm… well, Marleeeeteeee. You were the onnnne who brought the enchantmennnnt to the Princcccce. Oftennnn, there is a bonnnnd created between the onnnne who bringssss the enchantmennnnt and the onnnne who receives it. He is likely to assssk for your hannnnd in marriage withinnnn the day."

I don't really like the thought of that. I want to ask more, but I feel too uncomfortable with the topic to ask. Instead, I decide to avoid it… somewhat. "So, what do we do about all this?"

"That, my deeeear, is a very good questionnnn."

4

The Proposal

We all work hard to get ourselves ready to leave. My mama and papa each have many meetings every day and face countless issues which must be addressed, but they still manage to help pack along with our servants.

I hadn't realized this, but most of our servants live in the same quarters as us, just in various caves throughout the area. Once everything in our area is fully packed up, my mama and papa, begin to help pack up Rint and Mildren's quarters. They both grew up in my family's service, fell in love, and were married over forty years ago. They truly are like family to us.

Most of the servants insist that my parents not help out with their packing, but my papa, in his way, sticks out his head at them and begins to ask questions like, "And whyyyy wouldn't I do thissss? And whyyyy wouldn't I hellllp? And whyyyy do you have a rug on the walllll? And whyyyy do you have fourteen salt and pepperrrr shakers? And whyyyy is my sock bunched uuuup within my left shooooe?"

After he does this for a bit, they thank him for his help and continue their packing with us working alongside them.

By the end of the fourth day, we are ready to go, as my papa promised the Prince. Many of the people in the caves are soldiers or support to the army. As such, they're able to pack their belongings in little time. That left them free to pack up much of the common needs such as the kitchen, the armory, the training grounds, the library, and more.

As we're about to leave our empty chambers for the last time, two soldiers arrive. I don't recognize either of them. It turns out the Prince has summoned me and requested that my parents meet with him.

My dad smiles at the men. "Yessss, my friennnnds. You may tell the Princcce weeee will all arriiiive together in a matter of minutessss."

The one soldier shakes his head. "I'm sorry, Lord Yune. The Prince has ordered that we return with the Lady Marleet. You are welcome to join them soon."

I'm worried that this might be the time when the Prince asks for my hand in marriage. I can't imagine that someone can refuse a request like that. I haven't talked to either of my parents about this. I'm afraid they won't be able to stop it. But one thing's for sure. I don't want to go with these soldiers without my mama and papa.

"Of courssse," my papa says. "The Lady Marleeeeteeee must go with you right awaaaay. So, we will all join youuuu. But, my friennnnds, we must move slooooowly. I am not as young as I used to beeee."

My papa has his ways. I hope he can manage to get us through this, because I have no ideas. I wish Ellcia and Caric were here. Ellcia is smart, and Caric would find a way through it all.

We slowly move toward the Prince's chambers with the two soldiers from the Prince ahead of us and our own guard behind. Soldiers are everywhere in this section of the cave system. All the walls have been stripped of any decorations, and the caves we pass sit empty.

When we reach the royal chambers, the guards pull the curtains aside, and we enter. On the other side is Captain Frindor, Captain Granel, many of my parent's friends, Nobles living in the caves with us, and Rulf. All the decorations and furniture are gone, except for one chair in the center of the room. In it sits Prince Roran.

He looks at me with even greater affection than before and smiles sweetly at me. I don't know what to do, so I curtsy, causing my mama and papa, who are each holding my arms, to stumble beside me. I then trip and roll forward, right over, coming to a stop on my butt.

It's not the best entrance into a formal situation I've made so far, but it's far from the worst. Rulf rushes to my side and pulls me to my feet. I see concern in his eyes, but I don't think it's for me.

Once everyone is back in place, the Prince smiles again at me. I resist the urge to curtsy a second time. It just seems like the right thing to do when I'm uncomfortable.

"Lord Yune," the Prince begins. "I have good news for you."

"Allll news from my Princcccce is good neeeews."

My heart sinks at the next words.

"Lord Yune and Lady Aldora, I have come to the realization that I must have a Princess who might become my Queen. It is also my firm belief that I cannot have a better bride than the Lady Marleet. And so, it is with great joy, my dear Lord Yune and Lady Aldora, that I ask for your daughter's hand in marriage."

My papa got me out of that kiss on my hand, so I'm hoping he can get me out of this as well.

"Ahhhh, my Princccce," my papa says. "Ahhhh, my deeeear, wonderful Princccce. You have honorrrred the Lady Aldora and myself faaaar more than we are worrrrth." At this my mama curtsies and my papa bows. My back begins to sweat, and my hands shake. "You have chosen wellll, my Prince. With my daughterrrr by your side, youuuu will be the wisest Kingggg, the proudest Kingggg, and the strongest Kingggg Sevord has ever knownnnn. You will be the envy of allll the people, for no mannnn will have a briiiide more beautifullll than my daughterrrr."

I am uncomfortable with where this is all going. I wish my dad would just say "No!" and storm out with my mama and me. I don't know if he can do that, though.

"And whennnn do you wish to take my daughterrrr's hannnnd in marriage?"

"I wish to be wed before we leave for Sevord."

The feeling drains from my face, and I think I'm going to be sick. If my papa doesn't stop this, I wonder to myself if I can make it out of here if I run. I glance at Rulf. He might help me get out. But then he'd have to turn against Roran. Rulf would never do that.

"Beforrrre we leeeeave!" my papa says with a large grin as he clasps his hands together to declare his joy. "The Ladyyyy Aldora and I are noooot worthy of such an honorrrr! To thiiiink, our daughterrrr, the Queeeeen of the greatest nationnnn in all the lannnnds!"

My heart races. I glance at my mom, and she smiles at me as if she's thrilled with the news, but she mouths the words, "Trust your papa."

I turn back to my dad, and he is grinning. He holds out his hands to Roran and adds, "We are honorrrred by our future Kingggg's requesssst."

"Thank you, Lord Yune." The Prince turns to me and is about to say something when my dad cuts him off.

"But alaaaas, we cannoooot give our blessingggg to this marriaaaage, my dear Princccce."

Prince Roran's eyes flash with anger. I've not seen that look from him before.

He regains his composure and then smiles. "Thank you, Lord Yune, for your honesty. May I ask for the reason for your refusal?"

"Of coursssse, Your Majestyyyy. It is myyyy and the Lady Aldoraaaa's wish that our dear Marleeeeteeee not be wed before her eighteeeeenth birthdayyyy. We would preferrrr she be at least twentyyyy, but we could not accept a wedding for herrrr at this aaaage. I think, my Princccce, that you are also of a youngggg age. Perhapssss, it might be betterrrr for you to waaaait until youuuuu are at least eighteennnn as well?"

Prince Roran's eyes seem to bore into my papa. He may have gone too far with that last statement. The other Nobles in the room appear quite nervous, while both the Captains look bored.

Finally, Roran composes himself and says, "Thank you, Lord Yune. I will honor your request for our marriage to wait until the Lady Marleet is eighteen, and I will take your counsel on my own age under advisement."

"Thank youuuuu, my Princccce. May I recommennnnd that we all move downnnn to the villaaaage? It would be prudennnnt, I think, to beginnnn our journey on the morroooow."

"Yes, Lord Yune. You are wise." Prince Roran frowns, but quickly tries to cover it with a smile. "We will move down into the valley and leave first thing tomorrow morning."

My papa bows to Roran, and my mama and I give deep curtsies. We turn, and my papa offers me his arm. Once out of the room, our guards walks before and behind us.

"I didn't know what was going to happen there," I whisper.

"I learned a long time ago," my mama begins with a light laugh, "to never question your father when it comes to politics."

My papa chuckles and places his hand on mine as I hold his arm. "My dearest Marleeeeteeee, if it is your wish to onnnne day marry the Princccce, I would be honorrrred to grant such a thingggg. But firsssst, I would never do such a thingggg whilst he is under an enchantmennnnt. And seconnnnd, your mother tells me you look at that young Milterite boyyyy in a… hmmmm… shall I saaaay… special waaaay?"

I feel my face grow red, and I don't answer. Instead, my papa chuckles again.

"Do not worryyyy, my child. For nowwww, you are saffffe."

"For how long?"

My mom answers. "My dear, it is difficult to say. With an enchantment, anything can happen. We do believe he is enchanted—and so do the Nobles and many of the officers. The General has not returned yet, but we have sent word to him of this. We know the enchantment is for ill, as all enchantments on people are, but we do not know for what end this enchantment might have been placed."

I remain silent. I can tell she has more to say, but is taking her time. She is a well-educated, extremely focused woman. In the short time I've been with her, I've found there is little she does not know.

"You are safe for now because not one of the Nobles will stand for the Prince to marry someone without full agreement. A marriage among royals and Nobles is not always for love, but often for benefit. For it to happen apart from the full support of all parties will cause distrust to grow and eventually tear the kingdom apart."

I didn't realize it could have that kind of effect, but I nod my head.

"So, for now, we do not have to worry. But the affection that comes from an enchantment transfer such as we have here is strong. The Prince will only hold to this restriction for so long."

"Can we prove he is enchanted?"

"It issss," my papa says, "Rulf's word againnnnst the Prince's worrrrd. For nowwww, we cannot prove anythingggg."

5

The Journey

And then your father flips completely over, landing on his head, with his undies showing!"

Rint is laughing so hard by this point that he nearly falls over. Mildren gives him a scornful look, but I see her smile.

My mama just shakes her head, saying nothing.

My papa, the slowest laugher in the entire world, lets loose. "Ha… hhha… hhhhha… hhhhhha. If I recaaaall correctlyyyy, my kneeees were showingggg, but my undiiiies did not make an appearanccccce that dayyyy."

"No, Yuney, I was there! I saw it all."

I find it surprising to hear how Rint and Mildren speak to my mama and papa in times such as this. In moments of formality, they speak as proper servants, but times like this, they speak like old friends.

My papa lets loose with another of his agonizingly long laughs. "Ha… hhha… hhhhha… hhhhhha."

The four of us walk at the moment. We spend much of our day walking, actually. We have a cart in which we can travel, but few people ride, so my parents insist that we walk when we can. According to my papa, "Thissss is a time to be unifiiiied, not to be separaaaate."

Mildren waves to my mom. "Aldora, can you hand me an apple?"

"Sure, my dear." Mama grabs an apple out of the pack in the wagon trundling along beside us and tosses it over my head to Mildren. My parents are never what I expect.

"But that's not the worst of it!" Rint continues now that he's composed himself. "King Hartor then comes in just at that moment with Prince Roran, who has just turned four years old. As soon as the Prince sees your father upside down, he squeals with joy, runs up to your dad and kicks him right in the butt!"

I shake my head, trying not to laugh for fear that I'll embarrass my papa, but then I hear his slow chuckle and lose control.

"King Hartor, of course, always the proper gentleman, is horrified. Had it been anyone else, I would have stepped in… I mean, not to kick your father, but to hinder further embarrassment, but it was the Prince, so I just holler out, 'Goal!' and that's when the King starts to laugh."

"What happened next?" This was something that had happened while we were all still at the castle as a family, but I have no memory of it. I assume I wasn't around.

"Well, the King hears someone behind him. It turns out a dozen soldiers led by Captain Tilbur were on their way into the hall, and the King, despite the fact that he's laughing so hard and that your father is still upside-down…"

"Iiii was meditatingggg…"

"Yes, meditating!" Rint lets out another loud laugh. "As your father is still meditating with his undie-covered butt up in the air, Captain Tilbur has a dozen soldiers about to enter the hall for an award ceremony. The King slams the door shut to protect whatever dignity the undie-meditator has left, and bolts it, laughing the entire time. But Captain Tilbur sees the door close and lock, hears a bit of the laughter—which he mistakes for arguing—and assumes the King is under threat. So, he orders his soldiers to break down the door to rescue the King and Lord Yune!"

I shake my head. I can't believe this kind of thing happened.

"So, once the door is bolted shut, King Hartor and I work to get your father back up on his feet, but just as we do, your father slips again, comes crashing down on top of King Hartor, and I slip and end up kicking the King in the face."

"What?" I can't imagine that's a good thing.

My mom puts up her index finger. "Pardon, dear. You are a Lady. You say, pardon, not what.

"Pardon?"

"What we didn't know," Rint continues, "is that soldiers move fast when their King is threatened. By this point, two of the soldiers have climbed along the outside stone wall of the castle from their window to ours and are just climbing in as my foot connects with the King's face."

"Oh my!" I feel stressed just listening to the story, but I must know how it ends.

"So, they tackle me, and by the time the King gets back on his feet, my hands are bound behind my back."

"Didn't you tell them that it was an accident?"

Rint laughs. "First, they wouldn't have believed me. Second, it makes for a better story not to."

"Ha… hhha… hhhhha… hhhhhha. Youuuu left something out, Rinnnnt."

"Oh, right!" Rint gives me a look and explains, "I figured it would all be cleared up soon, and I do so love to mess with soldiers, so I scream out, 'You'll never take me alive!'"

I'm nearly gasping for air by this point, and my heart is raging in my chest. I love the story, but it's also quite stressful. "Weren't you worried they would attack you if you fought back?"

"Oh, I didn't fight back. I'm no fool. I just knelt there calmly as they bound my arms behind my back, screaming, 'You'll never take me alive' and then I broke into a song about my beautiful Mildren and her world-famous cabbage soup."

"Ha... hhha... hhhhha... hhhhhha. That was a funnnn day."

"So, did the King order you released?"

"Well, eventually. King Hartor was quite a gentleman, but he was also quite a joker. He asked Captain Tilbur if the gallows were available that afternoon or if they had been booked for a party. None of the soldiers questioned such a request, but the good Captain figured it out at that point and joined in. He said something about how an early surprise retirement party was set to use it that afternoon, but it should be available by early evening, just after the monks use it for their soup kitchen."

I want to hear more, but Ellcia's brother, Captain Granel, approaches at this point. Papa has requested that the Captain keep us posted on everything going on. My papa has other means of gathering information, but he learns what he can from whomever he can.

As we walk, my papa asks, "Yessss, Captain?"

"Lord Yune, I have just received word that our messengers to the General were killed."

"Hmmmm… that is troubling newssss, Captain. He is yet unawarrrre, thennnn, that the Prince may beeee enchanted."

General Lirnal, third in line for the throne and leader of the Free Armies of Sevord, has gone to meet with the leaders of the four cities. As my papa has explained to me, if the cities do not get behind the Prince, it will be difficult to take the throne. It wouldn't be an issue if we didn't have to travel past the cities, but because we do, we need their support. I find the politics to be annoying, but my papa seems to thrive on it.

We've been traveling for three days. I still have no idea where my friends are, but my papa figures they've gone to Haner. He thinks it's the only option that makes sense.

The Prince has asked to meet with me every day and sent four requests for my hand in marriage, but my papa has managed to find solid reasons why we cannot do either. I don't want to be anywhere near the Prince right now. I trust Roran, but no one trusts an enchantment.

"I believe we would be wise to appoint a personal guard for your daughter."

That statement pulls me back to the conversation, and I lean in. They're whispering, so it's a wonder I even heard that part, but I did.

I step up close. "Why do I need a guard? Is it because of the Shaloomd?"

I look up briefly but can't see any in the sky. We haven't had to worry about them too much as we are still near the mountains, but the farther we travel across Sevord, and the closer to the cliffs on the edge of the Talic Region we get, the more there will be. At the moment, archers are stationed all throughout the people traveling across the plains. If any Shalloomd do show up, the archers shoot them as soon as they come within reach of the bows.

"No," the Captain says. "It's not the Shaloomd."

"What is it then?"

The Captain looks to my father, who turns to me. "My dear Marleeeeteeee. The Princccce is a threat if heeee is enchannnnted. He is a good young mannnn, but enchantmennnnts are not. But the biiiigger threat appears to be Captain Frindorrrr. Captain Granel hassss, I believe, noticed our friends not too far awayyyy?"

My papa keeps his eyes on me as he speaks, but Captain Granel whispers, "Yes, my Lord Yune."

"Our friends?" I look around, but don't see anything out of the ordinary.

"Soldiers, my Lady, appointed by Captain Frindor. They are not far away, but they have been following you for the last two days."

"How do you know they are following me?"

"Do you recall how your father asked me to take you to inspect some of the troops yesterday?"

I did. I thought it was odd, but I figured it was something a Lady was supposed to do.

"We did this to see if they would follow you or remain with the Lord Yune and the Lady Aldora. They followed you, my Lady." Captain Granel casually glances around as we carry on. "They are not far away now. Different soldiers today, but they are definitely Captain Frindor's men."

"Will youuuu, my dear Captainnnn, seeee to it that my daughterrrr is safe?"

The Captain turns back to my papa and meets his eyes. He can be quite intense when he wants to, and right now I feel like the Captain is about as intense as he gets. "I will, Lord Yune. I will have a guard assigned within the hour."

He turns and moves off through the crowd. I worry for a moment that he will not be safe, but a half-dozen soldiers meet him a short distance away, and they climb into their saddles. I'm glad he's not alone.

6

The Giant Guard

Mid-day on the fifth day of travel, General Lirnal arrives.

He approaches my father with a grim look on his face, and my father waves for him to join us. I take my seat among them—I assume that's okay. So far, I've been involved in most stuff.

My personal guard, which I haven't quite gotten used to, wanders a short distance away. They watch me constantly and scan the area. We have a lot of space around our camp as it is and plenty of our own soldiers, but these ones are focused on me.

I don't mind them so much. There are nearly a dozen of them in total, since they have to be on guard at all hours of the day, but the two main ones, Denner and Billot, are my papa's personal guard. Denner is in charge, and Billot seems to be… I don't know… maybe the second in command. I don't know how it all works. I just know that anywhere I go, my guard—Denner and Billot—are usually around, plus a few others from Captain Granel.

The General has arrived with next to no fuss. He's not only a General, but he's also a Prince, third in line to the throne, so I'd think there'd be a lot of attention given him, but he just… arrives. Quite a few soldiers follow him, but I don't recognize any of them. Most stay back, but two join us. A tall woman and a very large man.

The General sits and frowns at the fire for a moment. We've stopped for the night, and we've finished our meal, but Mildren arrives with a quickly put together plate for the General and each of his two companions. Mildren smiles at the woman, and they embrace. It seems just about everyone knows everyone else.

While the General eats, we all remain silent. There's nothing about his demeanor that suggests he's anything but disappointed.

My papa leans forward. "Are thingssss that baaaad, Lirnallll?"

The General nods. "It's worse than I thought, Yune."

My mama leans forward and focuses the conversation. "What have you heard about what's gone on here?"

He shakes his head. "I have heard nothing. I've had soldiers arrive and tell me all is well, letting me know the movement of the army out of the mountain and more, but nothing else." The look on his face tells me he does not believe the reports. "Is all truly well? Where is my nephew?"

I let out a little whimper at that question. I've been trying not to think of Caric, Ellcia, and Hemot. I feel sick every time I do.

My papa looks over at my mama. She is better at summing things up than he is.

"We believe all the soldiers we have sent to give you messages have been killed. The soldiers you've received messages from are likely all either traitors or have merely been given less information to pass along than would be proper."

The General nods. "I thought that might be the case. I sent soldiers back to get an accurate report, but no one returned."

My mama continues. "Shortly after you left, there was an attempt to kidnap Prince Roran."

The General's eyebrows shoot up, but he doesn't say anything. Instead, he merely waits.

"Your nephew, Prince Draydon, was accused of the crime, although the evidence didn't add up, nor was it realistic to assume that he had done this on his own. Captain Frindor intended to push the trial through within hours of Draydon's arrest, and it became clear that he had no intention of allowing your nephew to live. We intervened, and the Lady Ellcia, the Milterite boy, and our daughter escaped out of the mountain with him. Your nephew, Ellcia, and Hemot are, we hope, safe, but we have no idea of their location."

General Lirnal's eyes skip to me, but he doesn't say anything. I know he sees the problem.

"Yes, our daughter." My mama pauses for a moment. "This is where things become dark."

"Darker than what you have already told me?"

My mama frowns. "Far darker." She shakes her head. It's hard to believe all that's happened in such a short time. "My daughter then appeared back in the mountain, and Captain Frindor found her. She asked to be taken directly to the Prince—without Rulf's presence."

The General makes a growling noise in his throat at the comment about Rulf not being there.

"When she arrived, she approached the Prince… and touched his face."

The General turns to me. His eyes seem to pierce right into me. "Lady Marleet, what do you remember from before you touched his face?"

"Not much, Sir."

"Do not call me, Sir, Lady Marleet. You are a Lady. You may address me as General, General Lirnal, or in an informal setting such as this, merely Lirnal. Only those under me call me 'Sir'. I may be a General, and I may be a Prince, but you are the daughter of a Duke and Duchess." He then adds, "Describe a memory from just before you touched his face—any memory."

"I… um… it's hard to say. It's… blurry, General."

He nods. "And tell me what you saw on Prince Roran's face and, particularly, his eyes, the moment your memories ceased to be blurry."

"His eyes… changed. They refocused. It was as if he left and someone else took over."

"And, Lady Marleet, what are his feelings toward you now?"

I hesitate, but my mama gives me a nod. "Be open and honest, my dear."

"He wants to marry me."

General Lirnal growls again but nods his head. He turns to my mama and asks, "And Rulfor?"

"He claims there is an enchantment, but of course, there is no evidence. All we have is the testimony of two people who have only recently joined us."

General Lirnal nods again. "When I returned, the Prince refused to see me. That is why I am here." He turns to the two people with him. They haven't said a word, but they look as grim as the General.

"What are your orders?" The man's voice is deep and gravelly.

The General glances back at my parents. "No idea where Caric and the others went?"

My papa shakes his head. "Weeee suspect, Hanerrrr, but noooo, we do not knoooow."

"That is what I suspect as well." General Lirnal leans toward the two. I haven't looked closely at them, but I see now that the woman is missing her left leg, and the man is missing his left hand. They look like they've been in a lot of fights.

"Terr, I want you to go to Haner and find my nephew, the Lady Ellcia, and Hemot. I recommend you speak with Lord Hillbin. He has to be careful, so try to avoid notice as much as possible. If he doesn't know where the young ones are, check with Phil at the Horse and Bow. There's not much Phil…" at this point, the General makes a strange face and in an odd voice says, "du'nnt nuh."

Terr and the woman laugh, and my dad lets out one of his slow chuckles. I just decide to ignore it. It's one of those jokes that I'll likely never understand.

"What's the message?" the woman asks.

"Bring him up to speed on what's happened here, especially with the Lady Marleet. Feel free to ask her questions before you leave. Then tell him he cannot return to the army. Instead, he is to head to Nimville. They should settle in and await further orders. He'll be safe there. Nordin's people are good people, and they are loyal."

They each nod their head, and then the woman makes her way over to me. I assume she's going to pelt me with questions, and she does while my parents continue their conversation with the General.

Two days later, we reach Leito. Well, the front of the army reaches Leito. We're a long way back. Our family would normally be up near the front, but we've stayed back to keep me away from the Prince. My papa fears the Prince might just ask me for a visit, and I might suddenly find I'm in the middle of a wedding.

It would not hold, legally, of course, but it's not something we want to face. It turns out an enchantment attraction is powerful indeed.

In the distance, I see the walls of Leito. It's not much different from Haner, at least at this distance.

"You can't go near her!"

"I have orders. Outta my way!"

I hear a crash following the argument, and swords are drawn. I turn and run back to the wagon in the center of our camp. I'm not sure what else to do. I figure that will give my guard time to protect me.

A large man moves through the soldiers. My guards, along with many of my family's soldiers, push back and strike him with their swords, but it doesn't appear to be hindering the man at all. I see Denner hacking at the man.

I look around for my mama. She's rushing to my side. My papa is already gone. He's moved to the front of the army just this morning to be near the Prince in their talks with the city.

I wish I still had my sword, but I lost it at some point during my time with the spellcaster. The enchantment on it gave me such skill, but I have to make do with normal swords at the moment. They're heavy, bulky, ugly, and aren't as easy to use.

"Trust the soldiers to do their job, Marleet," my mama urges when she reaches me.

"Wait!" I holler, finally getting a good look at the man. "It's Rulf. He's okay! He can come through!"

The soldiers hesitate for a moment. Denner calls back, "Are you certain, Lady Marleet?"

"I'm certain. Please let him approach."

Through all of this, Rulf has not slowed down at all. Soldiers hang off him as if they're trying to make it harder for him to walk, but it's like he doesn't even notice them.

When they let go, he looks back briefly, but continues on at the same speed. He reaches me and grunts.

I run in and wrap my arms around him. He smells. He smells bad. Really bad, actually, but I don't mind. I've missed him, and it's so good to see a friend.

After a few seconds, however, I realize that I do, in fact, mind the smell. Every second it gets worse.

I pull away and take a big step back, trying to pretend I'm not about to gag. I wonder briefly what someone would have to eat for their body to make a smell like that, but push the question aside.

"Rulf, I've missed you!"

Rulf grunts.

I shake my head. "Please, tell me more than that, Rulf."

"I…" Rulf is not good with words and things like communication. "I… think I might have missed you as well. You're Ellcia, right?"

"I'm Marleet."

Rulf grunts.

"I know you're joking about not knowing my name."

Rulf gives the barest hints of a smile.

"What are you doing here?"

"Mic doesn't want me."

I frown. I'm pretty sure I don't want to spend every minute I get with Rulf trying to convince him to speak. "Rulf, please, tell me everything you need to tell me. Don't do this thing where you keep it all inside."

Rulf pauses for a bit and stares at me. I know he's always liked me. Not... not like I like Hemot, but he's always been kind to me. Even when I would bump into him in the streets of Sevord, before we even became friends, he would give me what I think might be Rulf's version of a smile and even sometimes help me get a better deal at the market.

He takes a deep breath and grunts again before saying, "Mic doesn't like it when I say he's enchanted. He looks at me like I'm the bad guy. I keep trying to get him to draw his sword to cancel the enchantment, but he just gets mad at me. This morning, after we reached the city, he sent me away. I'm not part of his guard anymore."

My heart goes out to him, and I want to give Rulf another hug. I just don't think I can manage with the smell. I know how much Mic, or Prince Roran, means to Rulf. Rulf has practically raised Mic from just such a young age. The big guy is actually younger than Prince Roran, but with his magical giant blood... he grew up faster than everyone else.

"So, what are you going to do now?"

"I'm guarding you."

"But I already have a guard."

"I know. Captain Granel assigned me to join the guard."

"You mean the guard that you just pushed through?"

"Yeah, that one. I'm supposed to report to the lead guard for duty."

"Perhaps," I say slowly, "that might have been a better idea than to push your way through them."

Rulf looks back and examines Denner, who's currently watching Rulf like a hawk. Rulf slowly nods. "Yes, I think that would have been a better approach."

He turns and walks back toward the guard. I move off to join my mama. I don't really want to hear how Rulf's conversation with Denner will go. It'll frustrate me.

A little while later, Rulf joins me. "He tells me I'm on duty in an hour. So, while I'm waiting, I'll stay here and eat your food."

My mama laughs at that, but then frowns when she realizes he's not joking. "You're definitely Traltor and Nareesa's son."

Rulf just grunts and then asks, "I look like them?"

"Yes, that too," my mama says with a bit of a smile.

We sit down by the fire, and Rulf stares into the flames. Without looking at either my mom or me, he says, "Mic's enchanted."

"I know." My voice comes out so quietly, I wonder at first if he can hear.

"Do you know that you gave him the enchantment?"

"I do." I feel the tears well up in my eyes. "I didn't know what I was doing."

Rulf nods. "Not your fault, girl."

"Rulfor!" My mama does not raise her voice often, but I think Rulf has a way of pushing people. "My daughter is not to be spoken to in such a manner. You will call her the Lady Marleet. I recognize that you were responsible for bringing her back to me, and I will not deny your courage or kindness in doing so, but I will be pleased to hear you speak to her with respect. At the very least, you will call her by her given name. But 'girl' will never do."

Rulf slowly looks up at my mama as if seeing her for the first time. As he moves his head, he reaches down into his pocket, pulls something out, shoves it into his mouth, and begins to chew.

My mama is a patient woman, so she just sits there and waits. I'm surprised at how long it takes Rulf to finish that mouthful.

When he finally swallows, he nods. "Yes, Lady Aldora. I will respect that. Please accept my apology. Neither the Prince nor I have lived among Nobles for many years.

He has adapted well. I have not. I will do my best to speak with respect to you and your daughter.”

My mama smiles. “All is well, my dear Rulfor.”

I didn’t know Rulf had it in him to speak in such a manner, but I’m pleased. I prefer this Rulf to the grunter-Rulf.

“I am sorry, Rulf. I would never want to pass on an enchantment.”

“You are not to blame, Lady Marleet.”

Somehow, I don’t like being called Lady Marleet by Rulf, but I have to accept it now. Instead of commenting on that, I ask, “Can you really tell if there’s an enchantment on someone?”

He grunts.

“Can you tell if there is still one on me?”

He looks me up and down and shakes his head. “If there is one, it’s not a strong one anymore.”

I don’t like the sound of that. I want a yes or a no. “How can we know for sure?”

“I only know one way,” Rulf explains. “I can smell it on someone.”

My mom begins to protest, but Rulf just stands up, leans down, pushes his nose onto my head, and sniffs as hard as he can. I’m surprised by how long he can suck in air, but I just stay still. I have to know.

When he finally finishes, he goes back to his seat. He settles down and stares into the fire.

I wait while he collects his thoughts or whatever he’s doing. I’m sure my hair is a mess, and I want to use my fingers to fix it, but I’m also sure some of my hair went up his nose.

I don’t want to touch my hair. Perhaps ever again.

I continue to wait for a long time before I realize that Rulf has no intention of telling me if he smells an enchantment.

"Rulf, tell me if you smelled an enchantment on me!"

"Oh, sorry Mar... Lady Marleet. I didn't smell one on you. I thought you knew because I didn't frown."

"I thought you were frowning."

Rulf looks down as if he can see his own face. "No. This is my happy look."

My mama lets out a quiet laugh. "There's an easier way to tell if you're enchanted, my dear. I did not realize this was a concern of yours. I would have helped you with this."

"What do we have to do to confirm that I'm free?"

My mama gives me one of her sweet smiles. "No enchantment leaves room for it to be questioned. The very fact that you're wondering if you are enchanted is proof that you are not. To question it is to have power over the enchantment. If you can say out loud that you might be enchanted, you are not enchanted."

"I might be enchanted."

"Do you feel any struggle inside?" my mama asks.

"I feel a lot of worry and fear."

"If you were enchanted, you would feel a struggle inside—as if you are fighting against yourself."

"I don't feel that."

"Then, my dear, you are not enchanted."

I smile at my mama. I am so happy to be with her. I love her so much, and I can't imagine my life without her. As much as I want to be with my friends right now, I'm glad I'm here with her.

Unfortunately, this is the last I see of her for a long time.

7

The Soldiers

Three soldiers gallop toward our little encampment. Not many soldiers on horseback gallop, as the risk of trampling someone is so great. This must be an emergency.

They dismount near my personal guard. One of the new arrivals speaks quickly, waving his arms. I don't recognize any of the three who just approached our camp.

Finally, Denner comes to me. "Lady Marleet, I apologize for the intrusion, but your father, the Lord Yune, has requested your presence. He is to the northwest of us. With your permission, I will lead you to him."

Rulf grunts and announces, "I'm going too."

Denner frowns at Rulf. "No, you will remain here until I return."

My mama steps forward. "Perhaps Rulfor should go with my daughter as well. It is, of course, your decision, Sergeant, but I would consider it a personal favor if you were to allow him to stay close to my daughter."

The man bows. "Of course, my Lady." He turns back to Rulf. "You may join us as the Lady Marleet's personal bodyguard."

Rulf grunts his approval. Or disapproval. Who knows?

My mama embraces me and gives me a kiss on my cheek. She then leads me to a bag which Mildren had packed. My parents insist that whenever I go anywhere, I always have a small pack with a few supplies with me. I suit up with my armor and sword, and then go with the men.

My armor fits well over the dress. It's beautiful yet simple and fairly easy to walk in.

The men who have just arrived offer me the horse, but Denner refuses. He explains that if I were to sit a little higher than everyone else, I would be an easier target for the Shaloomd. It seems a little paranoid since the skies are clear, but my dad explained that I need to listen to their direction.

We walk for hours. It was already late in the day when the orders came for me to go to my papa, and now the sun has nearly set.

Due to the hundreds and hundreds of encampments spread throughout the area, we have to weave back and forth among the people, and it takes a long time. When we finally reach the edge of the massive procession of people, the sun has completely set. We stop at one of the last fires to get a few torches, and the men lead us out, walking a short distance in front of us.

Away from the people, we might be in greater danger from Shaloomd, but the creatures don't hunt at night. As we move, I find my personal guard moves closer to me. I see Denner growing more nervous by the second.

After another few minutes, Denner calls out, "Soldier, how far is the Lord Yune from the encampment?"

The soldier calls back, "About half a mile."

"Why is he so far?"

"I am unaware of his reasons. I didn't feel I should question a Duke. Are you questioning the Duke's orders?"

"My orders are to keep the Duke's daughter safe. If that means questioning the orders of the Duke, then that is exactly what I'll do!" Denner comes to a halt along with the rest of my personal guard. Rulf grunts next to me. I glance over and see his hand on the hilt of his sword—not that Rulf needs a sword.

The soldiers who came to fetch me come back—the one who had been doing all the talking is in a rage. I see he's the same rank as Denner. I don't know if that means one has to listen to the other or what.

He stands in front of my guard for a moment, and his eyes flick quickly to Rulf before he nods. "Then stay here. I'll go meet with Lord Yune and ask him to come back to see you. Perhaps he will think that's a good idea."

He walks off shaking his head, mumbling something about soldiers thinking Dukes will come to them.

Denner turns back to me and stares at me for a moment. It makes me uncomfortable.

Finally, he hands his torch to one of the other soldiers and asks, "Lady Marleet, will you give me your counsel?"

I've never been asked for my counsel before. I can't imagine that I might give good counsel, but I don't think I have any choice but to do it.

"Yes, Sergeant."

"My Lady, I don't feel good about this. If it is your father requesting this, then I should take you to him, but I think… something is not right. I would recommend we ignore the Sergeant's orders and return to the camp. The soldiers guarding the boundaries will offer extra protection for my Lady, and we can remain with them until we have further clarification from the Lord Yune. But, if you wish, we will remain here."

I have no idea what to say. I wish he would just make the decision. But I know I have to say something, so I say, "We should return to the camp." I feel good about that. I will feel safer with more people around.

"Yes, my Lady."

I start to turn but feel myself pulled out of the way as one of my soldiers lunges for me. Rulf's bulky torso blocks out any view of what happened for a moment, but then I catch sight of the man. He hadn't lunged for me. A crossbow bolt sticks out of his back.

"Protect the Lady!" Rulf bellows as more of my guard goes down.

He wraps his arms around me, and I feel my feet leave the ground as he turns us back toward the camp. A bolt slams into his shoulder not too far from my own shoulder, and he turns to the right, away from the camp, rushing past the bodies.

I can't make out anything as Rulf runs. My body just flops around as he jumps and leaps and bounds along. After a while, he drops me and orders me to run.

I don't see any of the rest of my papa's soldiers. It's just the two of us now.

Rulf runs behind me. I don't believe it's because I'm faster than he is. Now and then, I hear a thud, followed by a grunt. He's acting as a shield for me. The only way he's surviving is because of his giant blood. The skin of a giant is better than most armor.

I hear the sound of horses in the distance. They can't move fast along the rolling hills of the Talic Region, but they will certainly outpace us soon.

I try to get my bearings. We seem to be heading northwest. I can't tell that from the stars—I've never been able to read that kind of thing. But I see the lights of Leito. It's to the west of us and we're heading on an angle that will take us to the right of the city.

There should be plenty of soldiers all through this area. If my papa's waiting for me, we might even come across him.

Rulf grunts again as he runs. He doesn't struggle with running like full-blooded humans do. I'm sure he gets tired, but it's like he doesn't notice it.

"Oooph!" Again, another grunt.

"Are you okay, Rulf?" I want to do something to protect him, but I know he doesn't need it. I'll just end up getting myself killed.

Confusion floods through me. I suddenly come to the realization that I have no idea why they want to kill me! I try to think about it, but then lose my concentration and trip.

Strong hands yank me to my feet, and in another moment, I'm running again. I'll focus on running for now.

The hard part of traveling through the Talic Region when you're not on the roads is the grass covering the rolling hills. It's very thick, and if I'm not careful, my feet tangle in it with just about every step. I have to concentrate to lift my feet high.

"How many are there?" I call back.

"Too many."

"That's not an answer—at least not a proper one! Rulf, tell me how many are back there!"

"At least fifty. Maybe more."

"Fifty! How are we going to survive? We can't run forever, and we can't fight that many!"

Rulf grunts. I think he agrees with me.

We run on. I still have my endurance from running across Sevord just a week or so ago, yet I'm gasping for air. I think I feel pretty good, though. The more I run, the less tired I am. I think I just need to move!

It's a good thing, too, because a few more crossbow bolts whiz by me.

Rulf grunts as another one hit him. "This isn't going to work."

"It's not going to work?" I don't know what he means. "Are you talking about running? What other choice do we have?"

Sometimes Rulf frustrates me. I wish he would just say when he means.

"Yes."

"Ahhh!" I focus in on my feet again. I don't want to trip. "Rulf, what are you talking about?"

"We can't keep running. You need to go ahead. I'm going to go back and deal with the soldiers."

"But you can't deal with fifty soldiers!" A moment of doubt passes over me. "Wait, can you?"

"Don't know. Never dealt with so many at once. The most I've fought at one time is about twenty."

"How did that go?"

"Fine, until they all piled on top of me."

"What happened then?"

"They held me until I promised not to hurt them if they let me go."

"Did you hurt them?"

"No. I wanted to, but I promised."

I don't want him to leave me. And I don't want him to get hurt. But then, I'm not sure if he can get hurt.

"Listen, Marleet. I have to go back. You can't. You have to keep going. We don't know how many soldiers are trying to kill you."

"Why are they trying to kill me?" My voice comes out in a panic. I'm desperate to get out of this whole situation.

"Listen! Don't interrupt! I don't know why they want you dead, but they do. I'm going to go slow them down, but you have to keep running. Try to get to Haner. I think Caric might have gone there. Find him. He's small, weak, and complains a lot, but he's got a good heart. Find him, but don't come back. Not until you know it's safe!"

"Wait…" But it's too late. He's turned around, and I already hear him charging the soldiers behind us, his guttural growls blocking out the sound of even the horses.

I have no choice but to run on.

I wrap my cloak around myself and shiver.

In all the times I slept outside in the Talic Region, I guess I never found out how cold it could be.

Without a fire burning nearby, it's cold.

Alone in the dark, it's cold.

Afraid I'll be found and killed, it's cold.

My cloak doesn't quite cover me.

I pull off my pack, and the cold reaches the spots previously covered. I quickly find my blanket, seal up the pack again, and wrap myself up. I cover my face and hope I'll be okay.

I've cried a lot in the last few hours. The soldiers haven't caught up with me. They're either dealt with, or they can't track me in the dark.

I hope Rulf finds me.

I hope Rulf is still alive.

8

The 'orse and 'ow

I push on until I reach the road leading north and south between Leito and Haner. I hope maybe I can find Terr and Gerr along the way, although I expect they're far ahead of me.

Gerr, however, is missing her leg. That might slow her down.

I can't believe I'm happy that a woman is missing a leg. I think that's the most selfish thought I've ever had.

I pass traders on the road, along with plenty of men and women heading south. In fact, hundreds of people head south along this road.

When we traveled this road a couple weeks ago, it was just for a short bit, but there had only been a few people on the road. Now, it's a steady procession.

At first, I didn't know why they're all out traveling. It seemed strange to me.

Then about an hour ago, I overheard one of the men talking about the Prince. I notice most people carry swords and wear old armor. They're going to join the Free Armies of Sevord to see the Prince back to the throne.

I'm glad about that, but I feel sick to my stomach about it at the same time. I'm afraid of what the enchantment did to Roran. And I'm afraid how it'll change him as a King. Whoever is behind this likely wants Roran on the throne so they can control the King.

As I walk, I try to think things through. That's what Caric and Ellcia would do. I know it's a smart way to do stuff.

I try to figure out why those soldiers would want to kill me—ME? I'm nobody. I mean, I know I'm somebody, but until recently, I was just a servant girl from the castle. I don't know anything. I don't have any power or anything.

Now… my mama and papa… they have power and influence. But the soldiers can't be killing me because of them. I'm worth more to my parents alive than dead. Besides, none of them even knew I was alive until a couple weeks ago. Killing me would have no benefit to anyone. Other than to make my parents mad. But what would that accomplish? What would it accomplish to have an angry Lord Yune and Lady Aldora?

I step in something unpleasant and decide I no longer want to walk behind that horse. I move off the road, pick up speed, and get in front, then go back to a normal walk.

Unless it has to do with the Prince. He's acting strange and definitely under an enchantment. What do they want… wait… Prince Roran is attracted to me because of the enchantment. If I were to die, it wouldn't just be an angry Lord and Lady… Roran would be angry.

I don't think it would benefit them to make my parents angry. They are influencers, not decision-makers.

But Prince Roran. If he were angry, he might hunt down the killers with the army.

The soldiers who tried to kill me wouldn't be interested in being hunted down themselves, but if they could frame someone…

I'm almost at Haner. The gates are just a short distance away. There still aren't too many people moving toward the city. Most move south toward the army. I haven't seen Terr and Gerr yet. They must have made it there already. Could I have missed them on the road coming back this way?

Now the soldiers… They couldn't frame my parents. That wouldn't make sense. They couldn't frame the Prince. He would be the last person right now to try to kill me.

Who is a threat?

I stop in my tracks as it comes to me, earning me a few loud insults from the two men walking behind me. They pass by, and I start up again.

There are two… no, three threats right now.

The first is Prince Roran. They tried to take him out, and that didn't work, so they enchanted him. Then they tried to get rid of Caric, but we got him out of danger. Now, an attempt on my life would cause the Prince to ask who would do such a thing. The General… General Lirnal… if the General is accused, the Prince might turn on him.

Those are the three who stand next in line to inherit the throne. Once they're all out of the way, there's only the Regent.

I understand. This is about the throne.

It's always been about the throne.

I don't know what to do about it yet, but I do know this: I have to survive to let them know the General was not one of the soldiers who attacked me. I guess they could always argue he had ordered the murder, but I don't know what to do about that. I won't accuse General Lirnal.

I pass through the gates.

The guards might have glanced at me at one point, but no one pays me much attention. It's one advantage of being small. It's late in the day, and I don't want to be caught out in the streets at night, so I find a soldier and ask for directions to the Horse and Bow. He gives them to me, but I can't seem to understand how to follow them. So, I ask for how to find my way to Lord Hillbin's home. Those directions seem a little easier to follow. It's just straight north.

Apparently, I can't miss it.

Apparently, I can.

I find myself in an area of the city that seems dangerous—and there's not much light left. I ask a soldier how to find Lord Hillbin's home, and he laughs. It's a long ways away—way behind me. I decide to ask where the Horse and Bow Inn is, and he laughs again.

"You mean the 'orse and 'ow!"

"Sure." I'm not in the mood for silly conversation. I'm really tired.

"It's just over there. If you're looking for a room, though, I think they're full. Phil's been busy lately."

I thank the soldier and head where he pointed. When I enter, no one even glances my way. I find a pretty young woman cleaning one of the tables. She smiles at me.

"Excuse me, I'm looking to speak with the owner of the inn—Phil. I need to speak to Phil."

She smiles again, but looks like she's about to laugh at me. She whispers, "We don't get too many of your kind here."

"My kind?"

The woman leans in. "Nobles."

I glance around. For the first time, I realize that it's probably not a smart idea to let people know that I'm Nobleborn. I have heard rumors of the children of Nobles getting kidnapped and ransomed back to their parents.

"Don't worry, my Lady," the woman says quietly with another smile. "I won't tell anyone."

"How did you know?"

"Under your cloak, I can see a bit of your dress. You also carry yourself like a Noble. And… I'm just good at recognizing such things. You weren't born a commoner, that's for sure."

I don't know what to say to that, so I hold my tongue.

"Come with me."

A few of the patrons call out for refills, but the young woman just waves them off. They don't sound pleased, but they also don't do anything else other than complain.

She steps through a doorway into a short hall, but stops before she enters the kitchen. "Where's my pa?"

A man growls back, "He's upstairs."

The woman waves for me to follow, and we climb some well-worn stairs. When we get to the top, she wanders down the hallway until she finds an open door. "Pa?"

"Eh?"

She leads me into the room, and a large man with an odd look on his face stands in the corner, pulling a shelf apart. The room is in shambles.

The woman looks around as if to confirm no one else is here and then whispers, "Pa, this is a Noblewoman. She's looking to speak with you."

The man turns around and gasps. He charges toward me, and I nearly turn and run away, but he gets to me too quickly. He drops to his knees and cries out, "ou're ali!"

I just stare at him. I think he's a little on the crazy-side of things.

"Pa!" the woman says. "You're going to need to speak clearly. This is a Noblewoman. You can't expect her to put the effort into finishing your words for you."

"Oh, right. Sorry." He stands up and smiles at me. When he speaks, he looks like he's putting a lot of effort into it. "You are Lady Aldora's daughter. There's no doubt about it, my Lady. You look so much like her. I see your father in you as well, but your mother's beauty has blessed this world by gracing you with its presence."

I think to myself that I almost prefer his previous way of speaking. I decide the best response is simply to stare at him with a confused look on my face.

"Pa!"

"Oh, right. Sorry again, my Lady. Thank you for your visit. How may I be of service to My Lady?"

I want to stare at him again with that look of confusion. I'm not really sure how to say what I need, but I just dive in and hope for the best.

"General Lirnal believes you can be trusted, so I have come here. There was an attempt on my life, and I barely escaped. I'm trying to find my friends, and I think they might have been here recently."

"May I ask the names of your friends?"

"Hemot, Ellcia, and Caric, or Prince Draydon."

He bows to me and gives me a big smile. "They were here, the young Prince Draydon and his friends, although I had to pretend I did not know them. Then Terr and Gerr, old friends from long ago came, spoke with Prince Draydon, and he and his two friends had to leave the very next morning."

My shoulders slump, and I feel the tears in my eyes. I missed them. I've come all this way and missed them.

"When did they leave?"

"Ah, my poor dear Lady. Do not weep. It breaks my heart to see you in your grief. They left only the morning of yesterday. If you rush, you might catch them. But you cannot travel west on your own. The Shaloomd will take someone of your size without a second thought.”

“I have to. I must reach them.” I pause for a moment before asking, “Do you know where they were going?”

He shakes his head. “Forgive me, my Lady. I did not ask for details. I knew they were heading west from here toward Sevord, but I don’t know anything else. I did not ask as I did not feel it was my right to know the business of royals.”

The tears begin to flow freely down my face. I know I can’t leave right now. It’s getting dark, and I cannot travel through the night. My only hope is to leave first thing in the morning, but by then, they’ll be two days ahead of me. I’ll never catch up. And when I get to Sevord or even to Switcher Pass, assuming I make it past the Shaloomd, I won’t have any idea of where to look for them. I was there when the message was given, but I just don’t remember. They were to go somewhere to settle in. To await orders…

“My Lady,” Phil says in his odd way, struggling to get every word out in a clear manner. “I will give you a room for the night. It will be far from what a Lady of your status deserves, but it will be the best I can give. Tomorrow, I will purchase a horse for you. Perhaps with the horse, you will catch them. I will also provide you with a bloom.”

I don’t know what a bloom is, but I’m hoping it’s helpful.

Phil and his daughter lead me out the door, and his daughter runs downstairs for a moment. I hear her yelling at the men in the tavern, and she comes back up a moment later.

“Wha’ the ‘oblem?”

Phil’s daughter scowls. “Oh, they want refills! I mean, how impatient can you get?”

Phil growls. "Ah dea' wi' 'em." He trundles off down the stairs and disappears out of sight.

"My name's Laanna."

"I'm Marleet."

"Yes, my Lady."

"No, I mean, please call me Marleet. I only just found out that I'm Nobleborn a couple of weeks ago." I pause for just a moment. I don't know why I'm asking Laanna this, but it seems right. "I'd just like someone to call me by my name."

Laanna smiles at me. "Okay, Marleet. I'll call you by your first name when we're alone, but if there are other people around who know your identity, calling you by your first name is a good way to get in a lot of trouble."

Laanna waves me to follow her. We wander down the hall to a small door which looks like a closet. Laanna pulls out a key and shoves it in, unlocking the door, and then pushing it open.

When we step in, I'm shocked to see a beautifully decorated room. I've never stayed in a room like this before. I've helped clean rooms like this in the castle, although they were much larger, but never thought for a moment that I could actually stay in one.

The door closes behind me and locks. I spin around and go for my sword, but Laanna puts her hands up. In a whisper, she says, "I'm sorry, Marleet, my Lady. I didn't mean to threaten you. This room is secret. It's only used for Nobles staying on business when they do not wish to be found. I believe that is the case for you, no? I locked it just in case someone comes by and happens to push open the door."

I relax, but I still feel a little on edge. I let go of my sword, and Laanna lowers her hands.

She calms down her breathing a bit before continuing. I hadn't realized how much I scared her. "You are welcome to eat downstairs, or we can bring a meal up to you. Do you have a preference?"

"I'd like to eat up here, if I can."

"Of course, my Lady. Would you also like a bath?"

I look around and, off to the side, is a bathtub. I'm a little surprised. I can't imagine how they could secretly get hot water in here and then out again. That kind of thing takes a lot of work and makes a lot of mess. I've done it enough times to know.

I'm about to say yes—I do love a good bath—but then I politely decline. Something about taking a bath in a place I don't know seems awkward. I smell, there's no doubt about it, but I feel uncomfortable with it.

"I will bring your meal up in about an hour. If there's anything else you need, just come down and find me, but please lock the door when you leave."

I take the key and see her out. I lock it behind her and drop my pack on the floor, then make my way to the bed. It's soft. Not just a little soft, it's like I'm sinking down inside and may never stop sinking.

9

The Leaving

I awake to the sound of quiet knocking on the door. I feel like the knocking has been going on for a while.

I'm shocked that I fell asleep. I didn't know I was that tired.

I reach the door and hear Laanna's voice. "My Lady. Are you ready for your meal?"

Once the door is unlocked, Laanna slips inside, motioning for me to lock it behind her. In her hands is a small tray with a lot of food.

She walks it over to a small table and curtsies to me before asking if there's anything else I need.

"Will you join me? There's enough food for two."

Her eyebrows shoot up at the request, and her mouth drops open, but after a moment, she smiles and says, "Yes, Marleet. I will join you."

We sit down at the table and begin to work through the meal. It's good—really good. I have to show some restraint, though. I'm hungrier than I realized, and I'm afraid if I don't hold back, I'll eat all the food and maybe the tray as well.

Laanna smiles at me. "Now, if I didn't need to keep it secret, I could brag to people that I ate with a Prince, a Noblewoman, and a Duke's son, and now I'm eating with the daughter of the most powerful Noble family in the kingdom."

I laugh. "I'm no different than I was before I found out I was Nobleborn."

"But before you found out, you were still Nobleborn."

"Didn't make much difference."

"No, maybe not. I don't know why you didn't know you were Nobleborn before, but it will one day be fun to brag about this."

I laugh. "Were the others… were they okay?"

"They were. The boys were quite cute."

A wave of jealously comes over me, but I catch myself. "Did they mention me?"

"I'm sorry, Marleet. I don't remember them mentioning you. I'm sure they were thinking of you all the time."

"Did you talk to them much?"

She shakes her head. "But…" A wicked smile comes over her lips, and she looks at me in a funny way. "I did have a lot of fun with them, at least until the end."

"At the end? What do you mean?"

"Well, the Lady Ellcia is quite protective of Prince Draydon, and I don't mean because she thinks he'll get hurt. She has her eye on him. So, I kept pretending like I was interested in the Prince, just to annoy her."

"What happened at the end?"

She smiles, but she also seems embarrassed. "I put my hand on the Prince's arm, and she was… not happy. I crossed a line somewhere, so I backed off."

"And what about Hemot?"

"The Milterite? What about him?"

I realize I don't actually have anything to ask. I know Hemot's always liked Ellcia more than me. I… I don't have anything to ask at all.

When I look up again, Laanna has that wicked smile on her face again. "Ah, I see."

I feel uncomfortable. "Well, I think I should probably head to bed now. Thank you for eating with me, Laanna."

Laanna laughs and gets up. When she reaches the door, she stops. "Marleet, I'm sorry I made you uncomfortable. I didn't mean anything by that. You're asking about the Duke's son. Hemot, right?"

I nod.

"What is it you wish to know?"

I shake my head. "I don't know."

"Lady Ellcia and Prince Draydon are quite close—I can see they have strong feelings for one another." Laanna smiles at me. "But the Duke's son… it's normally the four of you, right?"

I nod.

"And that means that you and Hemot likely spend a lot of time together."

I nod yet again.

"And you have your eye on Hemot?"

I don't know what else to do. I just nod.

"Does he know how you feel about him?"

I shake my head, and tears roll down my cheeks.

"What's the problem?"

I'm about to just ask her to leave, when it all comes out. "I don't just have my eye on Hemot. I love Hemot. I want to marry him. But he has his eye on just about every other woman—even Ellcia. He's never been interested in me, other than as a friend. And now, Prince Roran wants to marry me and make me his Queen when he becomes King, but he doesn't want me, it's just an enchantment, and if I marry the Prince, then I'll lose any chance I'll ever have of getting Hemot to notice me."

Laanna stares at me for a moment. I see she doesn't quite know what to say. After a bit, she comes in close and hugs me. It's actually just what I need, and the tears and sobs just come out.

When I've calmed down a little, she steps back and puts her hands on my shoulders. "Listen, Marleet. I don't know Hemot. I don't know the others, either. But I can tell you that you are one of the most beautiful women I've ever seen. If Hemot hasn't noticed that yet, he's walking around with his eyes closed. But you… you shouldn't worry about that kind of thing. Just get back together with your friends. And as for Prince Roran wanting to marry you, but it being an enchantment, I don't understand that. I've never understood enchantments. I'm not really even sure they exist." She takes a deep breath and gives a sad smile. "Not everyone gets exactly what they want in life. I don't know if you will or won't. But here's what I've learned from my pa and his war buddies: the goal is not to get what you want; the goal is to do the right thing. Walk the road that's before you to the best of your ability, and let the rest work itself out. There's nothing you can do about Hemot right now, other than find him. So, that's what you need to do right now."

I give her a smile, and she gives me another hug. When she lets go, she walks to the door but stops. "Is it your desire to leave first thing in the morning, Marleet?"

"It is."

"Then we will wake you early."

Once she leaves, I lock the door, then sit on the bed, thinking about what she said. She's right. I know she's right. There's nothing I can do about any of it, other than to find Hemot and the others. So, that's what I'll do, and I won't worry about Roran right now—other than to stay away from him.

I change out of my dress and into something easier to sleep in. Once I lay back, it's not long before I'm sound asleep.

Laanna doesn't wake me early, for which I am grateful. The sun is well up by the time she knocks on my door with my morning meal. I would have thought they'd get me on the road at first light, but they likely know what's best.

She leaves my meal with me and tells me that when I'm ready, I should come down into the kitchen.

I get myself all packed up again and my dress back on. When I'm ready to go, I head downstairs and find Phil waiting for me with a big smile. There's also a big man hard at work in the kitchen, but he just focuses on the meal he's making.

"My Lady Marleet," Phil says, struggling with every word, "Would you like to leave immediately?"

"Yes, I would, thank you." I don't like ordering people around. I'm used to other people telling me what I should do, but I'm trying my best to be a Nobleborn. It's hard.

"Then follow me, if it pleases you."

I follow him out the back and find a horse, saddled and ready to go. I'm thrilled with this at first, as it means I'll make better time, but then my stomach drops. I have never actually ridden a horse, and from what I've heard, it's not easy.

Phil pulls out a strange contraption and brings it to me. "Have you ever used a bloom?"

I shake my head.

He comes around behind me and straps it to my back. It's not the most comfortable thing I've worn, but I'm hoping it has some decent purpose. Maybe it'll keep the sun off me.

When he comes back around, he smiles. "This is designed to protect you from the Shaloomd. If you see one above you, and from here on out, there will be plenty, you simply pull that cord on your shoulder, and it will give the illusion that you are larger than you are.

"The Shalloomd," Phil continues, "rarely bother someone while they are on a horse as they appear too large, but sometimes they do. This will help in those times."

I pull the cord, and the bloom spreads out on either side of me and above my head. It's like a giant umbrella—or a big ugly flower. The Shaloomd will only try to take someone if the person is small enough. If this fools the creatures, it will help get me through.

"Well, my Lady, mount up, and I will lead you to the gate."

I turn to the horse for only a moment, then back to Phil. "I would prefer to walk until we reach the gate."

He bows and says, "Certainly, my Lady."

I take the reins of the horse and am pleased that it moves along with me. I wouldn't know what to do if it didn't come right away. I've heard some horses are easier to ride than others. I hope this one's not one of the hard ones.

Laanna comes out and tells me the pack behind the saddle contains food and water, along with oats for the horse. I'm glad about that. I hadn't thought of actually needing to feed the horse until this moment.

We move out from behind the inn, and I find the streets quite busy. Many of the people wear armor and swords. Most of the men in armor are older—although a few are young. I think these might be old soldiers from wars gone by who are heading out to join the Prince for his return to the castle.

We reach the gate, and Phil whispers, "When I leave you, I will just leave. I won't say anything, as I don't want anyone to know your identity, unless you wish that."

I nod. We take a few more steps and an older soldier waves at Phil.

"Eh! Co' by the i' someti', Gilla'."

I didn't know they spoke a different language in Haner, but fortunately, the guard responds in the language of the capital. "Sounds good, Phil. I'll stop by tonight or tomorrow evening."

I move through the gate, and the horse continues with me. I keep walking, deciding that I'm going to avoid mounting the horse until I'm out of sight of the walls. There are enough hills in the Talic region that it shouldn't be far. I keep my eye on the sky, though. Shaloomd show up when you least expect them.

So far, I don't see any people on this road, and it's not long before I come down behind a hill and can't see the city or anyone. This road is smaller than the main road. I expect it rarely gets a huge amount of traffic.

I bring the horse to a stop and take a good look at it. I think it might be a beautiful, strong horse. There seems to be a lot of muscle on it, and it's tall, but then again, I don't know what makes a horse beautiful. I've seen people talk about horses, though. I know others can tell the difference.

I examine the seat... or... the saddle, I think. It's really high, but I'm thinking if I can get my foot in that little loop down below, I can maybe grab something and use my arms and my leg to get myself up there.

I lead the horse off the road. The ground in the Talic region is soft due to the grass. There's no way I want to fall on the road.

I put my foot in the loop, grab the saddle as best as I can and pull myself up.

I'm very grateful that I moved onto the grass. I stand up from where I've fallen on the far side of the horse and come back around to the same side I started on. I try again, but this time, I manage to stay in the saddle.

I know there are things called reins, and I look around for them. Unfortunately, when I find them, they're hanging off the horse's mouth. I climb down, swing them up toward the saddle, and climb back up again.

Okay, now, I'm on the horse.

I think for a moment. There has to be a special way to get it to move when you're not pulling on the rope—or reins.

I use my hips to lurch forward a bit, hoping that'll help. The horse doesn't seem to notice.

I tell it to go. The horse doesn't seem to speak the same language as me.

I yell at it. The horse doesn't seem to hear. Perhaps it's deaf. Or… it doesn't respond to yelling.

Finally, in frustration, I snap the reins down, and the horse moves forward. I almost fall off again, but I laugh as the horse just moves back onto the road on its own. I think it's maybe done this kind of thing before.

I think at first that I might be able to do this, but then I realize that we're barely moving. The horse will help to protect me from the Shaloomd, but it's also supposed to help me catch up to Hemot. At the moment, I can walk faster.

I lurch my hips forward to speed it up, but I remember that didn't work the last time. I snap the reins again and holler, "Faster!" and the horse picks up speed.

That's great and all, but now I'm bouncing all over the place in the saddle.

I try to grip a bit tighter with my legs, and it helps.

At this speed, I should catch them. Well, maybe. It might take me a day or two.

18

---•---

The Shaloomd

I pull the cord on the bloom, and the contraption spreads out.

Above me, two Shaloomd circle. They haven't approached yet. I don't know if that means they don't think they can pick me up with the bloom and the horse, or if they're just waiting for the right moment.

I think the horse can sense them. It's starting to get upset.

Since I started out a few days before, the Shaloomd have rarely bothered me. I've seen a lot of them flying overhead, but few of them have stayed above me for long. Unfortunately, as they've flown above me, I've seen at least a half-dozen people in their grip.

I expect they're hunting among the soldiers and people moving toward Sevord. I hope none of them are my parents. There are archers spread throughout the army, so I assume it's only those who have wandered away by themselves. My parents wouldn't do that.

I stop that line of thinking. Even if none of the victims are my parents, they're still important people. When I saw the first person in the clutches of a Shaloomd yesterday, I wept for over an hour. I just don't want to think about any of it anymore.

I nearly fall out of the saddle as the horse lurches forward. My legs are so tired, and I think the insides of my legs are worn raw. I'm grateful for the extra speed, but it's so uncomfortable.

At first, I don't know why the horse lurched forward. It does all sorts of strange things.

I listen to its breathing, and I can't help but think it's scared. I look back. There's no one behind me. I look up as best as I can, but there are no Shaloomd in sight.

It's hard to see with the bloom above me, though. I reach up and push it back just a bit. I twist around in the saddle and scream as a Shaloomd swoops down.

The horse lurches forward again. I lose my grip with my legs, and the reins pull out of my hands. I hit the ground hard and roll. It hurts more than I think anything I've ever felt in my life.

I scramble onto my feet. My bloom is torn and hangs in pieces from my back. If I don't get back on the horse, I'll be picked up in moments.

I spin around. The horse is nowhere in sight. I check out the small hills around me. If I run the wrong way, I might never find him.

I run in the direction of the cliffs—the direction I was heading in the first place—and up the side of another of the thousands of small hills in the Talic.

A Shaloomd circles around. I think he's coming for me.

At the top of the hill, I cry out in despair. The horse is not ahead of me. Spinning around, from my height on this hill, I can see my horse. It's heading back toward Haner. Even if I had run that way, I'd never have caught it. A Shaloomd swoops down on it, and the horse runs like it's in a panic.

Something black catches my eye, and I dive off to the side, landing on the soft grass. I try to spread out my bloom, but it just falls back down again. I unclip it and run.

My legs ache—not from running, but from riding. My back hurts too, but it feels good to be off the horse.

A glance over my shoulder drives me to roll onto the grass as the giant bird comes for me. I jump up again and race down the road. I don't know how long I can keep doing this, but if I can catch up with my friends, I'll be safe.

Something grabs me, but I twist out of its grip and hit the ground hard. I keep trying to land on the grass, but this time I hit the road. It hurts.

Two Shaloomd are after me. I can't outrun two. I'll dodge the one, only to be taken by the other.

I go for my sword, but I'm not fast enough.

My feet leave the ground. I scream, but there's no one around to help. Even if they were, what could they do?

I reach for my sword, but the Shaloomd has me with its talons, gripping my shoulders in a way that keeps me from reaching my blade. I can touch the hilt with my left hand, but I'd never get it out.

Looking down, I see it doesn't matter. Even if stab the creature and get out of its grip, the fall will kill me. It's too late.

My heart races. The creature is huge. Its wings spread out on either side, feathers mostly black with streaks of gray. If it weren't about to eat me, it might be a beautiful bird.

The height we've reached is terrifying. It just seems to get higher and higher. I've never imagined what the world might look like from this high up.

I wish I still didn't know.

I decide to think things through. I think that's what Ellcia would do. And Caric. Hemot would just take it as it comes, but I don't think that's a smart move right now. I think following Hemot's way will leave me eaten.

I go through my options.

I can't hurt the Shaloomd as it'll drop me.

I can't climb up, around and onto its back, because that's just ridiculous.

I don't think I can find a way to force it to land. Anything I do could make it drop me. That'll leave me very much dead, and that's what I'm hoping to avoid.

The nest…

I heard that the Shaloomd take you to their nest and feed you to their babies. If that's the case, then that's the place to fight. I'll have to make sure I get my sword out really fast as soon as I'm dropped. I can attack all the birds and drive them away. I'll likely have to kill them. I don't know if I can do that, but I'll try.

We're getting close to the cliffs, and the Shaloomd flies a bit higher still. I can't see any nests, but truthfully, I don't know what to look for.

I make the mistake of looking down again and wish I hadn't. I'm up far too high.

But something below catches my eye. Three people move in a clump down on the road. They're trying to avoid the fate that has taken me.

I recognize the armor and the cloaks. There's no doubt about it. It's my friends.

I almost call out to them, but I catch myself. They can't do anything about the danger I'm in. That just means they'll be upset, but will have to watch as I'm carried away. If I don't survive, it's best if they don't know.

I keep quiet. I think they're looking up at me, but I bring my hands up to cover my face as best I can with the limited movement I have.

Shame washes over me. Since I'm above them, they'll be able to see up my dress! I think through what I might be able to do about that, but none of my ideas will work.

I close my eyes and feel my face grow red. I just hope I'm high enough that they can't see well.

I open my eyes and scream out involuntarily. We're almost at the cliffs and dead ahead is a nest! We're moving fast, but I can see a bunch of creatures scrambling around.

Now's the time to act.

I bend my right arm at the elbow, just enough to move it a little closer to my sword. With my left hand, I feel the sheath of my knife. I'll need to reach over with my right hand for the sword and reach up with my left hand for the knife, pulling both weapons out at the same time.

The Shaloomd hovers over her nest, and I look down to see six of the ugliest creatures I've ever seen in my life. Each one with a sharp beak snapping up at me.

I feel the talons release, and I drop.

Before I've hit the nest, my knife is out. My sword comes out just after I land, and I slash at the little Shaloomds coming for me. One drops right away, and the others back off, snapping and hissing.

I run behind them and put my back to the cliff face. I don't know what the adult Shaloomd is going to do, but I want to see it coming.

Swinging my sword again, I instantly kill a little Shaloomd and injure another. That's two down, one injured; three to go, plus a big one.

The birds are smart—smarter than I would have thought. They split up, and one goes around to my right while the other two go around to my left.

Before I can do anything about the little ones, the adult Shaloomd lands and lets out something between a squawk and a roar, but loud enough to shake the entire nest.

I fight down the urge to cover my ears. Instead, I charge at the two little ones coming at me from my left, stabbing the one through its chest and slashing at the other. The one I miss jumps back, but loses its footing, dropping off the side. A moment later, the adult Shaloomd goes after it.

Only one more little Shaloomd plus the injured one.

I turn around just as the little one that had gone to my right reaches me. It sinks its teeth into my arm, but my armor protects me from the sharp beak. The only thing it doesn't protect me from is the pressure, and I cry out, dropping my sword. I stab at it with my left hand and drive my knife right into its side.

Without thinking, I toss this little Shaloomd over the edge, pick up my sword, and bring it down on the injured one.

Now there's just the adult Shaloomd to worry about, unless it manages to catch the little one.

I rush to the side of the nest and look over. The height makes me dizzy, but I force myself to focus. I see it coming back up. I can't tell if it's alone.

I turn around and look to see what I can do to help protect myself. I can't imagine the big one will be as easy to kill as the little ones.

There's not much to use, other than a lot of sticks, both brown ones and white ones. I quickly look away from the white sticks. Thinking too much about them will make me sick.

I grab two long, sharp, solid looking brown sticks and take them to the back of the nest. I hear the sound of the Shaloomds's wing beats. It's close.

I run the sticks into the back of the nest, driving each one in as far as I can and leaving the sharp edges pointing out. I set them in far enough apart that I can stand between them and not have to worry about hitting them, but the adult Shaloomd will have trouble with them if its wings are out.

The Shaloomd lands, and I'm pleased to see it's alone—although it seems quite upset about that. It walks toward me with its wings stretched out, letting loose with its squawk and roar combo.

Standing firm, I hold my sword in front of me. My heart races in my chest, and my breaths come out in rapid gasps, but I find if I focus my thinking on just dealing with it, I can get through. I want to just hide somewhere, but that's not an option. I killed six. I just have to kill one more—one really big one—and I can survive.

The Shaloomd hesitates for just a moment, then charges at me. I step back without thinking, tripping on the edge of the nest and slamming back against the rock wall of the cliff, but the two sticks I set up work perfectly. The Shaloomd roars in agony as each stick pierces a wing.

I take my chance and charge forward, driving my sword into the Shaloomd's chest. I pull it out right away and slash at the creature, but I miss as it stumbles back. I refuse to wait for it to recover and go at it again. This time, when my sword enters the giant bird, the creature meets its end.

The Shaloomd slumps to the ground, and I pull my sword out. After cleaning it on the creature's feathers, I turn around, looking for a way out of the nest.

I run to the side of the cliff, but stop.

It's so quiet. There's the wind noise, but that's it. The creatures are all dead. They're truly dead.

My hands shake, and dizziness overcomes me, dropping me to my knees. It all happened so fast. I feel guilty for killing the Shaloomds, but then again, I don't. I'm not sure what I feel, but I don't like any of it.

I wonder if this is how Caric felt when he had to kill the giant. I hate what I've had to do.

What makes it worse is that I'm hundreds of feet up in the air on the side of a cliff. My eyes are on the floor of the nest, but I know there's no set of stairs leading down… or up. I may have stopped them from eating me, but I only have a limited amount of food. What will I eat?

And I can't believe I fought off seven Shaloomd and survived!

"I can do this!" My voice is quiet. I take a slow, deep breath. "I CAN DO THIS!"

I expect my voice to echo, but it doesn't. The sound just fades away in the wide-open space behind me.

Still on my knees, I look around. The cliff face goes up for a long way—a LONG way. Going to the side of the nest and looking down doesn't make me feel any better. I see the ground far below me, but that's the problem—it's FAR below. Even if I had rope, I'd never make it.

But I'm pretty sure I can't climb up. I examine the cliff face again, running my hands along it. There's no moss growing on it, although I would have thought there might be. There sure was a lot of moss on the cliffs in Switcher Pass, but maybe that doesn't happen here.

But what there is… are cracks…

The cliff itself goes up for a while, but I think I'm a lot closer to the top than to the bottom. I'm sure I can't climb down if I can't see where my feet are. But if I get to the top, maybe I can find a safe way down from up there.

I pull off my pack and dig inside. I eat a bit of food and drink a bit of water. Then I change out of my dress and into some pants and a comfortable shirt—something I should have done at the inn. I feel embarrassed to change out here in the open, but I'm assuming no one can see me.

I don't like wearing pants. I always prefer a dress, but I can't climb with all that material around my ankles.

When I'm done, I empty my pack of everything I don't think I need. I drop all the food, except for enough for two more small meals. I pour out some of my stored water, hoping I can find more on top of the cliff. I even leave my dress. It's just a traveling dress, but it's beautiful. I don't want to leave it, but it weighs too much.

I keep my traveling cloak, my sword, and my knife, even though they're all heavy. At least I'm carrying less now.

My hands hurt almost immediately once I start up the rock cliff. I find enough handholds and footholds that I don't have a problem climbing. It's just everything scrapes my fingertips and my knuckles.

I climb until my hands feel almost numb, then make the mistake of looking back down again. At this height, if I landed right in the nest, I would still die. If I missed the nest, I would have a long fall.

I heave myself up a little farther, and when I look up, I see something different about the cliff. I can't quite tell what it is yet, but in a moment it should become clear.

Another few minutes, and my hand lands on something different—a handhold that's larger than most. I push with my legs and get my face higher until I see a ledge. I heave and pull and find that just getting onto that ledge seems harder than the entire climb so far.

Once I've settled on the small landing, gasping for air, I close my eyes. My arms feel like they're ready to fall off.

Maybe just a little nap.

I shake myself awake. I still don't know how safe I am from Shaloomd up here. Besides, the ledge I'm on isn't much deeper than a chair. It's great to sit on, but if I slip at all in my sleep, I'm gone.

After climbing to my feet, I shuffle along the side of the cliff. The ledge leads along for a short distance and then stops, so I head the other way. After a few minutes, I find it slants upwards. I hope this is a good thing. With my back to the cliff, I shuffle along, doing my best not to slip.

As I come around a bit of a corner, the wind picks up. I hadn't realized the cliff was blocking the wind, but I'm glad I had the cover until this point.

I shuffle along for another moment or two, pushing my back up against the rock, until I find myself falling backward.

I scream as I grab wildly for anything that can stop my fall, then I hit hard and twist around. I'm not sure what's just happened. It takes me a moment to realize where I am.

It's not a cave so much as a crack in the side of the cliff. Above me, I see sky, but it's visible through a thin opening way above my head. Behind me, the crack runs into the side of the cliff.

I don't really want to go back out onto the narrow ledge, especially with the wind blowing, so I move deeper into the crack. It's a tight squeeze, but I've always been thin. At one point, I have to take off my pack and push it through ahead of me, but so far, I've been able to make it through.

The ground slants upward, and I climb, hoping I can get out onto the top of the cliff soon. And I'm nearly at the top when I come to a dead end.

Leaning against the side of the rock wall, the tears flow freely. Just a couple days before, I was safe and happy with my parents. I was worried for my friends, but I knew Caric would keep them safe. He always finds a way to get things done.

Now, here I am, just a few days later. I've lost my parents again. People are trying to kill me—I think because they want to upset Prince Roran—and I still didn't catch up with my friends. On top of that, I was captured by a

Shaloomd, almost eaten, had to kill seven of them, climbed the side of a cliff to get to the top, and now I'm stuck just a few feet away from getting out.

It's all too much.

I want to drop to the ground and cry some more, but when I try, my knees hit the sides. There's not enough room. I turn back the way I came, sit down, stretch out my legs, and weep.

11

The Fuzzy

It's dark. Really dark. And cold.

I reach up without taking off my pack and pull out my cloak, wrapping it around myself. I kept it to keep myself warm and to sleep in at night. I left my bedroll behind. I hope that wasn't a mistake.

I'm not sure how long I've slept. I think maybe a few hours at least. It was getting dark when I sat down to have my little pity-party. I can't see the moon, but then again, I can't see much of the sky at all.

I climb back to my feet and take off my pack so I can put on my cloak properly. In such a tight space, it's hard to get the pack on and off, but I manage to put on my cloak and get the pack on again. I make sure I have everything and that my sword and knife are firmly in place before I focus on getting out of here.

I can't really see much. Part of me wants to wait until the sun rises, but ever since I figured out they were trying to frame the General, something has changed in me. I don't want to sit around waiting. I want to act. I want to change things. I want to change the world and do my part—no, I want to do more than "my" part. I want to do something HUGE.

And I can't do that, sitting in a crack on a cliff.

I feel the rock walls on either side of me. It's pretty smooth, and I don't think there are many handholds. But… maybe there are enough.

I put my foot in a small indent and try to push off, but my foot comes down pretty hard. I try again, but this time I lean up against the opposite wall.

My grip holds, and I push up. Using my hands and shoulders to brace myself, I slowly make my way up. It's not far, so if I can just keep this up for a few minutes, I'll be out.

I find a decent handhold, but my foot slips, and I drop down. I feel like my arm has just about ripped out of its socket, but my grip holds, and I find another foothold.

I push and pull and brace myself, squeezing my way to the top. When I finally manage to get my head out into the open air, I want to cheer, but I don't dare just yet.

I push some more, brace myself, and manage to get my arm up out of the crack and onto the ground. In another moment, my upper body is out, and I roll onto the ground.

I lay there for a moment while I catch my breath. I want to cry and sing for joy, but instead, after a moment, I sit up and look around.

The area is flat. With the light of the stars and moon, I can see the cliff not far from my position. I look back the other way, behind me, and see a tree line just a short distance from my position.

That's the direction for me.

I get up and walk toward the trees, but I'm careful to keep an eye out for more cracks in the ground like what I just climbed out of. If I fall up here and hurt myself… well… as far as I know, I'm the only one up here.

I enter the forest, but stop about two steps in. This is not a good idea. The trees are far too thick in here, and I can't see a thing in the dark.

I step back out and walk along the edge of the trees, heading south. At least that's somewhat the direction toward Sevord. I'm not sure where my friends are heading exactly, but I have to pick a direction.

Maybe I can catch them on the other side of Switcher Pass… if I hurry and can find a way down…

I push on. So far, it's just a steady line of trees on my right and a cliff not too far away on my left. The wind isn't quite as bad as it was earlier, but the more I walk, the more it seems to cut through my cloak. It's not long before every part of me shakes.

I look out to the east, back toward the mountains, and I see the first bit of light from the rising sun. It won't be long before I can see clearly, and maybe I can make my way among the trees.

As the light increases, so does the wind. I find myself shivering even more, and as soon as I can see well enough, I head west into the forest. At first, the wind isn't any better, but the farther in I go, the more the trees offer cover.

Once I've warmed up a bit, I find a fallen log and take a seat. I have to be careful to rest. I can't just push myself, so I take a drink of water, careful to conserve what I have. The trees obviously have enough water, but it might come from rainfall. I don't want to have to wait until the next rain for my next drink.

If all goes well, I'll find another route down within a few days.

As I sit, I take in the sights and sounds. It's a beautiful forest. In fact, if I didn't know I was up on top of the cliffs, I could easily believe it was one of the forests down in the Talic Region, or even among the trees of Switcher Pass.

But something's off. Something doesn't fit with what I know about where I am. At first, I can't quite place it, but then it comes to me. It's faint, but it's definitely there.

Smoke. There's the smell of smoke. And something else. Food. Those are cookfires.

I get up and move deeper into the forest. There's no way to tell for sure which direction is the right direction, but I know the people aren't back the way I came.

I try to be quiet. I don't know if these people are good people or bad people. I tend to think everyone is good, but the last month has taught me how foolish that view is. I think most people want to do the right thing, but I've met enough dangerous people to learn that I have to be careful.

The light of the flames catches my eye. The sun's coming up, but it's still dark enough in the forest that it stands out quite well. I creep through the trees and bushes until I can get a good look.

About a dozen men sit around the fire. They all have bows with them, along with knives. I'm guessing they're not out to do bad stuff, otherwise they'd have swords. The bows make me think it's a hunting party.

I listen in. Their accents are strange to me… well, some of them. Some of them speak just like me, but others talk like their speech is fighting to get out of their mouths—like they're punching each word. I heard a lot of accents while working in the castle in Sevord but never anything quite like this.

So, it's a mix of people from different places. They're likely a hunting party with families back at home. No one wears armor, so they're not fighters—or expecting a fight.

But, I still don't know if I can trust them.

I decide to sneak around their campfire and see if I can find their village. Maybe with more people, I'll have more safety.

I stop breathing as I feel a cold blade on my throat. I dare not move. I dare not say anything.

A loud voice, a woman's voice, booms out behind me. "Well, honey, why you don't stop spying and stand up you?" A little louder she shouts out, "Hey boys, we have visitor yes!"

The woman grips my hair in her fist as she pushes me along. I feel pressure on my back now and then and assume that's the knife. It doesn't hurt me with my armor. I don't know if she hasn't noticed it since I'm wearing my cloak, or if she doesn't care.

"Look like spy!"

I glance at the man who said that. I can't turn my head with my hair held the way it is. The man has a mean look on his face, but that's no different from anyone else in this group.

I had figured they were hunters, and they are, but they seem quite willing to leave the hunt while they deal with me. They keep talking about taking me to someone named Fuzzy.

"What are you going to do with me?" I don't want my voice to come out with so much terror, but I just can't control it. Maybe I should just stay quiet.

"Quiet!" one of the men screams.

I take that as an indication that yes, I should, in fact, just stay quiet.

Only one woman moves with this group. I think she's married to the man who's carrying my sword and knife. Everyone seems so angry at me, but then happy to see me, but not in a good way. I thought I heard someone mention something about throwing me off the cliff. I'd really rather not take that route down.

We walk for another hour or so, and by that time, my neck aches. I want to ask the woman to let go of my hair, but I'm pretty sure she'll just hold tighter if I do.

When we finally reach their village, it's just as rough of a place as the people I'm with. Dirt and garbage lay everywhere. Along the main street, or whatever it is, lines of laundry hang across the road and people just zigzag in and out of the pants, shirts, and unmentionables.

When we're noticed, people gather around, asking where I came from and what the hunters are going to do with me. Most have that same punchy accent that I heard earlier, although a few speak a little more like me. But whether I recognize their accent or not, they're all rude and mean, and everyone wants to throw me off a cliff.

The man with my sword and knife calls out, "Get Fuzzy."

A couple of boys run off looking for this Fuzzy, or I assume that's where they're going. I have a brief rush of fear that Fuzzy might be something like a bear or some big hairy creature.

We make our way to what I think might be their town square. It's small, covered in garbage, and smells like feet. Well, that's not a kind thing to say. I think most feet would be offended by such an insult.

It smells like this is the place where stinky feet go to die.

They push me down onto the ground. The angry woman lets go of my hair and pulls off my pack.

I try to look around, but the moment I turn my head, she screams at me. I do manage to stretch my neck just a little, though. My back is so tight, and my hands shake.

When Fuzzy comes out, he's not at all what I imagined. He's small, skinny, and has no hair. As he gets closer, I lean forward a little just to confirm. Nope, not even eyebrows.

"Well, what we have here?"

I just stay silent, but no one else speaks. I'm afraid to say anything for fear that I'll anger them more.

Fuzzy comes a little closer. He leans down in an odd way and says again in his punchy voice, "Well, what we have here?"

"I'm Marleet." I'm sure there's something better to say, but that's all I can come up with.

Fuzzy nods. He gives a wicked smile and says in the most sinister voice I've ever heard, "Good meet you, Marleet. I Father Zeke."

I almost respond with, "Oh, Father Zeke! I thought they called you Fuzzy," but I hold my tongue. It's a good thing, too.

"Most people don't like syllables, so call me Fuzzy on account of hairy eyebrows."

I nod slowly. I think it would be good to be far away from these people. A lot of fear is growing inside me—and not just for my eyebrows.

I don't know why I do this, but in a teary voice, I ask, "Why is everyone so mean to me?"

Fuzzy stares at me for a while. He moves back and forth a couple times as if he's trying to get a better look. In a fast, angry voice, he says, "Because, Marleet, we know why you here you. You here you to find all about us. You here you to learn our secrets. You here you to kill us all."

I'm so scared, but I just can't help it. I laugh. I laugh, and I laugh, and I laugh. So much so, that I fall over onto my side. I think they might start kicking me for laughing so hard, but I just don't care.

"Why you laugh you?" Fuzzy screams.

I sit back up and try to control myself. "Fuzzy, look at me!"

"I ams. I look at you. Look at my eyes!"

"No!" I laugh again. "Look at me! I'm the most harmless person in the entire world! I'm not here to kill you!"

Fuzzy looks at the man with my sword and knife. I think maybe carrying weapons might give the impression that I'm actually dangerous, but that doesn't seem to be the issue.

The man with my sword says, "She caught scouting out land."

"Scouting?" I say. "I was trying to find my way down!"

"Down where?"

"Down to Sevord."

"Sevord? You mean Lower People?"

I nod. "I guess so."

"Then why you scouting you?"

"I wasn't. What makes you think I was scouting?"

Fuzzy looks at the man with my sword again. The man nods and says, "We found her on sunside, yes."

"Ah, yes, that's it!" Fuzzy says. "Sunside, yes. If you not scouting you, how you get on sunside, yes?"

At first, I have no idea what this sunside is, but then I realize it's likely the side with the sun in the morning—east.

"That's the side I came up."

Fuzzy scrunches up his nose and leans in close. For a second I'm afraid he's planning on kissing me, but he's just weird, that's all. When his face is level with mine, he says, "You came up sunside? The side of Shaldoomsies, no?"

I furrow my brow, then think to myself that doing something like that might make Fuzzy feel insecure, what with his obvious limitations in that area. We always pronounced it Shaloomd, but they pronounce it Shaldoomsies. I'm no longer sure who's right.

I just nod, hoping that works.

"How you get past Shaldoomsies, Marleet?"

"Well, a Shal... Shaldoomsies picked me up and carried me to its nest. When I landed, I drew my sword and fought them off."

"You killed a Shaldoomsies, no? All just you? You just you?"

I think maybe the answer to those questions is "yes," so I try going with that answer. "Yes."

Everyone takes a big step back, and they give out a loud "ooooohhh."

I don't know what that means. None of them look like they want to be my friend.

"So, you must be toughun."

I stare at Fuzzy for a moment. I'm pretty sure I'm done with this conversation and with these people, but I don't really have a choice but to stay here longer. I take a bit of a guess. "Yes, I'm a toughun."

"None us kill Shaldoomsies." Fuzzy looks around, and everyone shakes their heads. "So, if you such toughun that you kill Shaldoomsies you, you can fight any us."

I hold my tongue. I think I'm in a worse spot than I had thought.

Everyone laughs, and Fuzzy sends a man to a hut at the side of the village. He comes out with two swords and drops one at my feet. It's not my sword, but I've learned a lot over the last while. I pick it up. It's rusty, heavy, and ugly. I'm also really, really tired. This may not work out well for me.

"If I win, will you show me the way down to the Lower People?"

Fuzzy's eyebrows shoot up… I think. Or that area of his forehead moves up. It's just hard to know for sure what's happening on that face without a clear landmark. "Agreed."

Everyone growls at Fuzzy's response, but he waves both hands at them vigorously like he's quickly washing a window, and they calm down.

I shift the blade around in my hand, trying to get a feel for it. Fuzzy grabs the other one for himself and swings it clumsily back and forth. I take a quick look at his weapon. The good news is, it's not going to be all that sharp. The bad news is, it can still kill me.

My face goes numb as I come to grips with what I'm about to do. I can't believe I just agreed to fight someone for my freedom.

I open my mouth to ask if we can find another way when Fuzzy lets out a wild scream and charges.

12

The Shaldoomsies

I jump into action and use my sword to deflect his, then step out of the way to let him stumble past me. I wish I had my enchanted sword, but one of the advantages of using an enchanted sword like mine for a week or two, training every day, is it increases your skill with any sword—fast!

My papa explained that every day using the enchanted sword was anywhere from two to four weeks of regular training. After a couple of weeks with the enchanted sword, I'm actually as good as a swordsman who has trained hard for the better part of a year.

As Fuzzy lunges again, I deflect his blade again. Less than a year of training is not great, but Fuzzy obviously hasn't had any.

He brings the sword down hard toward my head. His sword is big, almost like a club, and he's much bigger than I am. I can't stop his blade, but I step off to the side as I use my blade to slide his to the side and away from me.

I take the opportunity and lunge forward, bringing the tip of my blade right up against his hand. Fuzzy's sword drops to the ground.

I didn't mean to cut him, but I see blood. I'm still learning and can sometimes be a little sloppy.

I raise the tip of my blade to his throat and ask, "Do you yield?"

"What this yield mean?" Fuzzy barks at me with a large scowl on his face. "What you yield you?"

"To yield means to give up—to me—that I win."

"I no…"

I push the tip of the blade a little closer. This man is not going to stand in the way of me getting to my friends.

"I yield you! I yield you!"

I lower my sword. "Now show me the way down."

Before I know what's happening, my sword is yanked out of my hand, and a couple men have me by my arms. I want to struggle, but I know there's no point.

"You no go Lower People." Fuzzy steps in closer and glares at me while he holds his bleeding hand. "No one go down. Lower People no hear us. You no tell them."

The two men drag me off, and a moment later, I find myself locked in a room in a small hut.

I spin around. I know I should be crying right now, but I'm too angry to cry. Part of me wants to break out of here and attack Fuzzy to teach him a lesson for lying to me. I know that won't accomplish anything, but it might make me feel good.

The wiser part of me, however, knows that I need to get out and get to the western edge of the cliffs. If I'm to find a way down, I'm pretty sure it'll be on that side. The eastern side is just straight cliffs—it's open to everything—and the Shaloomd are on that side. Even if I make it down, I'll likely just get picked up by another Shaloomd and this time I might not survive.

I explore all the edges of the room I'm in. The floor is dirt. The hut is secured down to the ground, but if it came to it, I might be able to dig my way out.

A window sits on the side of the building, but it's boarded up. Even if I could break through, it'll make too much noise. But that doesn't matter. I can see right away that I don't have the strength to break the boards.

The ceiling is open to all the supports and beams. If I got up there, I might find a way through the roof. It looks like a vent or window or something up there. But I'd need a ladder.

A table and two chairs are the only furniture in the room, and I move one of the chairs out a bit from the wall. I get behind the chair and start to dig.

The boards go down only a few inches, which is thrilling, but I find the digging slow. The dirt's packed down really hard, and it's not long before my nails are full of dirt, and my fingers, which were already scratched and sore from climbing, now ache a lot. But I keep going. I don't think I have any chance of getting out of here unless I make it happen.

I jump as I hear someone at the door and quickly make sure the chair is well positioned to hide the hole—at least a bit. I then stand against the back wall, hiding my hands in case they notice the dirt on my fingers.

When the door opens, it's the woman who caught me in the forest. She has a tray in her hands and a bundle of something under her arm. Someone outside closes the door and locks it.

"Sit down, girl!"

"No." I'm not normally defiant, but I don't think it's good to let these people order me around.

The woman simply nods and moves to the table. She sets the tray down and on it is food and water. Once that's down, she pulls out the bundle from under her arm and unwraps it. Inside is a little statue of a Shaloomd. She sets it on the table.

"Eat!"

I shake my head. "How do I know it's not poisoned?"

The woman's face scrunches up. "What is poisoned?"

"It's when you put something in the food that either makes me sick, makes me die, or makes me fall asleep or something."

The woman looks at the food, then back at me. "We no have that."

"How do I know?"

The woman growls and says, "Point at food. Anything on tray. I eat it. You see no poisoned."

I point at the bread. Without any hesitation, she picks it up, shoves it in her mouth, chews for far too short of a period of time, and swallows. "See, no poisoned. You eat!"

I still don't want to do anything they say, but they've taken my food, and I'll need the energy. I rush to the table and start to eat.

"Why you fingers dirty?"

I frown at her. "Why you face dirty?"

The woman doesn't look offended. Instead, she just nods and says in the punchy speech of these people, "You make good point."

I keep eating, and the woman just stands there. When I'm done, I'm quite full, and I step back and wait.

"Pick up the Shaldoomsies!"

I shake my head.

"Pick it up and make your promise!"

"Tell me what's going on!" I'm not going to just do whatever these people want. They're dangerous—that's for sure.

"That Shaldoomsies enchanted. You make promise. Promise you never leave Top People. Promise you never tell Lower People about Top People. Promise."

I don't know what she means by the Shaldoomsies being enchanted, but I can't very well promise all that. I have no intention of staying here my whole life.

I smile. I just realized something. If they want me to promise never to leave, that means there's definitely a way down. But why would she want me to hold the statue?

"Why the statue?" I ask.

"Statue enchanted. Every promise holds. Holds forever. You promise now."

I've heard of this kind of thing. It's not something I want to do. If you try to lie, not that I would lie, it'll hold you to your promise—possible or not. I once heard of a man who promised on one of these kinds of things to fly like a bird. He couldn't fly, of course, but the enchantment held him to it, and he ended up falling off a high balcony.

I have to find a new way out of this. "I have an idea."

"What? What you idea you?"

"Why don't you leave the statue with me for a bit and come back in an hour?"

"I don't know why I don't!"

These people are hard to work with. I shake my head and try again. "Leave this statue with me for an hour. Come back in an hour."

"Will you promise then?" the woman asks.

"You'll find out."

The woman gives one big nod, moves to the door, knocks twice, and leaves when the door opens.

I grab the statue and run to the hole I started. The wings will work well as little shovels. I think I can dig my way out of here quickly with this thing.

I go at the hole with the shovel, careful to keep myself from saying anything or even thinking anything that might come close to a promise. I almost say to myself at one point, "When I get out of here, I'm going to have myself a nice hot bath!" but I drop the statue. I picture myself running naked through the village screaming, "Where's a hot bath?"

Once my mind is clear again, I dig quickly, doing all I can to make sure the hole is big enough. I'd hate to get it all done, then get stuck half-way through. It's a good thing I'm the only one here. If Rulf was around, we'd need to dig a hole about three times the size.

Then again, if Rulf were here, he would have just thrown the villagers around, and we would have run out of here.

The farther I get into the hole, the harder it is. All the dirt I dig has to be scooped out of the hole and set aside. After a bit, I have to climb into the hole, then dig, then slowly wiggle back out, pulling the loose soil with me. Not easy.

When I see the first bit of light on the other side, I nearly scream with joy. I think I have to be getting close to that hour mark. I hope the woman doesn't come back early.

I start clearing the way on the other side, and pretty soon I'm sure I can fit through. I toss the statue to the side and dive into the hole, squeezing my way through. Just as I'm nearly there, I realize my problem. The hole goes down, then up again. That's fine and all, but my body doesn't bend like that. If I go on my back, I'm good until I get to my knees. If I go on my belly, I can't bend my back enough.

I pull myself out and use the statue to dig some more to allow my legs to slide through. I think going through on by back is the best way, so I need to extend the hole a bit more on my side. When I'm done, I slide through.

Outside, I find I'm right next to the trees. Unfortunately, I have to get to the other side of the village, so I step into the cover of the forest and creep around, keeping an eye on the villagers. I'm also on the lookout for my sword and pack. I don't know how long the food in my belly will last, but it'll take a few days to get to the other side, then it might take me a long time to find the way down. I'll need my supplies.

I can't see my stuff anywhere, but I do remember the one man ran to a certain hut and retrieved that sword.

I go to that hut and sneak around to the front. No one's looking my way, so I slip in through the front door, hoping there aren't any villagers inside.

Once my eyes have adjusted, I gasp. In the hut are dozens of swords. I'm not sure why the villager grabbed the rusty ones he did because most of the rest are nicer. There are also jewels, piles of gold, and even some armor. I think these people have been capturing others for years.

I find my pack and check inside. Sure enough, my food is still there. That causes me to pause for a moment. I look around and see a couple other packs. I'm curious if any food was left in them as well, but I don't dare look. What I find might be quite gross.

I strap on my pack, followed by my sword and knife. When I'm ready, I move back to the door and check to see if anyone's looking my way. A moment later, I'm out the door and back in amongst the trees.

13

The Hope

I circle around the village and then move straight west. It doesn't look like there are any paths, and from what I learned about tracking from Rulf, no one has moved through these trees and bushes for a long time. I'm beginning to wonder if they just avoid heading toward that side of the cliffs.

It makes for slow progress, especially since I'm trying my best not to leave a trail, but I'll get there, eventually.

After a few hours, I settle down for a small snack by a river. I don't want to eat much. I have no idea how to hunt. This might be all the food I have.

When I start up again, I hear shouts in the distance.

At first, I don't know which way they're coming from. I can tell, though, that they're angry, and I hear the same accents I heard before. I take off through the trees, hoping I'm running away from them. I try my best to be quiet and hide my tracks, but who knows how that's working out.

Now and then I stop to listen. I still hear them, definitely behind me. At least they're not in front of me. But the bad thing is, I don't seem to be getting away from them.

I find a small river flowing roughly to the west and follow it. The ground under my feet is firm, so I run along, careful not to get too close to the river, as I'm afraid I might leave a footprint.

Down along the riverbank, I'm making much better progress, but I soon find it starts curving to the south, so I climb back up into the forest and rush along. The trees are a different sort in this area. They have white bark, and they're growing a bit farther apart from one another. The ground is soft, though, so even though I can move faster, I'm sure they can track me.

The sweat starts down my face, and that's when I realize I should have washed when I stopped by that river. Now I'm just covered in sweaty dirt that's running into my eyes.

I run along until I find a dip in the ground. Below me, a small valley sits with a lake at the bottom. I almost decide to run around it. My first thought is if I go down there, I'll get stuck out in the open when my pursuers catch up, but then I notice something a little different. All around the lake are little cracks and crevices. They seem too small to call them caves, but whatever I call them, they look like good hiding spots.

I see a rocky area not too far from me and rush to it, brushing off as much dirt as I can before I climb down so as not to leave a trail.

When I get to the bottom, I find a large crevice in the rock that I can climb in. Once inside, I find it turns a little to the left. It's out of the way, but the spiders are horrendous. I hate spiders. But then again, I hate the thought of living in that village the rest of my life more.

Once inside, I find there's enough room to sit down. I pull off my pack, and it's not long before I fall asleep.

When I awake, I don't know where I am. My butt's cold, but the rest of me is warm. Aside from the ground, it's actually quite nice in this cave.

I stand and find I'm sore. When I make my way toward the light and reach the entrance to my little nook, I'm looking out over a small lake, barely visible in the dim light of the evening. I wonder where my friends are, but then it all comes rushing back.

I'm all alone.

The good news is, the people from the village didn't find me. The bad news is, I slept for the rest of the day. It's now dark, and I don't think it's smart to travel at night. Who knows what holes I could fall into? And nighttime is when many of the nasty animals come out to hunt.

In the fading light, I pull out some food and eat just a little. I'm trying to make sure I keep myself fed, but not overfed, so I don't run out of food too soon.

When I'm done, I sneak up the side of the hill and wander around the entire area. I think the people from the village are gone. I don't hear them anywhere.

I head back down. It's dark enough now that I don't have to worry about being seen, so I strip down to my undergarments and wash up, cleaning my clothes as best as I can. When I'm done, I ring them out and lay them on some large rocks, still warm from the sun's heat.

I head back into my new little home and wrap myself up in my cloak. I'm still so tired that I'm out in a matter of minutes.

My clothes are still a little damp, but it's not a problem. This area of the forest is pretty thin, so the sun beats down on me. In the midday heat, my clothes will finish drying in no time.

But damp or not, I'm happy to be finally clean. The water had been cold, but refreshing, and I no longer have dirty sweat dripping in my eyes.

I've come across many campsites. I assume they camp in these spots when hunting. I've checked each one, and the fire pits are all cold, so I don't worry too much.

But I'm tired. And I'm hungry. And the bugs are bad. But even so, for some reason, I'm really happy. I think for the first time in my life, I'm able to just do something—and do it well.

I can survive.

Sure, I don't know how to hunt.

Sure, I don't know how to find more food.

Sure, I don't know… well… there's a lot I don't know.

But I can run fast—faster than I could a month ago.

And I can fight off these people with my sword.

And I can escape from a locked-up room.

And I can make sure I'm clean and feeling refreshed and moving in the right direction.

I can survive.

Two days later, I'm not so sure about the surviving part.

They found me earlier this morning. I didn't see them coming, I just heard a twang followed by a thud. When I looked toward the thud sound, an arrow sat only inches from my head.

I've been running ever since. I'm glad they don't have horses, although it might be hard for a horse to maneuver in this area. But if they did have horses, I don't think I'd be able to keep away from them.

They have one guy who's fast. He caught up to me a few times, but he can't turn very fast. Each time, I eluded him long enough, changing directions back and forth, until he got tired. Then I ran hard.

I glance back. They're not close, but they're not far either. When I first saw them, there had to be at least a dozen, but only three now follow me now.

Unfortunately, if those three catch me, I'll be done. I can fight with my sword, and I might drive them off, but I'll likely have to kill them. I'm not sure I can do that.

Ahead, through the trees, I see the ocean. I'm finally at the western edge of the cliffs! But that means I can't run west anymore. I have to head north or south.

I turn south far before the edge of the cliff. I'm afraid if I wait until the last minute to turn, they'll catch me.

I don't know where the way down might be, but I keep angling toward the cliff. When I get within twenty feet of the edge, just outside the tree line, I run along there. I'm hoping I'll see some area that slopes down.

I'm not surprised that they keep chasing me. They don't want anyone to leave. I doubt it's because they're lonely. I think it has to do with fear. They don't want anyone to know they're up here. I was always taught that there was no way up onto the cliffs. The fact that there are people here tells me there is—unless, of course, they were all carried up here by Shaloomds.

The other thing is the promise. They wouldn't make people give that promise if there wasn't a way down.

I run for another hour or so. By this point, only two guys still chase me. They're struggling, too. When I glance back, they stumble more than run.

And the gap between us is widening.

Something catches my eye off to the left—back among the trees. It's a mound of dirt and rocks. That in itself is not entirely unusual, but I'm sure I see lumber on it—cut pieces of wood. I run in that direction and hear the men behind me yell and scream.

That's a good sign. I'm pretty sure I've found it.

The mound of dirt is almost entirely unimpressive. It's just a mound, after all. Of dirt. And rocks.

But as I come around, I get a better look at the lumber. On each side, a couple of posts of wood are set down into the ground. Secured by nails to the posts are boards, covering up what appears to be a cave.

I grab one of the boards around waist height and pull, yanking it back. It gives a little, and I pull harder. I yank over and over.

I glance to my right and see the men still stumble toward me, and they're getting closer. I give another pull, and the board comes loose.

The boards are old, and I think they've been in this spot for a while. If they weren't a little rotten, I don't think I'd be able to pull it open.

Once I have one board off, I try to get through the hole, but I can't. I grab the board below it, but it just won't budge. I grab the one above it and feel it give just a little.

The men are almost on me. If I can't get this open soon, I'll either have to run again, or be caught.

I yank once again, and the board comes loose. I pull it out of the way and scramble through. When I'm just about entirely in, I feel a man grab the bottom of my pants. I pull with my leg and try to get away, but his grip is like iron. I briefly consider slipping out of my pants, but that's all I have to wear. I'm not going to trek across Sevord looking for my friends in my undies.

I draw my knife and try to cut away a section of the pants, but it just doesn't work. The knife doesn't cut fast enough, and it won't be long before he gets a grip on my leg. Then I'm done.

I grit my teeth and do what I don't want to do. I bring the knife down hard on the man's wrist, and he screams.

He pulls away, and I stumble back. My knife is still in his arm.

I turn away from the hole and try to get out of reach, but neither man comes close.

"Pull out!" the injured man yells at the other.

The other man grabs the knife and yanks it out, and the man I stabbed drops to his knees.

"We no go there."

The other man just nods. "We promised. We go back. Tell Fuzzy. This might be end."

I pull away even farther from the door. I want to say that I won't tell anyone. I want to be nice and considerate of their privacy, but I'm pretty irritated with them at the moment. I think I might just tell everyone about this place for no other reason than because they imprisoned me and then chased me for days.

They turn slowly and move off through the forest. I feel a little bad about scaring them like this, but I'm still upset at them for locking me in that hut.

I wish I was more like Ellcia. She doesn't have to feel so conflicted all the time. She knows what she wants—always.

Once they've moved off, I turn around and examine the area. The cave is small. In fact, it's really small. It's a little hard to see due to the forest, the boards over the entrance, and the fact that it's a cave, but even so, right away I see the cave goes nowhere.

I cry out in frustration. After all this running and chasing and more, I'm just in a little hole in the ground!

I'm about to climb back through the boards when I stop myself. Why would anyone board up a cave that doesn't go anywhere? They're either trying to trick people, or… maybe the cave does go somewhere.

I drop to the ground. On the outside, it's just a large mound of dirt. If the cave leads anywhere, it has to be down.

The floor of the cave is soft dirt, for the most part. A couple of large rocks sit in the corners, but most of the ground is just soft. Mushrooms grow everywhere. I'm tempted to stock up on them, but I remember Tereese once spoke about mushrooms that weren't mushrooms. Poisonous things. I don't know if these are the good ones or the bad ones.

I brush them aside carefully, not sure if I should even touch them.

I'm pretty filthy again. If I do make it down, it'll be hard to clean myself up. At least up here there's privacy if I have to bathe in a lake at night. Down below, there are too many people. Maybe if I find my friends and the village they're going to, I can clean up there.

What a strange thing to worry about at a moment like this—dirt! I guess I've spent most of my life… clean. I don't like dirt.

I'm at the back of the cave, looking, digging. I almost miss it. In fact, I move right past it, but then stop. As I slide my hand along the floor of the cave, my finger catches on something.

I move back and find a small hole, about big enough for me to fit a few of my fingers inside.

I dig, hoping I haven't found some kind of animal home—like a snake. The image of a snake lunging forward and biting my hand is making it hard for me to continue, but I push the thoughts away.

The more I dig, the bigger the hole gets. That seems obvious, but it's more than that. I'm not just pulling dirt out of the way; a lot of the dirt is falling into the hole, making it larger every second.

It's about big enough for me to get my head down there, but I kind of want more than that. I also don't want to just dive in. Who knows if this really is the way down.

"She in there!"

I spin around and rush to the boards. The two men who just ran away a moment ago are back. With them are not only another eight men and women, but Fuzzy's coming as well. He looks both angry and happy. I'm not sure how that's possible. It may just be an effect of the lack of eyebrows.

Fuzzy sees me, points, and shouts, "Grab sharp sticks!"

The people scatter. A moment later, they have sticks in their hands. I'm not sure what they're for, but I don't want to find out.

I crawl back to the hole and dig fast. In just a few seconds, the hole is big enough for me, although I still don't know what's down there.

I hear a grunt behind me and turn around. A woman crouches with her face up against the opening I created. It looks like she's letting her eyes adjust.

When she sees me, she takes a large, sharp stick and shoves it in the cave at me.

I duck just in time, and the stick slams against the rock where my face had been a moment before.

These people are insane!

I don't give it another thought. Feet first, I jump into the hole.

Into the unknown.

Into the blackness.

Into whatever lies below me.

14

The Way

I hit and then tumble.

I don't know what's happening.

I can't see a thing. I feel like I'm being trampled by a horse.

When I figure out what's going on, I'm simply tumbling and sliding. I cover my face, not out of fear of seeing something—I can't see anything—but out of fear of smashing it against something hard and breaking my nose or losing teeth or an eye.

I'm mostly sliding on my butt, but now and then I slip onto my back or belly for a bit. Sometimes I roll and have to use my hands to get control again.

I'm slowing down. Not much, but a bit.

My feet slam into something hard and my whole body crumples up against it. I want to just lay there, but dirt and rubble have followed me down, and if I don't move quick, I'll be buried.

I scramble on top of the landslide. At first, it's nearly impossible. I find my feet sink into the rubble sliding around me. I climb on top, but my feet get buried, then again get my feet out on top, then buried again.

When it finally settles, I'm gasping for air, but coughing in the dust, dirt, and grime that fills my mouth and lungs. I plop down on my butt, but then cry out and twist off to the side. Everything back there hurts. When I reach back to see if I'm bleeding, my hands are so raw and numb that I can't feel properly if there's the wet of blood. I can't even feel if there are still pants back there or if the slide on the dirt and rock ripped it all open.

This is really turning out to be a bad day.

But, even so, I made it out of Fuzzy's grasp. I got away. Now, it's just a matter of finding my way out of this mess.

I laugh out loud, despite the pain, but my laugh sends me into another coughing fit. When I'm done, I'm still smiling. This has been a terrifying week, or however long it's been, but I'm not sure I've ever felt so alive!

I might not be the person I thought I was. It's not that I didn't like the person I was while living in Sevord. I loved my life. But I always saw myself as someone who should wear beautiful dresses and do beautiful things.

I still think that's me. I still think I want to wear beautiful dresses and do beautiful things. But now I think I'm also something else. I'm a fighter. I'm a survivor.

I decide to say it out loud. "I'm… a warrior."

I giggle at that. The giggle that comes out is far from a warrior's giggle. It's a little girl's giggle. Cute, adorable, and gentle.

That's me. I'm a gentle warrior. I'm not going to be a threat to anyone who isn't a threat to me or my friends.

I'm not going to fight just to prove myself. I'm not going to make a point to show people what I can do. I'm not going to impress anyone. I'm going to be me. I'm going to be content to be a warrior.

But I don't need anyone to recognize that about me. I can just be a warrior. That means I can giggle like a little girl… and be okay with that.

The giggle comes out again as I stumble toward the wall that I slammed into a moment ago.

I run my hands gently over the rock, doing my best not to scrape them any more than they already are. The wall I hit is a little taller than I am—I can feel the roof of the cave, but the wall comes to an end on my right.

I head to the left. I really don't know where I am, but I think I tumbled and fell roughly in the direction of the cliff. That means I might only be a few feet away from the outside, but if that's a few feet of solid rock, it really might as well be the other side of the world.

In the darkness, I continue to move to the left. Aside from a few rocks and dirt still tumbling down, there's no sound apart from my own feet shuffling through the soft dirt. Every step is difficult. Not only do my legs, ankles, and feet hurt, but I'm sinking in. It makes it hard to move, but I'm not stopping. I have to find my friends—or at least get out of here.

A moment later, I crack my head on something hard and lights flash before my eyes. I lean against the wall while it settles. My whole body's tense. I want to scream in pain and frustration, but I'm not going to. If I give in to my frustration, I'll be angry until I find my way out.

I have a moment of panic. What if there is no way out? I shake my head and refuse to consider that. Of course there is. Fuzzy's people blocked this way off. They know there's a way through.

I feel a little in front of me. The palms of my hands remain numb, so I feel with the back of my hand. The ceiling of the cave slopes down here.

Crouching, I move forward, trying my best not to crack my head again. I feel like there's something wet pouring down the side of my head. I think I hit that rock hard.

It's not long before I'm on my hands and knees. The cave has come in on either side of me as well. I gather if a big guy with broad shoulders tried to get through here, he'd have to slide through on his side. Rulf would have a tough time in this area.

I miss him. I really grew to like him on our journey across Sevord. He irritated me with his lack of answers and inability to speak, but I know deep down inside he's a really sweet guy. I also know he would do anything for anyone of us. He's mean on the outside, but he would die for us if needed.

I stop thinking about Rulf. There is no benefit to it right now. I'll just start wondering if he survived his fight with the soldiers. I'm sure he did, but I'm also not sure.

The back of my head scrapes just slightly against the top of the cave, so I lower my head. It's getting tight in here.

My hands drop out in front of me, and I hit hard on my chest. I'm not falling, but my hands found a slight drop. Well, maybe it's slight. I don't know. It's dark. It feels like it's a rock slope—like a slide. Not too steep, but certainly too steep to crawl down. If I start down that, I'll slip in no time.

I pull back and feel around for a loose rock. When I find a decent sized one, I toss it forward. I hear it bounce a bunch of times, then start to skid down the slope.

Well, I have my answer. However far it goes, it goes for a long time.

Off to my right, the area is a little flatter. I know there must be a better way down. People would never climb up such a steep incline—and I think some of the people on top of the cliffs likely came up this way.

I follow off to the right and, sure enough, there's another small passage. I continue to crawl along and find my path continues at a gentle slope down. Now and then there's a drop, but it's never more than a short distance, and I crawl down each one.

My belly starts to rumble. When I dig the food out of my pack, it tastes like dirt. I don't think it's the food, so much. My hands are likely caked in dirt, and my mouth and nose certainly are.

When I finish, I feel around and confirm that I know which way I was heading before. When I'm confident, I lay back and use my pack as a pillow. I can't help but think about the thousands of bugs and centipedes and strange creatures that likely crawl through these caves, but I won't survive if I don't sleep.

As I doze off, I smile to myself. I am a survivor. This is the kind of thing real warriors are made of.

When I awake, I cry out in pain.

Everything hurts. It's like half my body is on fire, and the other has been cut and bruised.

I look around for some idea of where I am. It takes me a moment to realize that it's far too dark to see anything.

It all comes rushing back—the journey across Sevord, my short life in the caves with my parents, my time on the journey back, the soldiers, the Shaloomd, the strange, dangerous people on top of the cliffs, and this… place.

My legs hurt so badly. My ankle feels like it's seized up. My back aches like I've been carrying a kicking horse. My head… it feels like it's three sizes too big.

I stretch and cry out again. I think some of my cuts have scabbed over. Moving has ripped them open again.

I pull out my canteen and take a drink of water. When I feel refreshed, I put it away, pull on my pack, figure out which way I was going, and set out again.

Every movement hurts. Before I slept, it stung and ached. Now, it's agony. It feels like my body is tearing apart with every inch of progress I make.

But, I'm alive. I'm also making it through.

The little cave I'm in is low enough that I need to get down on my belly now and then and slither through like a snake, but the entire time it slopes down.

I laugh at the thought that maybe I've missed my turn, and now I'm just going deeper into the earth. It's not really funny, but I think I've entered a state somewhat akin to insanity. I don't mind. In fact, I think I kind of like it.

I'm giggling again. I can't believe I'm thinking about going insane and enjoying the thought.

I push on until I find another steep slope going down. There's no other way, and when I drop a rock, it slides far enough that I don't want to do it on my butt. I'm still not entirely sure I have pants back there. I think the first slide might have ripped them open. The feeling in my fingers hasn't quite come back fully, so I still can't really check.

I pull off my pack and slide my legs through the loops. My pack is thick leather, and I suspect it'll hold up well. I launch myself off the edge and slide into the darkness.

After a few moments, I reach the bottom, but it's not at all what I expected. I land with a splash in a pool of water.

I gasp and jump to my feet, pulling my pack up with me. I don't want it to fill with water. The water itself is icy cold, and it makes my cuts hurt more.

I tip my pack upside down and try to drain what I can. Hopefully my food and supplies are still dry.

I'm glad the pool isn't deep. It's a little past my knees. Although it's cold, it's also refreshing.

But the good news is, I see something.

It's not much, but just a little way ahead, I see light.

I move in that direction, careful with each step. It's possible the pool I'm in might only be shallow where I'm standing.

I slowly wade over to the other side. When I climb out of the water, I can see even more. The ceiling is low, but still a bit above my head. The floor is fairly level, and the cave ahead turns sharply to the right.

When I get to the turn, I see why there's not much light coming through. First, the hole out is very small, which also explains why few people find their way up. Second, plants and bushes cover the hole. Third, it's nighttime.

It's a wonder I can see anything at all.

I push the plants out of the way and step out into the warm night air. It feels good to be out of that cave. I have no idea how long I was in there, but it was long enough to have a good sleep. I think I went in around noon the day before—which means I was probably in there for a good day and a half.

I'm in a forest, but the trees are sparse enough and the sky clear enough that I can see a bit. I twist around and get a look at my pants and breathe a sigh of relief. It all hurts back there, but my pants appear to be solid. I wasn't sure what I'd do if I was actually missing the back half of my trousers.

I'm tired, so I climb back into the cave. Part of me wants to stay out, but I'm alone. If animals on the hunt happen by, I might be a target. I'm also a young woman alone. I don't know who's around or who among them is safe.

Inside, I find a soft area and settle in for the night. My cloak keeps me warm while I struggle to get to sleep. I'm so tired, but I'm also in a lot of pain. Every movement adds to the agony and wakes me up. It's a long while before I fall asleep.

15

The Helper

When I awake, my hands are finally starting to get their feeling back. That seems like a positive in my mind. My hands, unfortunately, disagree.

It hurts to touch anything, and they sting all the time.

I spend a few minutes cleaning myself up in the little pond or lake or whatever this water thing is—large puddle? When I'm done, I at least feel like I'm a little more presentable.

I pull on my cloak and head out.

It looks like it's nearly noon. The shadows from the cliff behind me are just about gone. While it's warm, it's not uncomfortable with my cloak on. That's just as well. I don't want to be recognized by anyone but my friends.

I head toward the water. I can't actually see it, but I know it's to the west. In school, we studied all this. I remember learning a lot about the coastline and so on, but I don't think I paid attention, and I definitely don't remember anything that I might have learned.

So, I don't know how far the water is from the cliffs. I think I remember that it's different distances in different spots.

I walk for most of the afternoon, stopping for a meal around the dinner hour—if my guess of the time based on the sun's position is correct. I've tried doing that before and been quite wrong.

I've been careful only to eat small amounts when I've eaten. I'm just about out of what I had left, but I hope to find my friends soon.

Shortly after my meal, I catch sight of the water through the trees. The relief floods through me. I grew up looking out a window and seeing the ocean. I hadn't realized how much I'd missed it.

What scares me, however, is there are enough people on the road that it'll be hard to go unnoticed. All it would take would be for someone to ask who I am and insist on an answer, and things could get awkward.

I move back away from the water and out of sight of the road before I head south. That's the direction of Sevord, but it's also the direction of Switcher Pass. My friends should be coming through there, and I hope, by chance, to run into them.

The walk south is slow going. It would be faster to move along the road, but as I think about it, my friends will probably go through the forest. When the sun begins to set, I find a good place to sleep where I can't be easily seen.

No fire—I never really figured out how to start one.

No warm food—unless I sit on it first.

No one to talk to—except myself.

Despite how interesting I am to talk to, I decide to give myself the silent treatment and fall asleep within minutes.

I think part of the problem is I'm tired.

I'm not making much progress. I think I should have made it to Switcher Pass by now, but between how sore I am and how tired I am, I'm barely moving.

My feet just ache. My back and legs and hands and more all feel like they're covered in scabs, and some peel off with every step.

I have to be careful. This area is swarming with soldiers, but I'm small, and they miss me.

I laugh to myself. I'm not so sure it's my size that's causing them to miss me. My clothes and my hair and my face and my hands are all caked in dirt. I thought I'd cleaned myself up well, but I ended up just spreading it around. I'm disgusting. And I think it's hard for soldiers to see someone the color of dirt in a forest. All I have to do is crouch down, and I look like a clump of mud.

I'm the warrior mud-girl. The Nobleborn warrior mud-girl who giggles.

Nearing the dinner hour, I sit down and take a rest. I didn't know why I was so tired at first, but I realized something about myself. I realized it as I thought about Caric and Ellcia.

I love those two. Not like Hemot. I love Hemot in a very different way. But those two… they're two people for whom I would do anything. If they needed anything from me, I'd do it.

But they're weird. I've noticed over the years that when they get tired, they want to go hide. I've even found them in a quiet room, each of them, not talking to each other, just reading. It looks so exhausting! But that makes them feel better. It's like the quiet energizes them.

Me, on the other hand, and Hemot… we're normal. When we get tired, we spend time together and try to get Caric and Ellcia to join us. They do sometimes, if they're not tired already.

But being with us doesn't get rid of their tiredness—it makes them more tired.

They're weird; there's no doubt about it.

But all this has helped me to understand what my problem is. I need people. I'm so exhausted, but I don't have anyone to spend time with.

"Are you in need?"

I jump and spin around, drawing my sword.

Before me is a man I recognize, but I just can't place him. There have been so many people in my life lately. This guy is… something about him reminds me of the castle.

"Ah, a young woman. I don't see many female vagrants. I suppose you're hungry."

I nod. It's starting to come back to me. I remember him.

"What's your name?"

I'm not going to give him my name. I'm in the process of hiding from people, not announcing my presence. "I… can't tell you my name."

"That's fine. I'll just make up a name then. I'll call you Skunk."

I smile. "Do I smell that bad?"

He laughs. "No, it's the marks down the back of your cloak. You have dark and light stripes of dirt as if you slid down something."

I remember his name. It's Hob. Well, no, it can't be Hob from the castle. Hob is quite mad. This man is non-mad. I guess I would describe him as sane.

"You can put your sword away."

"How do I know I'm safe around you?" I now think he's definitely not Hob, yet he looks just like him.

"You don't," he laughs again, "but truthfully, you wouldn't be able to hurt me with your sword. I spent too many years as a soldier and have fought in too many wars. You hold your sword well, but I would say you have less than a year's training."

I'm surprised that he's able to figure that out simply from the way I hold my sword, but he's right. I think I'm out of my league here. I sheath my blade but remain careful.

"So, about the hungry thing?"

I shake my head. "Pardon me?"

"Are you hungry?"

I nod. "I ran out of food yesterday."

"Water?"

"I have some left. Enough to get me through until tomorrow—unless I can find a river."

"All right. Anything else you need?"

I just stare at him. I'm a little confused. Is he offering to get these things for me? If so, that's quite nice of him.

"You look like you have some scratches and cuts. Do you need bandages?"

"Yes, that would be quite helpful."

The man nods slowly. "You don't speak like a vagrant. They're often quiet—friendly, but quiet. You speak like a Noble, or at least like someone who has grown up around Nobles."

"Thank you," I say, avoiding giving away anything about who I am.

"I'll be back in a bit. Feel free to wait here," he says, "but there are many soldiers out. If you want to avoid being seen, you'll want to move east about thirty feet. There's a small dip in the ground, and you can hide there. I'll be back with some food, water, and bandages. If you're still unsure if you can trust me, that's fine. I'll just leave them at the top of that little dip, and you can find your way from there. Agreed?"

"Thank you," I say again and smile at him.

He turns and wanders off. I hadn't noticed it before, but he has a rabbit and three squirrels on his back—dead, of course. I don't think he'd want them on his back if they were still alive.

I head east and find the little dip he spoke of. It's actually perfect. Ferns grow all around it, and it's hard to see. A perfect spot to hide.

When the man returns, I barely hear him approach. I guess he's used to moving through the forest. He sets the food down and turns to leave, but I call out from my hiding spot. "Wait!"

"Yes?"

"Do you have a bit of time? I'm… lonely."

The man chuckles. "Sure. Do you want to stay down there or come out?"

I climb out of the hole and pick up the food. Some of the food is still warm, while other bits of it can travel well.

He points at a little bag. "In there, I put some bandages as well as salve for your cuts. It's not nice smelling stuff, but it works. Oh, and it also stings, but it's better than an infection. Just rub it on any area that needs to heal." He looks me up and down. "Just a little farther to the east is a small river. You can wash up there, then when you're dry, put on the salve."

I thank him. I don't really know what to say. I just don't want to be alone.

Finally, I come up with something. "What's going on? I don't know why so many soldiers are in the forest."

He smiles. "I'm Berin, by the way." He looks around as if to confirm that we're alone. "The soldiers are part of the Free Armies of Sevord. The Prince has been found and is returning to the castle. Did you not know this?"

I nod. "I knew. I just didn't know that's why they were here. Is that why so many people are traveling toward Sevord?"

"It is."

"Do you know when the Prince will reach the castle?"

"I expect, from what I'm seeing and hearing, that he'll reach the city by the day after tomorrow. It's just a guess, though. I expect the Prince will make it through Switcher Pass sometime soon. He'll move slowly since he has the entire army and a portion of the population of the four cities traveling with him."

"How far are we from Switcher Pass?"

"A few hours at a fast walk."

"And Sevord?" I ask.

"About a six to eight hour hike."

"Thank you." I've finished my meal, and I think I want to clean myself up. I just don't know how to politely tell the man to leave.

"Well, I don't think you're a vagrant," Berin says. "You're too proper. That means you're on the run."

My hand goes to my sword.

Berin shakes his head. "No, no, no. You're in no danger from me. I'm just making an observation. If it's true that you're running from someone, then I encourage you to keep your hood up and try to travel with the people. If you're heading to Sevord, stay out of sight until you can join a large group. That way, the soldiers won't pay any attention to you."

I smile at him. He's been very helpful.

"Well, I should be off. It was nice meeting you, nameless skunk girl. I hope you make it to wherever you're going."

I thank Berin once again, and he heads off through the forest.

I continue east until I find the stream Berin mentioned. It's barely anything, but it's enough. I wish I had a pond or large river to bathe in, but I have to make do with what I have.

I make sure no one is around and take off what I need to clean myself and apply salve to the areas with cuts and scratches.

I redress in my extremely dirty clothes. After eating and spending a bit of time with another person, I feel so much better. Returning to the little dip in the ground, I settle in for the night.

I hope to find my friends soon.

16

The Abdication

I sit with the crowd in the early morning. I'm with a couple I met yesterday on my trip to the city. I hadn't planned on actually getting to know anyone, but when I stepped into a group of people moving toward the city, these two spotted me, came up, introduced themselves, and we traveled the rest of the way together.

It worked out well, actually. At one point, some soldiers came by and asked us all our names. The man and the woman stepped close, stood on either side of me, told the soldier their names, and the soldier simply ignored me. At first, I didn't know why, but then I realized since I'm so small, with my hood up, he probably thought I was their child—or grandchild. They're actually older than my parents.

Since then, I've barely left their side.

They tell me everyone calls them Gramma and Grampa. I feel a little weird about that, but everyone actually calls them that—even the older people. In fact, they even introduced themselves to the soldiers by those names.

They're from a village called Grimmer. Apparently, a lot of people have come from the first three villages along the coast. They tell me those farther than that likely won't come. They might not even know what's going on until it's all over.

Everyone's excited. There are a lot of tears—tears of joy. I see everyone crying now and then. A little while ago, a man who looked kind of like a bear came up to Grampa. The man was as tall as Rulf and looked like he could eat me. He just held Grampa, and the two wept together talking about how happy they were that they could see their Prince take the throne.

I also have no shortage of food now. People just pull out food and share it with anyone who wants some. It's like a big party.

I had intended to move closer to the entrance of Switcher Pass. I figured I could keep an eye out for the others when they came through, but the closer I got, the more soldiers I saw. I moved west to try to avoid them and found myself on the road to Sevord, standing next to Gramma and Grampa.

"You need a little more bacon, dear?"

"No, thank you, Gramma."

She smiles at me with her nearly toothless grin. "You such a polite girl. I so happy to have met you."

"Thank you, Gramma. I'm happy I met you as well." I look around. "What's going to happen?"

She laughs and shrugs her shoulders. "That's what we all want to know!" She laughs again and sits down beside me, leaning her shoulder up against mine. "There be lots of different ideas, but here's what I think. I think the Prince'll come along, the trumpets'll sound, the people'll cheer, and either the Regent'll put up a fight or he'll recognize that he has to bow to the Prince or die."

"What if he resists?" I have no idea what he'll do. I just know he won't be happy to give up the throne.

"I think if he resists, the people'll turn on him or the Nobles will. The only reason he been allowed to rule is because he a royal and he never put forward a claim to the throne." She smiles at me. "I don't think we have to worry about any of that. The Prince'll take the throne today. Maybe he'll even get married!"

"Married?" I'm a little confused about that. I don't want to marry the Prince, but I'm surprised that he's found someone else so quickly.

"Rumor has it the Prince has his eye on Lady Aldora's daughter. He a little young to marry, but tradition has it that an unmarried King finds a Queen quickly—often marrying the day of his coronation." Her smile grows large, and she holds up her cup to everyone around. "Perhaps we have a royal wedding today!"

The people nearby cheer, and I give an uncomfortable smile. This will be a strange day, for sure. I pull my hood down a little more over my face. Gramma seems to notice but doesn't say anything. Enough people around have their hoods pulled. I think everyone's excited, but also a little afraid.

The gates to the city open at this point, and rows of soldiers march out, lining both sides of the road leading into the city. They wear formal dress, so I don't expect trouble. Banners drop from the top of the wall in rich colors, displaying the crests of the Noble houses. In the center is the Royal crest, Roran's family crest. I guess that's Caric's family crest as well.

I see my family's crest up there, and the longing for my parents floods my heart. I hope to see them soon.

In the distance, toward the east, I hear the shouts of the crowd grow. I expect that's the Prince approaching.

Everyone around rises to their feet, and the excitement grows. I feel it myself. I can't wait to see the Prince return, although I have mixed feelings about seeing him again considering he wants to marry me and he's enchanted.

Rarely in my life have I wished I was taller. I've always been quite happy with my height and size. But right now, with all the people around, I can't see a thing. The crowd comes in closer and I find myself pushed around a bit, but then Gramma and Grampa move up on either side of me. I think they actually think of me as their grandchild.

The crowd pushes in, and I continue to be jostled around, but eventually find myself at the side of the road. It's a perfect position. I can't believe we get to stand here. I can see everything!

Although, it also means it's easier for me to be recognized. I'll have to be extra careful.

The crowd begins to cheer even louder. I look up the road and see why. The Prince is within sight. He's on horseback, the only one. Everyone else is on foot and is dressed in fine robes, but it's nothing compared to Roran. He's dressed like a royal—and there's no doubt that he's the center of attention.

Gramma and Grampa cheer on either side, and I find myself cheering as well, laughing and jumping up and down. The Regent will finally be removed, and the Prince will take the throne!

They're moving slowly, as they should. It gives everyone time to see the Prince and allows the moment to receive the respect it deserves. But I just want him to gallop!

When he passes me, I keep my head low enough that I think he won't recognize me. He moves on without comment, so I relax just a little.

Behind the Prince is his honor guard. They move with serious expressions on their faces and their hands on their swords. I can't quite remember the tradition, but they walk as though they expect to run into battle at any moment. I remember learning something about the King's honor guard is never simply for show.

Behind the honor guard is General Lirnal. He walks alone, shoulder's squared and a big smile on his face.

Behind the General are my parents. I nearly scream out for them, but I catch myself. They both smile, but I see sadness in their eyes as well. I don't know what they're sad about, but then I wonder if it's because of me.

I feel my heart warms at that thought. I want to run out to them, but a soldier will probably kill me before I can identify myself. I also think they want me to stay away for now.

I look from my papa to my mama and realize she's looking straight at me. She looks afraid, yet relieved. I mouth the words, "What do I do?" and she gives me just the slightest shake of her head. I think that means she wants me to stay back and stay quiet.

Behind my parents walk Captain Frindor and Captain Granel. I keep my head down as they pass. Behind the Captains are a row of Nobles. Some of them I've met, others I saw in the mountain.

I hear the crowd begin to boo and hiss and others shout angrily. I look toward the gates and see the Regent has emerged along with a group of Nobles standing behind him. Among the Nobles are General Corter and Captain Tilbur—the two youngest sons of King Hartor.

The Regent—Parthun—stands in front. He's dressed in royal robes and has a large grin on his face. I feel a wave of dread come over me. I don't think he's smiling because he thinks he can talk his way out of this.

Oh no… the enchantment! This is what it's about! This is the moment! It might be to take down General Lirnal, but ultimately, this is the moment the throne moves to Parthun!

I glance over at General Lirnal. Caric is actually second in line for the throne, that's why Captain Frindor tried to kill him. General Lirnal also stands before Parthun. Lirnal is third in line for the throne. The enchantment… it will take care of Roran. Not sure about what will happen to Caric. And Lirnal will either be arrested now or killed within the day.

My heart fills with dread. I see it all.

Parthun is about to take the throne.

I don't know what to do about it. Even if I told everyone, it wouldn't change what's about to happen.

I turn back to the procession. Prince Roran has finally reached the gates. I'm not too far from him. I can see it all. From my angle, I can't see my parents' faces, just their backs, but I can see the Regent. He's still grinning. The Nobles behind him wear smiles as well, but their smiles seem more genuine.

Roran brings his horse to a stop and dismounts.

As he climbs out of the saddle, the crowd grows silent. It's not a silence of respect, though. Everyone's shocked. I hear many people gasp, including Gramma and Grampa.

I look at mama and papa, and she's got a hold of papa's arm like she's terrified, and he's stiff as a board. General Lirnal, just ahead of them, has his hand on the hilt of his sword. I don't know what's happening, but it's not good.

The Prince moves forward, and two of his honor guard go with him. Each man, even from behind, looks like he's ready to attack anyone who gives even the slightest indication of threat.

When the Prince comes within ten steps of the Regent, he stops. I fear I won't be able to hear what they say, but there's no worry about that. When the Regent speaks, his voice carries well.

"My dear Prince, we are filled with joy at your return. The people have lived with hopeful expectation all these years that you might return and take the throne, which is rightfully yours to do with as you please."

My stomach tightens. This is not right. I don't know what's wrong, exactly, but this is really not right.

"I have, in my wisdom, oh Prince," the Regent continues, waving his arms in his dramatic fashion, "kept the kingdom in anticipation of your return, ruling in my loyalty, always hoping to once again see your face. The throne is yours, my Prince, to do with as you please."

I don't like that "to do with as you please" part. It's come out twice now.

The Regent continues with a simple question. "My dear Prince, upon your return, what is your first order?"

The Prince doesn't say anything for a moment or two. Everyone remains silent, and I feel the tension in the air.

Then Prince Roran does what I never would have expected—despite knowing of the enchantment. He drops to his knees, places his hands on the ground, and bows so low to the Regent that his forehead touches the ground.

I can't help it. I can't hold it in. I scream. "NOOOO!"

One of the Nobles behind the Regent steps forward. In his hands is the royal crown. The tears stream down my face as Roran gets up, takes the crown from the Noble, places it on the Regent's head, then unbuckles his own sword and hands it over. Once finished, he moves to stand beside General Corter, behind the Regent.

I don't think I'm breathing. I feel like I haven't taken a breath the entire time.

I hear someone nearby holler out, "All hail King Parthun, Ruler of Sevord and the Talic!" Another one calls out the same thing, then men here and there begin to chant those words. The crowds, however, do not join in. The men are obviously hired by the Regent. This has all been planned for a long time.

The Regent orders, "Arrest the traitor!"

Soldiers rush out of the city and surround General Lirnal. They take his sword and his knife and bind his hands. They drag him forward, bring him before the Regent, and one of the soldiers kicks General Lirnal in the back of the knees. He drops to the ground.

"Lirnal!" the Regent says, loud enough to be heard by many in the crowd, "you are accused of taking part in the assassination of King Hartor and in leading a rebellion against the throne these last eleven years. You will be held until such time as I deem you worthy of a trial."

The soldiers drag him to his feet and through the gates. He doesn't fight back. I can see he's stunned, but there's nothing he can do. Parthun is King.

At this point, people begin to scream and run away. I don't know why they're running at first, but then it hits me. Parthun has been brutal to the people, but until this point, he's only had limited authority. Now, he's King. No one can question him aside from the Nobles, and their ability only goes so far.

Gramma and Grampa pull my arm, and Gramma says, "Let's go, dear."

I turn back to them just as someone bumps into me, and my hood drops. I reach for it to pull it back up again, but as I do, I see Prince Roran looking straight at me. The expression on his face is one of deep joy and affection.

He says something to Parthun—King Parthun—
who orders the soldiers to retrieve me.

I turn to Gramma. She looks scared. "Listen. They're
coming for me. You and Grampa have to run. Don't worry
about me. I'll be safe. You… run!"

I give her a little push, and the two run away as fast
as their old legs can move them. I turn back to the soldiers,
and they grab my arms. They're far rougher than I would
expect.

When I reach the Regent—the King… oh, this is
going to be hard to get used to—he smiles at me. It's not a
nice smile. "Ah, Marleet. I was so upset when I lost you a
short while ago, but it's good to have you back."

"Yourrrr Majestyyyy."

"Lord Yune!" Parthun says. "Welcome back to
Sevord. I see you have finally decided to rejoin the civilized
people."

"I have alwaaaays sought one thingggg, Your
Majestyyyy."

"And what is that, Lord Yune?" The venom is hard
to miss in King Parthun's voice.

"To lovvvve and remain loyallll to the thronnnne,
Your Majestyyyy."

"And will you remain loyal to me, Lord Yune?"

My heart races. I don't know how my papa will get
out of this.

"I willlll, Your Majestyyyy, love and remain loyallll to
the thronnnne."

King Parthun is not pleased with that answer, but it
is all he can ask. He turns back to me. "And your daughter…
I suppose you wish her to stay with you? I don't know why
we find her covered in mud and hiding among the
commoners."

"There wassss, Your Majestyyyy, an attempt on her liffffe. This is the firsssst I've seen her since she rannnn for safetyyyy."

He turns to me. "It is gooood to see you aliiiive, my daughterrrr. Are you wellll?"

"I am, papa."

King Parthun scowls but orders the soldiers to release me. He turns to Roran. I notice the Prince hasn't taken his eyes off me. "And Prince Roran, who is this Lady to you?"

"I wish to marry her, my King."

The King slowly turns back to me. A big, terrifying smile has broken out on his face, but his eyes are savage. "Marriage! How wonderful! The Prince and Lady Marleet will be wed." Turning to my papa, he says, "We will speak of the upcoming marriage of your daughter at our next meeting of the Nobles."

Without another word, King Parthun announces, "Let us return to the castle. I will take my seat on the throne of Sevord and begin my rule of our great nation!"

17

The Quarters

R innnnt."

"Yes, My Lord."

"I wish for youuuu to go ahead and preparrrre our quarterrrrs for our arrivallll. My daughterrrr will obviously neeeeed a bathhhh and chaaaanges of cloooothes."

"Yes, My Lord."

As we make our way toward the castle in the long procession of soldiers and Nobles, Rint heads off down another street with the rest of our servants and half our guard. It's a long walk to the castle, especially at this speed, but even if he rushes, I can't imagine he could get everything ready by the time we arrive. I don't know where our quarters are, but I expect they've been abandoned for eleven years.

People line the streets to see all of us. I get a lot of confused looks, but the rest of the stares are sad. I think no one knows what to do or what to think. We have, in just one day, lost the entire kingdom. And no war was even fought.

I'm sure the soldiers are questioning both what they should do now, but also what they've done the last eleven years. I don't think there's a simple answer to any of it.

"Are we safe?" I whisper to my papa. I'm holding his one arm, and my mama has his other.

"Nowwww is not the tiiiime to ask questionssss."

I hold my tongue. I guess he's right. We don't know who might overhear.

The one good thing, however, is that I catch sight of Denner, one of my personal guards from when we traveled across the Talic Region. I ask about him, even though it's not the time for questions, and my papa explains what happened. It turns out he and two others were knocked unconscious when we were attacked, and they stumbled back into the camp the next day.

Denner gives me a nod and a look as if to say he's sorry he wasn't able to protect me. I mouth the words, "It's okay" to him, but the guilty look doesn't seem to go away.

The walk to the castle takes somewhere around two hours. As we get closer, people cheer more, but I can see their hearts are not in it. As I examine the crowd, I see soldiers positioned throughout the people, watching them closely. The crowds have obviously been ordered to cheer.

When we enter the gates, we enter through the east side. That's the largest of the gates. Past the castle gates, a huge area with fountains, grassy areas, flowers, and more spread out before us. Hundreds of soldiers stand guard throughout this area, all with sashes across their chests and plumes on their helmets.

We move through the courtyard—it's not a short walk either—and enter the castle. At this point, most of the soldiers break off, but the rest of us move down the large, ornate hallway toward the throne room. When we reach it, we enter and Parthun slowly makes his way toward the throne. When he reaches the stairs, he stops for a moment, turns around and addresses the crowd.

"Thank you all for your trust in me. I am honored and humbled by this gift of your love. I take this crown and this throne, not as an expectation, but as a trust. I will serve the people of Sevord and the Talic with all my might."

Parthun then turns around, climbs the steps, and sits down on the throne.

My mind jumps back to a memory. Once, a few years back, Hemot greased down a chair. He covered it in pig fat, then we watched from a hiding spot as a Noble sat down in it. His feet shot out, and he slid off the chair, landing on the floor.

An image of this pops into my head, and I imagine King Parthun's feet shooting up and him sliding off the throne, bouncing on each step. I wonder if I'm a bad person for wanting this to happen.

He raises his hand, and General Corter approaches. When the General reaches the bottom of the stairs, he kneels before the King and swears his allegiance to King Parthun. When he's finished, Captain Tilbur approaches and swears his allegiance to the throne. After Tilbur, my papa approaches, kneels, and swears his allegiance to the throne.

This process takes a long time as a member of each family approaches and swears allegiance. I notice that very few people, my father included, swear allegiance to Parthun himself, but rather to the throne. Both approaches seem to be acceptable, but Parthun frowns anytime he does not hear his name.

When we're finished, a celebration is announced for that evening, and my mama and papa lead me away from the throne room.

"Let's go get you cleaned up and prepared for the celebration," my mama says.

Despite all that's happened, I'm looking forward to seeing our apartments. I wonder where in the palace I used to live.

I step into my family's quarters.

The servants are hard at work. They're moving our belongings into the rooms, and some of it looks like it's just been purchased. I think, perhaps, my parents had to leave much of their belongings behind. A lot of it was likely sold or taken to other rooms.

I've been in these apartments countless times over the years. I occasionally helped Ellcia, Caric, and Hemot clean these rooms after a visiting dignitary stayed here. I just thought it was one of the many available rooms for Nobles to use. I had no idea my family had lived here.

I also didn't realize that my parents owned a great deal of land in the northern part of the Talic Region. Apparently, we have a large manor house there. I'm only actually learning this now because Rint talks about it as he coordinates the setup of the apartments.

My mama leads me into a room that I had always liked. It's small and quite pretty. In the closet hang three beautiful dresses, none of which were there on any of the times I cleaned the room in the past. That's something I would have noticed.

"Do you remember this room, Marleet? This was your nursery, then when you were older, we converted it into a bedroom for a young Noblewoman."

I shake my head. "I've been in here many times over the years while working in the castle, but I didn't know this was my room."

My mama points to a doorway. We walk through, and I see a tub steaming with hot water and two women standing by. My mama explains, "These two women will help you undress, then they will bathe you, then they will take you to your bed. Before you dress, a nurse will examine you. Once finished, she will bandage any cuts and then you will be able to dress."

I stare at my mama in shock. I'm certainly not used to being a Noblewoman. The thought of someone else undressing me is bad enough, but then to walk to the other room to wait for someone to come in and examine me—all the while undressed—is a little too much to bear.

The two women take a step toward me, and I put my hand on the hilt of my sword. "Anyone who tries to take off my clothes will lose their hand."

My mama gasps, and the two women take a big step back. I wonder if I'm taking this whole warrior-thing a little too far, but then I think that I want to be a little different from a regular Noblewoman. "I'm sorry, mama; I'm not used to others undressing me. I'm a very private person."

My mama stares intently at me for a moment, then smiles. "I understand, my dear. This is a big adjustment for you. It's also a big adjustment for us. Are you able to bathe yourself?"

I find that a strange question and wonder if my mama is not. "Yes, mama. I have been bathing myself since I was six years old."

"And what of your cuts and bruises? Are they in private places?"

My face turns red. I can't reach my back to bandage up any of those cuts, and the ones on my butt are going to be hard to take care of. I whisper, "I might need help with some of those."

My mama smiles. "I'll help you with any area which you cannot reach."

"Thank you."

My mama waves the two women out. Their faces fill with relief as they rush for the door. Before my mama leaves, she brings in a beautiful gown. It's not a dress, and certainly not something I'd wear out in public. It looks like it's just something you might sleep in, but it's beautiful. She leaves it on a bench for me and then walks out.

The bath turns out to be just perfect. Not too hot, not too cold. I don't ever remember having a bath like this. There's also something in the water that makes it smell nice. I scrub myself clean, then dry off, pull on the gown, and head into the other room. When I get out there, I find a note which tells me to ring the bell when I wish for my mama to come.

I pull a cord near my bed, and a bell rings. A moment later, my mama comes in. I'm still a little shy around her, but I remind myself that she is my mother.

When I'm all bandaged up, she helps me dress in a beautiful gown. I'm glad she's here for that part. I actually don't know how to put on a gown such as the ones in my closet. It does take more than one person.

When we're finished, my mama orders a tray of food and a hot drink brought in, and we sit down. She speaks quietly, and I have to concentrate to hear what she says.

"Marleet, I am going to need to speak quickly. We are in a difficult situation right now. I wish to hear all that happened to you, but perhaps what happened among us is of greater importance for the moment."

I nod. I think she's probably right. I look forward to telling them about all that I went through, but I'm pretty sure that our situation right now in the castle is life or death.

"After you left, we searched for you, of course, but we had to trust you to survive on your own. We knew you would be killed if we brought you back to us. We suspect Captain Frindor was behind much of it, but of course, nothing can be proven. So, we had to focus on other matters, although that was quite difficult.

"The Prince eventually received the hesitant support of the three northern cities, but Rainer, the City of Thieves, did not commit. They decided to stay neutral until they saw how it all worked out.

"As we moved through the Talic Region, Captain Frindor took the lead. We suspected he was also hunting for you, and we managed to insert a few loyal soldiers among his own, but many did not make it back from patrols.

"The Prince's abdication of the throne is a surprise, of course. This creates new problems on many levels. Parthun cannot legally take the throne, even though the Prince has abdicated. If the Prince abdicates, it falls to the second in line, then the third, then the fourth.

"General Lirnal, of course, is third in line for the throne. He, however, has been charged with treason. At an impartial trial, he will be absolved, which means he will be in a position to make a claim for the throne. But King Parthun will not allow it to go to trial, unless he can guarantee a judge's decision."

I lean forward. "Who will the judge be?"

"Your father would be the obvious choice, but Parthun would never allow such a thing. There are other Nobles of various loyalties and various levels of integrity. It is hard to know who might be appointed to such a position. But it will not come to this anytime soon."

"And what about Caric?"

My mama closes her eyes for a moment. "We do not know with certainty the location of the second in line for the throne, nor will we speak of possibilities, even in private. But if the second in line for the throne was to arrive and lay a claim, he would receive it without question by the Nobles. Unfortunately, now is too dangerous a time for such a thing. If Prince Draydon, or Caric, as you call him, were to arrive, he would be killed before he could reach the castle, let alone lay a claim on the throne."

I shiver at that thought. I also let the idea of Caric as King settle in my mind. I can see that. He has always been a kind and thoughtful leader. But Ellcia will not be happy. I wonder to myself what she will do. She has always loved Caric, but even as a young girl, she hated the thought of being a royal.

My mama continues. "Until Prince Draydon and General Lirnal are out of the way, the Regent can be called King and may sit on the throne, but his rule is not established. Everyone—both Nobles and commoners—will live open to the possibility that Parthun might be removed from the throne at any moment. The people will await General Lirnal's trial, hoping he will be deemed innocent, then expect either him to take the throne or for him to abdicate.

"Now, for this evening, it will be an awkward celebration due to all that has happened. It is possible Prince Roran might ask for your hand in marriage yet again."

"What do we do about that?"

She shakes her head. "There's nothing we can do about that, but leave it to your father. He will work it out. He has a way."

My mama smiles at me. She reaches over and takes my hand. "Many strange days lie ahead for us, under difficult circumstances. Trust us. Trust us to do what is right."

"I will, mama."

"And tonight, my dear, is where politics and nobility meet. Tonight, much may happen. But trust your father." She smiles again, and a little laugh escapes her lips. "My friends, when I was young, wanted me to marry a soldier. They wished for me to marry a warrior. I chose your father instead. He may not be a soldier, but his words can topple kingdoms and raise men up to the throne itself. When tonight, things move in a direction that you do not wish, trust your father. This is his battlefield. This is where your father shines. It is in times like this, my dear, where you will see Lord Yune shake the world."

18

The Celebration

On the way to the celebration, I walk with my mama and papa. It's a long walk—not a long distance, but a long walk. Every few steps, someone stops us and wants to talk, wants to ask advice, wants to welcome my parents back to the castle, or wants to tell us how happy they are to be back here and no longer in the mountain.

The smiles are all fake—that is obvious.

I don't think the fake smiles suggest those we speak to are our enemies—or that they're fake people. My parents are well loved by just about everyone. I think the Nobles are trying their best to act with nobility in the midst of terrible shock and disappointment. Few are happy about Parthun's rise to the throne.

But everyone we meet is quite nice and respectful until Captain Tilbur shows up.

Captain Tilbur is sixth in line to the throne. That doesn't sound like much, but he's not some distant relation. He's actually the youngest son of King Trevolay. King Trevolay and Queen Marlina had six sons, no daughters. Hartor was their oldest, and he was Roran's father. Hartor reigned until Parthun had him killed.

While I grew up in the castle, believing I was a servant, not a daughter of a Duke and Duchess, Captain Tilbur had always been one to avoid. He was mean to me. He was mean to all of us. But none of us felt the full brunt of his wrath. That was always saved for Caric.

My parents had explained that Tilbur was loyal to the throne, yet remained by Parthun's side in order to support the resistance. His cruelty to us had all been an act to allay Parthun's suspicion.

So, now that we're back in the castle, I had assumed that Tilbur would be nice. I thought he would be kind.

I assumed wrong.

"Captain Tillllburrrr. So nicccce to seeee you. It is good to be baaaack togetherrrr in the kingdommmm." My papa gives a slight, yet very respectful bow.

Captain Tilbur steps up close to my papa. The rage is clear on his face, and my papa's expression is one of shock. When Tilbur speaks, it's just barely loud enough for some of the other Nobles to hear. He spits his words more than speaks them. "Yune! Don't think all is forgotten. You sided with the rebellion. You sided against the throne. You stood against King Parthun. None of us will forget this!"

"My dearrrr Tilburrrr. I am so sorryyyy that so much painnnn has been experiencccced by so manyyyy. Pleeeease, my dear friennnnd, may we put all thissss behind ussss? May we move forward in peacccce?"

Tilbur steps forward just a little more and drops his voice. I can barely hear him, but the tone is clear. There is nothing but rage there. "Peace, my *friend*, is not something I expect to be a part of our relationship for the foreseeable future." Without another word, he spins on his heel and moves off down the corridor, growling at anyone who tries to speak with him.

We begin to move again, and I whisper to my mama, "I thought…"

She stops me with a slight shake of her head.

Most people avoid us after that. I don't think it's us they have a problem with. I think they're too shaken. Despite only being the rank of Captain, Tilbur is a Prince. He has a great deal of influence throughout the kingdom, and he answers only to General Corter and King Parthun.

On top of that, if it really comes down to it… General Corter is a puppet. Tilbur is the real authority in Parthun's army. He has a reputation for… well, few people challenge him and live.

When we enter the banquet hall, I see Tereese, and I nearly call out to her. She's the head cook for the castle, and I worked under her for years. Before I can, however, my mom gives me another shake of her head. She leans down quickly and whispers, "Ignore Tereese. She will do the same toward you."

"Why?" I can't imagine what would cause me to do such a thing.

"We all have a part to play, my dear."

We move toward our seat as our names are announced. Many stand as we enter, and a few more come to speak with my mama and papa.

While we await the King's arrival, other Nobles are announced. A few of the names I recognize. Some I don't. I met many in the mountain, and many more I've seen over the years in my time in the castle.

Noticeably missing is General Lirnal. I wonder to myself what he might be going through right now.

"Lord Yune! Lady Aldora! It has been far too long, my friends."

"Lord Hillllbin!" My papa's smile is large and genuine. "It is soooo good to see youuuu!"

"Is this your daughter?"

He smiles at me. I actually look down on him. I don't mean I look down on him in an arrogant way. I mean, I look down on him in the sense that he's actually shorter than I am. The word that immediately comes to mind is the word "portly." I don't really even know what that word means, but it seems to fit.

"Yes, this is our beautiful daughter, Marleet," my mama says. "She has finally returned to us after far too long."

The man's face just beams as he examines me. "You are well, my Lady?"

"I am, Lord Hillbin," I reply.

He turns to my parents and asks, "May I kiss the young lady's hand?"

I'm kind of grossed out by that thought. I really don't want my hand kissed by anyone, let alone this strange, portly man whom I've just met. Unfortunately, my papa gives a slight bow and says, "You maaaay, Lord Hillllbin."

Lord Hillbin steps in close and takes my hand. He brings it up to his mouth, and my stomach begins to turn. I decide right there that I'll have a talk with my papa about this kind of thing.

But all that slides away as he steps in close. He doesn't actually even kiss my hand. Instead, I hear him whisper, "My Lady, your friends are safe. I helped them on their way in Haner. They miss you."

He pulls away, making a loud smacking noise as if he actually kissed my hand. The sound is quite gross, but not only am I thrilled with what I've heard, but I think I like the man a lot. And I'm beginning to see how many people in the kingdom are truly loyal to the throne and loyal to my family.

At this point, a quiet song is played on a lute, and everyone moves toward their seats. I know this part of the process, after serving a few times in a banquet hall. The music means the guest of honor is about to arrive, and everyone should prepare themselves.

We sit down, and a moment later the new King is announced. We all rise as King Parthun comes in with General Corter. Captain Tilbur and Prince Roran walk behind.

I hadn't realized we sit so close to the King, but it turns out we do. In fact, what makes it even more awkward is Prince Roran is seated beside me.

They're up to something. I hope my papa is able to deal with it all.

The King gives a speech in which he says nothing, other than he is honored by blah, blah, blah. I'm afraid that he might actually have said, "blah, blah, blah." I can't imagine that could be true, but it's what I remember.

Throughout the speech and then throughout the meal which follows, I sit tense and very distracted. Prince Roran, seated beside me, barely touches his food. Instead, he can't take his eyes off me. He talks to me about anything, asking all sorts of questions. I would be flattered if it were not for the fact that this is merely the result of an enchantment.

On top of all that, he keeps sliding his hand toward mine—forcing me to spend a lot of time needing to adjust my hair, straighten my dress, organize my cutlery. I'd just as soon be anywhere else but here. I think maybe General Lirnal, sitting in prison, might have the best situation of us all.

At first, I feel only disgust toward Roran. Then, as the night wears on, I begin to feel pity for him. He's stuck inside there, driven by this enchantment. The enchantment's intention was to bring about the abdication of the throne, but…

My heart goes cold. There's more going on here. Much more.

"Marleet?"

"Yes, Roran?"

My heart races. Not because Roran is speaking to me yet again, but because of what I just realized. We're in greater danger than I had known. I wonder if my parents know!

"I have never seen such beautiful hair. I think I could stare at it for the rest of my life and be happy."

I bite my tongue. I don't think there's any good reply to that.

"What did you do to your hair to make it so beautiful?"

"I… um… combed it."

"Wow, Marleet. You are the best comber in the kingdom."

I think to myself that Roran is going to be royally embarrassed when all this is over. Before he can go on about something else, the Regent, I mean the new King, speaks.

"It is with great pleasure that I celebrate with all of you today. Here in this room," the King says, waving his hand across the large assembly of people, "are many of my closest friends in the world. Some of you have been by my side through the many difficult years leading up to this day, while others have recently returned. I feel we are complete now as we are, once again, together."

Everyone claps, including me. I'm just happy to have something to distract Roran for a moment.

When the applause dies down, King Parthun continues. "I recognize that today is a day of joy. A day when we have seen the return of our beloved Prince Roran. It is also a day when we have experienced sadness as the Prince has expressed his desire to give the throne to another. This, of course, is painful for all of us. For me, however, the weight of grief is greater than for most.

"These last eleven years, I have searched the kingdom countless times to find our dear Prince, hoping to return him to the throne. To reach this day and hope to see my Prince take his place, only to find he wishes to remain in the background, is agony for me and will continue to be a constant ache in my heart.

"However, while I take this responsibility with hesitation, I am also humbled by the Prince's trust in me." Turning to the Prince, he says, "My dear Prince, son of the great King Hartor, I will lead your kingdom with humility and grace, hoping that I can live up to the standard set by your father."

Everyone applauds again. I feel sick to my stomach, but there's no choice but to applaud. To take a stand right now would be of no benefit—even I can see that.

"But, I have good news," the King continues. "Prince Roran has a wonderful announcement for us and wishes to ask something of our dear Lord Yune in the presence of our Kingdom's fine Nobility."

The King sits down, and Roran stands up, a large smile on his face. I know what he's about to do. He's going to publicly ask me to marry him. I want to get up and run out of the room, but my mama's words come back to me. This is my papa's battleground. I need to trust him.

Prince Roran steps away from the table, gently grabs my hand and pulls me away from my seat. I take a glance at my mama, and she nods. I can't imagine that this will turn out well, but I've never understood the way of Nobles.

We stand in the middle of the room with all eyes on us. I am thrilled to be wearing such a beautiful dress, but I don't know if I enjoy the attention as much as I would have thought.

Roran clears his throat, smiles at me, and then announces to the entire room, "My dear friends. It is so wonderful to be with you once again. I wish to say many things, but I have only one thing left on my heart—my love for this beautiful woman. Ever since I first saw her, I loved her, and I knew I wanted to marry her. I wish only one thing, to have her as my wife."

My heart feels like it's about to jump out of my chest and run away. If it doesn't, I think I might run away myself. I start imagining myself living in Switcher Pass or in the Talic Region—living off the land. I might even prefer to live up on top of the cliffs.

I look over at my papa, hoping he'll come to my rescue, but he just sits there with a large smile on his face, as if he's the happiest man in the world. A quick glance around the room lets me know that all the other Nobles appear more concerned than my own papa!

"Marleet," Roran continues, "you are more beautiful than all the sheep and cows in all the land."

That one gives me pause. I think perhaps he should have worked a little more on that particular compliment. It's not that I'm looking for him to tell me I'm pretty, but… sheep and cows? I glance around the room and find I'm not the only one who's a little thrown by that comment. I remember hearing something about how enchantments not only make people act in a strange way but also say strange things.

I hear a chair move and turn to see my papa slowly get to his feet. He has his arms spread out on either side as if he's about to come in for a hug.

"My dearrrr Prince Rorannnn." He stops and bows his head, a large smile on his face. "My dearrrr, dearrrr Prince. I am so honorrrred to know that my daughterrrr has caught your eyyyye. What a privvvvilege to find that my daughterrrr could be a Princessss. It is certainly true that sheeee would be the most beauuuutiful Princess this lannnnd has ever seeeen."

Prince Roran thanks my papa and then appears ready to continue his speech, but my papa speaks up again.

"As you knoooow, I would neverrrr give my blessingggg to anyone to marryyyy my daughterrrr before she is eighteeeeen. Until thennnn, all suitors must waaaait. Of courssssse, to have youuuu, my wonderful Princccce, as a soooon-in laaaaw, would be a gift, for surrrre. But you, of coursssse, are younger than my dearrrr daughterrrr. As such, you must waaaait, as wellll, until you are eighteeeen."

I glance at Roran. He seems annoyed, but also a little dopey. The enchantment has a powerful hold on him.

"Of coursssse, my dear Princccce, as you also knoooow, many of my friendssss would wishhhh to be at the weddingggg, but would also not be pleeeeased if my daughterrrr was marriiiied before the age of eighteeeen. It would raise questionnnns about their own childrennnn." Turning to Parthun, he added, "A concernnnn, of coursssse, for the Kingggg."

I see a flash of anger pass through the eyes of King Parthun, but then he quickly calms himself. When he speaks, he speaks with respect, but there is a thread of sarcasm present. "As always, Lord Yune, your wisdom is so desperately needed." The King stands up at that point and announces, "The Prince's love for the beautiful Noblewoman warms my heart, as I'm sure it does yours. Prince Roran, would you defer your affection for the Lady Marleet until you are closer to your eighteenth birthday?"

The Prince bows to Parthun and says, "To wait all that time would be but a pimple on the eyelid."

That one causes King Parthun's mouth to drop open, and a few grumbles spread around the room. I suspect if anyone had doubted an enchantment, they no longer do.

My papa, unfazed by the pimple analogy, comes to me, offers me his arm, and leads me and my mama out of the hall. I hear some movement behind me and glance back. All the Nobles have risen to their feet and are moving toward the exit.

"What happened in there?" I ask my mama once we are back in our apartments.

"Oh, the King is such a wonderful man and such a wonderful leader. We are blessed to have him," she says with what sounds like genuine affection for him.

"Ohhhh, and what an honorrrr to have caught the eyyyye of Prince Rorannnn," my papa adds.

My papa moves off into his study, while my mama leads me into my own chambers. Mildren is already in there. Before she leaves, she gives my mom a nod and closes the door.

My mama points to a chair for me, and she takes her seat across from me.

She smiles. "My dear, outside this room, I cannot guarantee our privacy. This room, however, seems to have been ignored. There are no listening spots in this area."

"Someone might be listening out there?" I ask in shock.

"They might. It's difficult to know. So, for the future, we will only speak openly in this room. In the other rooms and in the hallways, we will be very careful, and you must keep in mind the possibility of spies."

"Is that why you spoke so well of the King and the Prince in the other room?"

My mama smiles at me.

"Why did papa say all those things in the hall? And why did everyone leave after he said it?"

My mama laughs. "Your father and I have a lot of influence within the nation—and without. It is often the King who leads, but the Nobles who move the nation. And your father and I, not to boast, my dear, move much of this nation. Your father, in saying the things he did to the King and the Prince, has announced that to displease him or harm his family in any way would be to displease a great many Nobles. It will be difficult for the new King to lead as it is, considering the circumstances, but to move ahead without the support of the most influential Nobles will lead nowhere good."

I nod. That makes sense. "And why did all the Nobles leave after he spoke?"

"Part of the concern is that if the King and the Prince can force you into marriage, that means they can force any of the Noble's children into marriage. Not one of the Noble Families, even the dishonorable ones, wish to give the King that amount of authority. A marriage often creates agreements between two families, promotes peace, alliances, and more. If the King has the authority to force this, the Nobles become his puppets. When we left the banquet hall, we announced that we would not stand for such a barbaric practice. If the other Nobles had not also left, it would be their way of declaring that they stand with the King on such a move. Since they left, the King knows he is in a dangerous situation. He must be careful."

"The enchantment…" I begin. I'm not sure how to say this. "The attraction… I'm concerned about it."

"In what way, my dear?"

"I don't think it was unintended."

"It is a common consequence of an enchantment. There is a story of an enchantment given through a spider. The woman, who was enchanted, fell in love with the spider and wept when the spider would not propose. Then one day, she accidentally sat on the spider."

I laugh. "Is that true?"

"I don't know, my dear, but it's a good story." She smiles.

"In this case, mama, I think the attraction was an intended part. I think I was centered out to carry the enchantment. I think the Regent wanted the Prince to fall in love with me."

My mama studies my face for a moment, but then her eyebrows shoot up. She rushes to the door and calls out, "Yuney! Please come quick."

He arrives quickly and closes the door behind him. My mama says to me, "Explain to both of us what you are thinking."

I quickly bring my papa up to speed. "I don't think the enchantment on the Prince was only about making him give up the throne."

My papa leans in close. He does that thing where his neck extends out, and his face moves far closer than I think should be possible. It's very... turtle-like. For some reason, it makes me love him more. I like that he's so strange.

"I don't think I was a random choice—just someone to reach the Prince. I don't think it was only because I'm the daughter of the two of you and am more likely to be granted access to him. I think I was chosen because they knew the enchantment would cause the Prince to fall in love with me."

My papa's neck quickly pulls his head back, and his eyes grow wide while his mouth simultaneously opens and frowns in slow motion. No sound comes out. If it weren't such a serious moment, I think I would laugh.

He slowly turns to my mama. "Then… the endgammmmme…"

I look at my mama. She looks… horrified. I'm missing something.

"What is this endgame?"

"If the enchantmennnnt was to result in thissss, then they are not finishhhhed."

I look back and forth between the two. I'm definitely missing something. "What would they gain from…" It hits me. I know what it's about. I'm not used to politics, so it's easy for me to miss the obvious. "This part of the enchantment is not about the Prince or about me. It's about the two of you."

My papa slowly nods, and my mama wipes a tear from her eyes.

I piece it all together. "This is about removing the two of you. So, either you will refuse the Prince and offend the throne, or you will be forced into agreeing to the wedding, and we will all be killed."

My papa nods again. "My dearrrr, this is hard for us to hearrrr, but youuuu must learn these waaaays. Please continuuuue. Telllll us what you haaaave figured oooout."

I feel proud that they listen to me. I think, as strange as this is, I'm actually kind of good at this. "They don't care if you offend the throne. The two of you are too powerful, and the King's position is too fragile right now. They want you removed. So, if the wedding goes ahead, then at first the Nobles will be upset. But they can solve that problem by shifting the focus. If, either before or after the wedding, they kill the Prince, me, and the two of you, then the Nobles will all want justice. If the King can blame it on someone else, he, as the new King, will become the hero. It will strengthen his position and remove our family. He will win."

My papa slowly nods. "Youuuu are wise, my daughterrrr. Please, tell ussss what we might doooo about it."

This is what I'm confused about. I don't know how to fix it. My mind is going to two places. "The only things I can think of are to break the enchantment on the Prince, which might solve the entire problem, or to run."

"Runningggg, at this poinnnnt, is not an optionnnn."

"Then can we break the enchantment?"

My papa shakes his head. "I'm sorryyyy, my dearrrr, but the King's sworrrrd is the only waaaay we have right noooow of breaking the enchantmennnnt."

"Then what do we do?"

My mama leans forward. "For now, we prepare. I expect sometime in the next three months, you will be forced into an engagement. The Nobles will not be happy, but as you have pointed out, the wedding itself will never take place. Once the wedding is declared, we will find out how long you have until you are to be married, and that is the amount of time we have left. At that point, either our preparations will be in place, or we will somehow have to find a way to run."

19

The Torturer

I feel a great deal of stress.

The Prince constantly wants me to come and see him. He's sent five requests for a visit in the last two days. My parents always politely refuse for me, as they will not allow me to be alone with him. The reason we have given is that if I am to be the wife of a Prince, my education will need to be completed.

So, I have jumped into my studies. I have learned a great deal not only about who the Nobles are, but also how the politics of the kingdom work. My tutors have also taken the basic education I had received and taught me far more than I had thought there even was to learn. At the moment, I'm half-way through a book by a famous author who died over a hundred years ago.

If, a couple months ago, I had been asked if I would like to study these types of things, I would have politely refused. But now, I just can't get enough of it. I think I see how much I am related to my parents. I love this kind of thing. I hope one day that I can be just like my mama and papa: good and kind people who pour out their influence on the kingdom.

I'm also getting a great deal of instruction on battle. Captain Tilbur comes and teaches me sword fighting and strategy and more. When we're in a place of privacy, he stops growling at me, and I find he's quite nice. He's quiet and serious, but he is nice.

At the moment, I have a break from my instructions, but I'm using it to read in a small sitting room. Unfortunately, this peaceful time is interrupted.

I hear yelling out in the hallway, and a loud crash shakes the door.

My mama rushes into the room. I jump to my feet, putting the book down on a small table. I also carry a knife now always, and I draw it.

Rint rushes in along with Mildren. Neither of them are fighters—especially Mildren… she's tough, but not in that way—but they both take their stand in front of me and my mama.

We wait.

More yelling.

Another crash.

The door opens slowly, and we prepare for a fight. My heart races, and I don't know what to expect.

When the door opens wide enough for someone to step through, it's Denner, one of my personal guards. He looks annoyed.

"My apologies, my Lady," he says, addressing my mama. "Rulfor, the… guard… is here to speak with the Lady Marleet. He doesn't seem to think he needs an appointment, nor does he seem to think he needs to wait for us to let him in."

I put my knife away. I haven't seen Rulf in weeks—since shortly after we entered the castle. Without thinking, I call out, "Rulf! I'm in here! Come in, please!"

My mama gives me a scolding look. I stop myself and apologize. I have not yet learned to control my tongue. As my papa says, "Controllll of the tonggggue is a Noble's greatest weaponnnn."

The door swings open, and Rulf pushes past our guard. When he's nearly at me, my mama steps in the way. She stops him with a simple raised hand.

"Rulfor," my mama begins in a stern voice, "you need to learn how to act around a Lady. You cannot simply force your way into her presence at any time except in an emergency. Do you not understand this?"

Rulf grunts, but my mama merely waits. After a short while, he finally says, "I'm sorry, Lady Aldora. I am still learning the ways of the Nobility."

"You once knew these things, my dear Rulfor. Do you not remember? You were young, but you were bright."

He nods. "I remember, my Lady."

"Have you forgotten all my lessons, Rulfor?"

Rulf shakes his head. "No, my Lady."

"Then what is the problem, Rulfor?"

"I'm…" Rulf looks embarrassed. "I remember all your lessons, but I'm used to living on the streets. I had to set aside all you taught me."

"You set everything aside?"

He shakes his head. "No, my Lady. I used what you taught me to teach Prince Roran. I taught him everything you said. But I didn't use any of what you taught me on the streets."

Rulf's eyes are downcast. I think he actually looks embarrassed. I hadn't realized my mama had been his teacher. I can't imagine how she would have had time for such a thing.

"Rulfor?"

"Yes, my Lady?"

"You need to start applying what I taught you."

He nods.

Her voice grows firm. With a lot of authority, she says, "Start now!"

Rulf stays still for a moment, then bows his head. "Yes, my Lady. I must apologize to my Lady for my shameful behavior. Does my Lady wish for me to leave?"

"No, Rulfor," my mama says. "For now, you may remain, but I expect better behavior from you in the future. During this visit, I will require proper behavior and etiquette."

I find myself smiling. This is something I would like to see.

"Yes, my Lady." He clears his throat. "My Lady, I would like permission to speak with the Lady Marleet, if it is acceptable. I would like to speak with her in private."

"Rulfor," my mama says politely, "if you enter my daughter's chambers, my husband will have you killed."

My eye's bulge. First, I didn't expect my mama to say that. Second, I don't even know if it's possible to kill Rulf. He's part giant. His skin can stop a bolt from a crossbow.

Rulf, however, does not have any doubt. His eyes show genuine fear, and he bows his head. "Then I will not enter your daughter's chambers. Please forgive such an impudent request."

Truthfully, I'm not really sure what the word "impudent" means, but I get the idea. I make a mental note to remember that if I want a boy to live, I need to keep him out of my chambers.

"Would it be permissible for me to take the Lady Marleet for a walk, my Lady?"

I'm not really sure that Rulf actually said that. It sounded like he said it—it was his voice—but that was far too polite for him.

"Yes, Rulfor. That would be wonderful. Will you keep her safe?"

"Of course, my Lady."

Rulf turns somewhat and holds out his arm. I laugh. It seems so absurd, but he's acting like a real gentleman. I didn't know it was possible.

We move out of our apartment, and three guards follow at a distance. Denner is one of them, but Billot is not around today. My papa has kept our family's guard close. They are all loyal.

I encourage Rulf to head to the east corridor. As we move, we speak of our journey across the Talic Region. He also tells me stories from when he lived in the city with Mic. He shares a funny story of how he and Mic, or Prince Roran, were caught stealing horseshoes from a baker to sell to a seamstress, who sold them back to the baker for a profit.

The problem with the castle is it is full of secret passageways. At any point, someone might be hiding in one of these passageways, listening to our every word. We're not sure if any of our enemies even know about them, but it's a risk. A short while ago, no one would have been listening, but now that there is such division among the Nobility, there's no way we can trust that we will be safe to speak openly.

But the east corridor is a unique area of the castle. It is a long corridor where sound does not travel well, and there are no secret passageways—as far as we know. If we need to speak, this is the place.

Rulf seems to know that as well. As soon as we step into the area, Rulf drops his voice. Unfortunately, he slips back into the old ways for a second. "Listen, girl…" He frowns. "I mean, Marleet. We have to speak to General Lirnal. He's being tortured in the prisons."

I feel sick to my stomach. I know the General is being tortured. I also know that we can't do anything about it. To rescue him would put an end to our ability to stop the King, but to leave him there… it gives me nightmares. Maybe Rulf has a way…

"How do we stop the torture?" I whisper.

"Can't."

"There's the Rulf I remember," I say with a lot of sarcasm.

Rulf grunts. "We can't stop the torture. It has to happen. It's the only way to keep the King satisfied."

I don't quite understand this, but it's what my parents say as well. They know the situation better than most. I accept it for now, but I don't like it.

"When I said we have to speak to General Lirnal, I mean just that—we have to speak with him."

"What do we need to speak to the General about?" I can't imagine going down there. If I see him, I don't think I'll be able to hold back. I think it'll make me want to do everything I can to rescue him.

"There's an enchanted item," Rulf explains. "I don't know what it is or where it is, but it's in the castle. It can cancel enchantments."

"Like the King's sword?"

He grunts. I take that as a yes.

"And why do we need to speak to General Lirnal?"

Rulf looks annoyed. He gives me a look to suggest that I'm a little slow. I know I sometimes come across that way, but he just hasn't told me why. I don't think I'm missing anything.

"General Lirnal knows where it is. He can tell us where to find it."

"Then how do we get it to the Prince? I assume you want it to cancel the Prince's enchantment?"

Rulf grunts again. "I haven't figured that part out yet. We need to find the item first."

"How do you know the General knows where it is?"

Rulf comes to a stop and turns us around. We're at the end of the corridor. My guards move behind us and follow at an appropriate distance.

"It's something in the Royal family. Ever since a King fell prey to an enchantment, they have had an obsession with preventing further enchantments. They have this item somewhere in the castle. Only the King's oldest two sons know about it—not even the King himself. So Caric's dad would have known, and General Lirnal will know. King Parthun likely doesn't even know that it exists."

"What about Captain Tilbur?"

"The Captain knows about it, but barely anything. Years ago, he happened to hear it exists, that's all."

"Can't he ask the General? Does he ever get to see him?"

Rulf stops and turns to me. He looks at me in shock.

My guard calls up, "Is everything okay, my Lady?"

I turn back to him. "Yes, Denner, thank you. We are fine."

Rulf examines me for another moment before starting to walk again. "I'm sorry, Marleet. I thought you knew."

I shake my head. When it comes to General Lirnal, I make a point to know as little as I can. Knowing that he's being held in prison and tortured is more than I can handle.

Rulf explains. "Captain Tilbur sees General Lirnal every day. He visits him every morning and every evening."

"Why doesn't he ask him?"

Rulf speaks slowly. "Two reasons. First, when he visits General Lirnal, he is always accompanied by three or four men who are unquestionably loyal to King Parthun."

"And the second reason?"

"He's a little busy when he speaks with General Lirnal." Rulf glances at me again, as if he's deciding to tell me something I might not want to hear. He clenches his jaw for a moment before saying, "The reason he's busy is, Captain Tilbur is the one who's torturing General Lirnal."

I pace back and forth in my chambers. Here I am, feeling guilty that I'm not doing anything to rescue General Lirnal. It's been eating away at me all this time, but I've set it aside because I'm told it cannot be dealt with right now.

And all the while, one of my teachers, Captain Tilbur, is the one who's doing the actual torturing. He's torturing his own brother—an innocent man!

A knock on the door. I expect that's Tilbur. Rint opens the door, and I hear Tilbur's voice.

"Out of my way, Runt!"

In a respectful tone of voice, I hear Rint say, "It's pronounced, Rint, Sire."

"Are you still here?"

"I'm sorry, Sire," Rint says. "Please excuse me."

"Captain Tilburrrr, to what do we owe this honooooor?"

"I'm here to see if you have come to your senses yet, Yune! You willing to give up that worthless child of yours to marry the Prince? The King is growing quite impatient with you!"

I have heard forms of this conversation many times. It's their cover story for when Tilbur comes to teach me. It's always a short lesson, but it's intense. Tilbur does not go easy on me.

"Let me speak with her!"

"You may only speeeeak with herrrr if I am presennnnt, Captainnnn."

"I don't care if you're around, Yune! Where is she?"

My door opens, and I smile, give a little curtsy, and prepare for the insults. Until the door closes, there is no friendliness.

"Hello Marleet. Am I speaking too quickly for you? Should I slow it down so you can understand? Heeeeellllllloooooo Maaaaarrrrrllllleeeeeetttt."

The door closes behind Tilbur and my papa. Tilbur gives a respectful bow and says, "My Lady. Are you ready for our lesson today?"

I nod. I don't know if I can say much else without being rude.

"Have you practiced what I taught?" His voice is respectful. He is far from a friendly person, even when he's trying to be nice. It's like he just doesn't know how.

I nod again.

"Excellent." He grabs the practice swords from behind one of my wardrobes and tosses one to me. They're about the same length as a sword, but made of wood and covered in cloth to quiet the sound. It also adds enough weight to make it feel like a real sword.

As we hold our swords out, I notice his knuckles. They're cut and split. I've seen that before but figured he was dealing with criminals or those he had arrested for crimes in the city. But now I know. It's from striking General Lirnal.

I attack.

Tilbur easily blocks and lands a light blow on my shoulder. Not enough to bruise, but enough to let me know I let down my guard.

I attack again with all the rage and anger building inside me, but once again, he easily blocks and hits me on my side.

"My Lady Marleet," he says in his emotionless manner, "you are not focusing today. Is something on your mind?"

I don't want to lie. I also don't want to have this conversation. "I don't think I am up for lessons today."

"If you do not practice regularly and receive regular instruction, you will not improve, my Lady."

I glare at him. He doesn't seem to mind, but I notice my papa shift in his seat.

"Perhaaaaps, my dearrrr, weeee can put off your lessonssss for a day."

Captain Tilbur bows to me, then to my papa, then returns the practice sword to its place behind the wardrobe before leaving the room without another word.

I stand there, holding my sword. I hadn't realized I was breathing heavily and sweating all over. Without moving my head, I look over to see my papa.

He has a concerned look on his face.

"Are youuuu, my daughterrrr, okaaaay?"

I nod, but it's not very convincing.

"Do youuuu want to tellll me what is wrongggg?"

I just blurt it out without thinking. "Tilbur is torturing General Lirnal!"

My papa nods.

"And I saw the split knuckles on Tilbur's fists. He's hitting him hard."

"Yessss, he issss."

"Why are you allowing this?" I ask. I notice my fists are clenched, and I'm squeezing the handle of my practice sword so hard it's hurting my fingers.

"It is noooot my decisionnnn, my dearrrr."

"But you have influence!"

He nods.

"And howwww would my daughterrrr recommend I influencccce this situationnnn?"

"By stopping it!" I've never spoken to my papa like this, but I don't understand why he is acting so unconcerned.

He takes a deep breath and motions me to a chair. I sit—but I don't really want to—and lay my sword across my knees. "My dearrrr, listen closelyyyy. I cannot stop the torturrrre, I can only influence whoooo might do the torturingggg."

"So, you suggested Tilbur beat up General Lirnal?"

My papa shakes his head. "My daughterrrr, calmmmm your minnnnd. Whyyyy are you drawing that conclusionnnn. Think it throuuuugh."

I close my eyes, but get nowhere. Instead, I ask, "What did you do?"

"There is a mannnn named Grinnnnor. He is a most vicious mannnn. He is King Parthunnnn's chief torturerrrr and executionerrrr. I recommended himmmm."

"You recommended someone brutal and cruel?" I'm shocked.

"Does the Kingggg trust me, my dearrrr?"

"No!"

"Thennnn what might he do with my recommendationnnn?"

It all comes clear. "You recommended the chief torturer, and the King rejected the idea. Tilbur volunteered, and the King accepted." I look my papa in the eye. "Is it a good thing that Tilbur is torturing the General?"

My papa shakes his head. "Noooo. It is not a gooood thingggg. But someone wiiiill be torturing the General. Tilburrrr will hit hard enough to impressss the Kingggg, but not hard enough to do damage to a sooooldier." He smiles. "They agreeeed that this is what they would doooo in such a circumstanccccce."

"They planned for this?"

"Tilburrrr plans for everythingggg. And he is a most wonnnnderful actorrrr."

My head is spinning, and I drop my sword. I come in and give my papa a hug. I don't know if I'm cut out for this kind of life.

When I pull away, I say, "Rulf came to see me today. He wants to…"

My papa raises his hands. "My dearrrr, Rulfor is an honorable mannnn. He is rough and ruuuude, but he is honorablllle. If he cammmme to see you about somethingggg to do with Tilburrrr or the Generallll, then do not tell meeee. If I am questionnnned, I must say I do not knoooow. I must always speeeeak the truuuuth."

I nod. "Yes, papa." I find myself smiling. Not only do I understand it more—not that I'm happy about the torture thing—but my papa trusts me to just do what needs to be done. Now I know what my next mission is. Rulf and I will do what we have to do to save the Prince from this enchantment.

Rulf and I lean over a table. We're in the library, and we have two maps. We have a map of Sevord with the Talic Region. We have marks all over it for the path we've traveled.

But that's in case we're caught. Under that map, we have a map of the castle. Rulf knows this place better than I do, including many of the hidden passageways, but he never went into the dungeon as a child. It had always been off-limits for him. As difficult as he is, he has never disobeyed his parents.

We find there are only two ways down to the dungeon—at least, according to this map. One is the main entrance, which is guarded by five to six soldiers at the top of the stairs and a dozen or more at the bottom.

The other is a side entrance. It's not guarded as well—perhaps only a few soldiers, but it requires that we go through a solid oak door with steel bands for added strength. That is, if we can sneak past the soldiers.

"I could just plow my way through them."

I nod and give a smile. "I know you could, Rulf." I also know he doesn't think that's a good idea. Rulf acts like he's not too bright, but he's actually brilliant. We're studying these maps, but Rulf already has them memorized. He can look at something and remember it forever.

"Rulf, what can we do?"

"I think we have two choices."

I stop and think about that. I bet I can figure it out. Fighting our way through is not an option—or at least not a good option. It's a good way to get us our very own cells, but not a good option if we want to speak with General Lirnal.

"The one option is to find an excuse to speak with the General."

Rulf grunts. That's his way of saying, "Yes."

"The other option," I say, staring at the ceiling, "is to find another way down." I look over at Rulf. "But that's not the best idea."

"Why not?" He looks like he really doesn't know.

"Because if we find a secret way down there, we will still need to approach General Lirnal's cell. But if we are caught down there because we snuck our way in, we'll have no excuse. It'll be obvious we're up to something unauthorized."

Rulf grunts again. "I didn't think of that."

"It doesn't matter. I don't think we have another way down."

He leans over, and without explaining anything, drops his finger on the map.

I stare at the spot where he points. I don't really see anything. In fact, maps really aren't my thing. I can work with a big map that shows a large area, but when it comes to something like this which lays out the castle and the corridors and more… I really can't make sense of it. It just looks like a big mess.

Rulf growls. That's his disappointment growl. "So, no point in looking for a secret passageway."

I put my hand down on the map and cover the area he's looking at. He grunts and turns to me. "Rulf, what makes you think that?"

"Because… we might get caught. And I can't let you get caught."

I feel flattered. That was one of the kindest things I think I've ever heard Rulf say. "Thank you, Rulf. But unless we come up with an excuse to speak with General Lirnal, and to speak with him alone, then we have to choose that option. Besides, it might work out."

Rulf purses his lips in a particularly ugly way. I haven't seen that expression before, but I think it might mean he wants me to explain.

"If there is another passageway down, it might lead anywhere. Unless we come up with an excuse to speak with the General, we have to at least check to see if there's a secret way down to the prisons."

Rulf pokes my hand. I pull it back. He leans over the map and drops one of his sausage-sized fingers onto that same spot he pointed at a moment ago. I stare at the drawings until I begin to piece together that it's an area near one of the entrances to the prison.

I wait. I think sometimes Rulf likes to not share all the information he needs to for no other reason than to be difficult.

Finally, Rulf says, "Look at this wall here."

I nod. "I can look at it all day, Rulf. You know maps aren't my thing."

"Thick."

I frown and cross my arms. "Rulf, we're trying to work together to save the kingdom, and you start insulting me? I am good at some things, but reading maps and drawings of buildings is not my thing. Just because I can't read this map is no reason to call me thick."

Rulf furrows his brow, then shakes his head. "No. Not you thick. The wall." I let him examine my face for a moment in the hopes that he'll figure out that I need a bit more information. I like Rulf a lot. I just find this kind of thing frustrating. Finally, he says, "The wall's too thick. It's thicker than it should be. Not much, but I think there's a secret passage in here. One I don't know about."

I nod. I don't mind if he calls the wall "thick," but I don't really want him calling me that. "How do we get in?"

Rulf leans over the map for a moment and runs his finger along what I think might be walls. When he straightens, he explains, "There's a long section of the wall that's too thick. The entrance could be anywhere along there."

"How do we find the entrance?"

Rulf gives one of his rare smiles. "Leave that to me."

20

The Tunnels

We step around the corner. We're near the area where Rulf thinks there's a secret passageway. Unfortunately, I always need to have my guards with me. Rulf could act as a guard, but I have to have at least two with me, so there's always a second.

I know we can trust them, though. My papa always says he only keeps loyal people close.

We come to a stop, and I wave for the soldiers. I never know if we're being listened to, so I whisper.

"Listen," I say to Denner as quietly as I can and still be heard. "We're about to do something that's necessary for the safety of the kingdom. If we disappear through a doorway, we need you to return to my apartment and wait. In one hour, return to this spot, and we'll rejoin you. If we do not, then inform my parents of what's happened."

The soldiers do not appear impressed, but they nod. However, Denner adds, "I will have to inform your father of this either way."

I smile. "That's fine, but assuming I rejoin you, I'll need you to hold off on telling him for at least a week, if not longer."

He doesn't look happy about it, but he nods.

We move off down the corridor. Rulf tells me he's seen enough secret entrances that he'll recognize it if there is one.

He moves to my left side, and I take his right arm. It's the improper side for a gentleman to walk on, but anyone who sees will just think, "Oh, it's just Rulf."

A few servants bustle around the corner, but stop and wait next to the wall. Unfortunately, that makes it impossible for us to do what we came to do.

I bring Rulf to a halt, and I call out, "Thank you for your respect, but we are moving slowly. We would prefer if you passed by us and went on your way, so we do not hold you up any longer."

The two ladies curtsy, move along the side of the corridor, curtsy again when they reach us, and then rush off down the hallway past my guard. I feel a little awkward about that exchange. I know those two ladies. I've worked with them as a servant in the kitchens many times. I even worked under one of the ladies when cleaning some rooms. It feels strange to suddenly have them offering a curtsy.

Once they're gone, we take a few more steps, but then Rulf stops. He grunts at me and turns to the wall. I look both ways up the hallway, but no one is within sight. That can change any second, however, so we've already decided to move quick.

The area of the wall that seems to have Rulf's attention is no different from any other area—at least to my eyes. But he seems to think it's what we want.

He glances both ways and nods at the two soldiers who stare at him with confused expressions on their faces. Without another word, he runs his shoulder into the wall.

I've seen him do this before. The first time, I thought he was just being arrogant, thinking he could just push his way through a stone wall. This time, however, I'm prepared for it.

A section of the wall shifts, and he pushes it in. It's on some kind of hinge, so it opens like a door. I smile at the surprised-looking soldiers and slip inside. A moment later, Rulf slides the stone door closed, and we're in near darkness.

It's not a moment too soon, either. It's faint, but I hear a conversation coming through the cracks in the wall.

"Soldiers! What are you doing here?"

I recognize that voice. It's Captain Frindor. Of all people, it happens to be one of the most dangerous men in the kingdom.

"We apologize, Sir," the one guard says. He pauses, and I suspect he's bowing. "We are soldiers of Lord Yune."

"I didn't ask who you worked for, soldier!" Captain Frindor barks. "I asked you what you are doing here!"

"We apologize, Captain Frindor." My papa always insists his guards speak with complete respect to others, regardless of that person's honor or dignity. "We are unable to answer you as we are soldiers of Lord Yune. If you wish to know our orders, you will have to speak with the Duke."

I hear footsteps—a lot of them. I don't think Captain Frindor is alone. When he speaks again, he speaks so quietly that I can barely hear him. "I wonder," Captain Frindor says, "if Lord Yune is paying you well enough." I hear a few other soldiers chuckle. "If not, I think I might be able to find a way to help you make a little more gold, if you understand my meaning?"

I clench my teeth and ball my fists. I can't believe Frindor would try to bribe my papa's soldiers! But they're loyal, so there's nothing to worry about.

My heart goes cold as I hear Denner laugh and whisper, "We always like a little extra. Of course, it depends what you think we might be able to offer."

"Information, of course," Frindor says. "Nothing too serious. Just little details that might be helpful to me."

I hear Denner clear his throat, then say, "We're interested. But information doesn't come cheap. Especially information about the Duke."

"I am willing to pay well for the right information."

"Then when you know what you're looking for," Denner says. "Find either one of us, and we'll get you what you need."

I hear footsteps moving off. Once it's quiet, I whisper to Rulf, "I can't believe our soldiers would betray my papa! So easily, too! I have to warn him."

"Not important."

I want to punch Rulf in the arm, but I can't see anything and don't want to punch him in the throat or something by accident. "What do you mean? Of course, it's important."

"No, not important right now. What's important now is for us to find out where this passageway goes. Then we'll inform your father."

I don't like it, but Rulf's right. We have to do one thing at a time.

I focus on where we are. "There's not much light— not much at all. Some cracks lead out to the corridor, but not enough light comes through to see any detail. What's strange about this passageway, however, is how small it is. The other secret passageways were wide enough for us to walk comfortably down them, but this one's barely wide enough for me to walk. In fact, when I turn to go down the passageway, my shoulders actually touch either side.

That means Rulf will have to scooch along sideways. Actually, I will as well, if I want to keep my dress clean.

I nearly groan. There's no way I'll keep my dress clean! I should have brought a change of clothes. I didn't think ahead!

"Move toward that light," Rulf whispers, pulling me away from my thoughts. I look to my left and, sure enough, it's a little brighter in that direction.

We scooch along until we reach the end of this passageway. I get to the turn first and find three things. First, it's a crossroads—the corridor we've just reached goes both ways. Second, it's no wider than the area we're already scooching through. Third, the light we see is coming from holes along the wall.

I turn left and go to the first hole I see. It's a little hard for me to reach it as it's obviously made for someone taller, but I manage to see a bit. It's a fancy room. I don't recognize it at first, but then I remember cleaning it a few times with Ellcia. It's one of the rooms reserved for visiting dignitaries.

A quick look, however, tells me that someone has moved in. I gather one of the returning Nobles or officers has laid claim to it.

If I remember right, that particular apartment is in a hallway with three or four apartments, one after another. From the streams of light I see pouring in through small holes all along the way, each of the apartments has access for someone to listen in from this secret place. It looks like nothing is as secure and private as we might have thought.

"This way," Rulf whispers.

I follow him down the other direction. Now that there's more light, I see his belly pushed up against the stone wall. I can't imagine that's comfortable, but I guess it's what we have to do to get to General Lirnal.

After a few more minutes of scooching—I think I like that word. Scooch!

After a few more minutes of scooching along, Rulf stops. He turns his head back toward me and whispers, "The floor drops off here. Give me a moment."

He awkwardly bends down, doing his best not to scrape the walls too loudly. When he stands up again, he quietly tells me, "There's a ladder. I'll go first. You follow."

I grab his arm. "Rulf, I'm a lady."

Even in the dim light, I can see the confusion on his face.

I clarify for him. "I have to go first, Rulf. If you go first, I'm… well… I'm wearing a dress."

Rulf gives a quiet grunt. "But if you go first, then I have to climb after you. It'll be an awkward climb for me because it's a tight squeeze. If I fall, I'll land on you. Your dress won't protect you from my weight. I'll go first. I won't look up."

I shake my head. "No, Rulf, this is not right. I cannot climb down that ladder with you below me."

He grumbles, but starts moving back the way we came. We reach the crossroads, and I head back the one direction, while he moves down to the left. Once he's past, I slip out and head back toward the drop off. When we reach it, I almost fall off the edge. In the darkness, I didn't see it coming.

"Wait here until I reach the bottom."

Rulf grunts. "How will I know you've reached the bottom? You can't call up to me. It'll make too much noise."

He's right, but I won't climb down that ladder if he's below me while I wear a dress. I shake my head. "Then just come once you think I must have reached the bottom."

Rulf grunts, and I crouch down. I can't feel the ladder with my hand, but I know Rulf wouldn't mess that up. I get down on my knees and stick one leg over the edge, feeling around with my foot. After a few seconds, I hit the top rung. It's farther down than I would have thought. What a poor design!

I get my foot on it, but I feel like I'm going to slip. There's nothing to grab with my hands!

"There."

I look up at the dark shape of Rulf. "There?"

"On the sides."

"I balance myself on the top rung with my feet, doing my best not to slip as I feel along the side wall. Sure enough, little holes are set into the stone on either side. I gather they're there to help climbers start their climb down—and probably finish their climb up. Hard to believe Rulf can see so well in this darkness.

One more reason to climb down the ladder first. Rulf's an honorable guy, but it's just not proper and… it's awkward.

I grip the support holes as best I can and make my way down. When I'm able, I grab the rungs of the ladder with my hands.

After climbing about a dozen steps, I realize two things. First, I have no idea how far down this goes. Second, I may never have actually climbed down a ladder before. I'm proud of myself for doing so well, but I also feel very uncoordinated with it.

When I do finally reach the bottom, I step back. I hear Rulf on the ladder, but I can't see him. It's far too dark up that way.

Behind me, however, I can make out some details. Cracks and holes line this passageway as well, letting enough light in to see ahead. The corridor we're in now is far wider than what we were in before. Rulf and I won't be able to walk side-by-side, but we can certainly move without scraping the walls.

But the biggest change isn't the space.

Rulf reaches the bottom and whispers, "You okay?"

I nod. Somehow, he seems able to see even in the dim light.

"Stinks."

I nod again. I cover my mouth and nose, although I'm not sure that's going to help at all. The smell is a mix of mildew, sweat, urine, and something rotten. I'm hoping the rotten smell is food.

Rulf gets in front of me, moves ahead, and peeks through one of the higher cracks. After a few seconds, he pulls back and looks through one of the lower cracks. He then steps farther along and looks through another crack.

It's times like this that I wish he had a better ability to communicate.

I step forward and copy him, looking through whatever cracks and holes I can, although I know I'll never reach the higher ones.

The first hole I look through shows me… I'm not sure. I think it's a board or something, covered in dirt and dents and marks. Just before I pull away, it moves, and I realize with horror that it's someone's back!

Whoever I'm looking at is filthy, and he or she is covered in bruises and cuts.

I move down to the next crack and look in to see filthy feet. The person is likely trying their best to sleep.

I move down a bit farther and find a slightly larger hole that's not obscured by a person. From this point, I can see a bit of the cell. It's fairly small. The only feature I can see in the room are two small barred windows through which lantern light shines from outside the cell.

I realize our problem. We might be able to see inside every single cell, but we might never actually find General

Lirnal. He could be this person in this cell… or not. Unless we see his face, we have no hope of finding him.

I move to the next crack and find myself staring into the next cell. This one appears unoccupied at first, until I move down a bit farther. When I do, I see a man with shaggy hair and a long beard curled up in a corner. Blood is caked all through his hair and along his arms and legs. He wears only rags.

I feel sick. Not just because of the smell. These people are being tortured and abused. I don't know how long a beard like that takes to grow, but if it's anything like my hair, I would think that man had to have been in here for years. I think if I were in there for that many years, tortured continually, I'd be curled up in a corner like that too.

I force myself to move on. I want to whisper to him something that might encourage him, but I have nothing to say. I don't know why this is allowed or how long it will continue.

For the first time, I begin to hope that Caric takes the throne quickly. As soon as he does, he'll stop this.

I come to a halt.

If I can't find this item that cancels enchantments, then I know what I'll do. I know what my job is. I know what the giggling warrior girl is supposed to do. I'll do everything I can to make sure Caric sits on the throne. I'll make sure that Caric becomes King. And I'll tell him that this kind of thing is going on. I'll make sure he puts an end to it all.

I move on, taking a quick look through each crack, but refusing to linger. I know each of these people is important and worth my time, but I also know that unless we accomplish our mission, there's no hope for them.

All the cells have a man inside, except one. I can't see any of their faces, though. The only person I know for certain is not the General is the man with the long beard.

I catch up to Rulf, but he's stopped. He's looking through a crack in the wall, but very intensely and not pulling away. Perhaps we've found the General.

Before I can look through a crack near him, I feel Rulf's hand on my shoulder. He comes in close and whispers, "We've found him, girl… um… Marleet, but you might not want to see this. If you do, you have to stay silent, no matter what."

I pause. I know I need to look, but then again, I'm not sure I want to. I step up to a crack in the wall and peer through.

21

The General

I t's the General.

I recognize his uniform and his hair, but not his face. There's not much there that still looks familiar. He's swollen and bloody. I feel even more sick than I did a moment ago. It's bad enough when I don't know the person. Now that I do, I just want to scream.

I close my eyes and calm my heart. I need to be prepared to act when the time comes, but I can't act out of anger.

I open my eyes and examine the room. He's strapped into a chair in the center of the room. Across from him is a small table with… knives and sharp objects on it. Hanging from the ceiling along the back wall are chains and ropes. In the corner… long spears.

This is not a cell. This is a torture room.

I'm about to whisper through to him when two men walk in. I've seen them around. One of the men works with Captain Frindor. The other man is one of King Parthun's personal guard.

They come in and take up position on either side of the doorway. A moment later, Captain Tilbur comes in.

His face is expressionless, and he doesn't even look at his older brother, but instead moves to the tray and begins to look through some notes scribbled on a few pages. General Lirnal doesn't react at all when Tilbur enters. Instead, he just continues to hang his head. I'm not even sure he's conscious.

"Lirnal," Tilbur says in an emotionless tone. "Today we have the same questions as any day. I'm still curious as to how long it'll take before you give me the answers I want." He pauses for a moment and then says, "Do you remember them? The questions, that is? The first is, of course, will you confess that you and your brother Geran spearheaded the rebellion to remove our beloved King Hartor?"

I clench my fists. I'm still having a lot of trouble trusting Tilbur. I know my papa trusts him and says he's loyal, but it sure doesn't look like it. Especially when I know that the beaten, swollen man sitting near him is beaten and swollen because of him.

Tilbur continues to read through his notes as he says, "The other, of course, is, are you ready to admit that you killed Prince Draydon on the day of your rebellion?"

That's it. This is how they're paving the way for Parthun to secure his rule. Roran has abdicated. Caric, or Draydon, will be declared dead. And General Lirnal will be declared a traitor. No one will stand in the way of Parthun, and his right to rule will remain uncontested.

"And third, will you, Lirnal, brother of mine, in light of your rebellion and murder, abdicate your claim on the throne?"

At first, I don't think Lirnal is even conscious. There's no movement. No response. But then, as Tilbur turns around and faces his brother for the first time since entering the room, Lirnal's voice comes out, scratchy, but clear, "You know I won't do any of that, Tilbur, so let's just get on with it."

Tilbur nods and stretches his shoulder. "Well, this is day eight of my time with you, Lirnal. As you know, on even days, I forgo the tools, and just use my fists. Is there anything you need before I begin?"

"A drink of water would be nice."

"Excellent!" Tilbur says. "I was wondering how long before you noticed we're no longer giving you anything to drink. I was beginning to think one of the guards might be bringing you water now and then. Anything else you're lacking, my dear brother?"

"Nope, that's all, Tilbur." I see a bit of a smile appear on Lirnal's face. "But thank you for asking. I so appreciate your thoughtfulness."

Tilbur offers a mocking bow to Lirnal, and then steps forward, fist clenched, and pulls back his elbow…

I step back quickly, but I still hear the sound of the first hit. I turn and nearly empty my stomach, doing my best to be as quiet as I can.

When I calm down, I try to block out the sounds. It's horrible. Absolutely horrible. I grab Rulf and pull him away. "We have to leave. We can't do anything here. Let's leave." I grip his arm tight. He's not moving, so I hiss, "NOW!"

He follows after me. I can tell he's not impressed, but I'm not staying here any longer. We have to find a way to speak with General Lirnal, but that can't happen while Tilbur is beating him.

I reach the ladder and just point at it for Rulf to go first. Without a word, he begins his climb.

I don't really care that Tilbur is supposed to be a good guy. I don't really care that he's doing the torturing so he can be "nice" about it. I just don't care. He's an animal. He's not worthy of being a Prince. I know I'm not much, but I will be his enemy. The more influence I get as I grow older will all be aimed at taking him down.

When I think Rulf is at the top, I climb up quickly, not thinking about much other than destroying that man. I can't believe he would act in such a barbaric fashion!

When I reach the top, I grab at the holes on the side, and I miss. I gasp as my hands find nothing, and I fall backwards.

I'm just about to scream when I stop mid-air. Rulf has me by the front of my dress. A moment later, he heaves me up as if I weigh nothing.

I'm grateful to him for that, and it pulls me away from my anger. It also makes me think that my dress must be very high quality if it can support my weight. I'll have to compliment the seamstress.

"Why aren't you as upset as me, Rulf?"

"About what?"

"That Tilbur was torturing General Lirnal."

"You didn't watch?"

"How could I watch that?" I hiss. "And how could you watch that?"

"They're working together."

I pause. That's what I had been told, but I don't get how Rulf could see that. "What do you mean?"

"This is what they planned."

I frown. "Tell me more, Rulf!"

Rulf grunts, but takes a deep breath. "They trained for this years ago. My parents even taught them. Tilbur suspected something was coming. He didn't know what, but he had a gut feeling that there was a betrayal underway. Lirnal didn't believe him, but humored him. The two laid out a plan that they would do this. They even practiced torturing one another to protect each other." Rulf pauses for a moment, then adds, "They didn't know what was coming, but they prepared. If you had watched, you might have seen." He lowers his voice and when he speaks, he sounds impressed. "They're a good team."

"What do you mean?"

"Tilbur would swing, but at the last moment, Lirnal would twist his head and made it look like Tilbur hit him. But they were barely connecting. Lirnal obviously lets Tilbur hit him some of the time, otherwise he wouldn't have bruises, but they're definitely pretending."

I'm shocked. Maybe I need to trust my parents a bit more. "Wait, what about the days when he's not punching General Lirnal? What about when it comes to those torture devices?"

In the dim light, I see Rulf shake his head. "Don't know. Have to ask Tilbur or go down again on an odd day."

I'm feeling frustrated, but I know I have to focus. I decide I'm going to have to trust Tilbur, whether I like it or not. Maybe he is a good guy. "What do we do now?"

"Now," Rulf says, "we have to get back to your soldiers. It's been about an hour. Now that we know how to get to the prison, hopefully we can find the General alone at some point. So we find a way to communicate with General Lirnal and come back."

"A way to communicate?"

Rulf nods. "Yep. Maybe your father knows a secret code to use to convince him to trust us. I didn't think of this before, but the General likely won't speak with us without proof that we're loyal."

That makes sense, but the bigger issue right now is I'd forgotten about the soldiers and our one-hour time limit. Now I feel stressed. "We have to move."

We scooch along through the tight passageway, Rulf going first with me following. We reach the turn and follow it around to the left until we get to the point where we came in.

We listen hard for any sounds of people. I hadn't thought ahead enough to come up with a way to signal our soldiers. We can't see them, so once we confirm that we don't hear anything, Rulf pulls open the doorway, and we step out.

Two men stand nearby, and at first, I nearly scream, but it's my two guards. They look me up and down and frown at Rulf.

This is the first time we've been in any light, and I take a look down at my dress. I'm covered in dust and dirt and grime and spiderwebs. The dust and dirt and grime are disgusting, but I really don't like the spiderwebs.

Rulf brushes himself off once or twice and appears satisfied. I brush as hard as I can and get a lot off, but I'm disgusting.

One of my soldiers points to a room off the corridor. I step in there and find a simple dress waiting for me. My heart warms to them as I quickly change into it.

As I'm just about to leave, I remember. In all the excitement, I forgot that these men have been bribed by Captain Frindor!

And they accepted!

I step out into the corridor and find both men up against the wall, one in each of Rulf's fists. He growls at them and demands, "Tell me now what information you passed along to Captain Frindor!"

Neither man answers. Instead, they look at me. I'm not sure what to do. I'm glad Rulf is taking their betrayal seriously.

I realize they're looking at me because they answer to my family. "Put them down, Rulf."

Rulf drops the men, and they immediately come to attention. "My apologies, Lady Marleet," Denner says in a whisper. "I didn't know you heard that."

"I did. Care to explain yourself?"

Denner looks over at Billot, then back at me before he shakes his head. Once again, in a whisper, he says, "Not here, my Lady."

"Yes, here, soldier!" I don't like speaking with such authority, but I'm not going to let this go.

The man purses his lips for a moment, then says, "I will only whisper it in your ear."

"If you try anything, Rulf will..." I'm not sure what to say. When I do finish, it comes out awkwardly, but it scares them. "If you try anything, Rulf will break you."

Denner nods, looking quite scared, and leans in. "My Lady, your father has an agreement with all his soldiers. If we are ever offered a bribe for betrayal, we are to accept and speak only the information your father gives us."

I frown. That does sound like my father. "And the bribe itself?"

The man smiles. "One of the perks of working for your father is we get to keep all bribes, as long as we remain loyal."

That also sounds like my father. I whisper to him, "I will confirm this with him, soldier."

Denner smiles again. "Just don't do it in a place where you can be overheard. Please, let us move on before we lose our ability to accept bribes." He smiles awkwardly at me. "It's one of the many great things about being loyal to your family."

I find that an odd statement, but I understand what he means. I nod, and we move back toward our apartments.

We accomplished our first part of our mission—finding our way down there. Now we have to meet with

General Lirnal himself, get the information we need, find the item, and free the Prince from his enchantment.

I feel like I've taken on a lot lately.

22

The Location

Rulf stands outside my door, refusing to come into my chambers. I don't blame him. I'm pretty sure my mama was serious about my papa having him killed if he entered my room. My dad seems so gentle, but I guess when it comes to boys around my age, there's no movement on that issue.

My door is open so Rulf can hear our conversation. My papa sits across from me. I can't help but notice that he doesn't invite Rulf in—even though he's sitting right by me. I think it's kind of funny, but then I also appreciate my papa's care. I've never had that kind of thing—at least since I was little.

"My dearrrr, rememmmmber that I do not want much deeeetail about certain thingssss."

I nod. I've thought about how to say this. "Papa, I'm just curious about something. Is there a secret code or something that you might give to General Lirnal to confirm that he can trust you? Some way to prove that he should tell you something or give you what you want?"

"Ahhhh, my dearrrr, that is a gooood questionnnn." He smiles at me. At first, I think that's all he's going to say. Then he adds, "There is a phraaaase I use. Just with himmmm. No one elsssse."

I nod. I wait. Nothing. "Please, papa, would you tell it to me?"

My papa frowns. He does not appear to want to part with that information.

"Do you not trust me, papa?"

"Marleeeeteeee, this has nothingggg to do with my trust in youuuu." He takes a deep breath. "This is soooome of the most seeeeecret informationnnn I have. This agreeeement we have is for the Generaaaal to tellll me anything I wannnnt if I give himmmm this coooode."

I assume that means the General has one that he can use with my papa as well. "I understand, papa." I know I have to keep from telling my papa anything in case he's questioned, so I can't tell him that I actually need to know. I have to tell him in another way. "Papa, I really, really, really would like to know. It would mean a lot to me if you trusted me with this information."

My papa stares at me for a while. I feel like his eyes are burrowing into my soul. He has a way. After a long while, he turns and does the same with Rulf. I see Rulf shift on his feet. He actually looks uncomfortable.

Finally, my papa frowns, but turns back to me. "I willll give this to youuuu, my dear Marleeeeteeee, but you must understannnnd, that this is information I will diiiie for. If I give it to youuuu, you must treat it the same waaaay."

I feel the blood drain from my face. My papa is actually asking me to lay down my life for this information. It's that sacred. I can't… I'm…

The blood rushes back to my face, and I sit up straighter. My face just beams. I'm actually becoming a woman—no longer the little girl. I'm taking part in my parent's great work. I'm a part of it! I'm trusted enough to lay my life down for this cause!

"Yes, papa, I will lay down my life for this. I will not give it to anyone, no matter what." I mean that, too. In that moment, I know I will die rather than tell a single soul.

He leans in close, and I do the same. When his mouth is right next to my ear, he whispers, "Hartorrrr wears yelloooow underpannnnts."

Truthfully, I expected something else. Perhaps something serious. Perhaps something confusing. Perhaps something… less… silly.

He pulls back, and I see a twinkle in his eye. He whispers to me, "No onnnne would guessss that, my dearrrr Marleeeeteeee, correct?"

I smile. He's right.

He leaves the room, and I call my guards. I think they're still a little irritated at me for climbing through that wall earlier. However, I appreciate the dress they brought for me. But the dress…

My guards stand in the doorway, refusing to enter. They only have permission to enter my chambers if there is an emergency. I ask quietly, "How did you get one of my dresses to bring to me?"

"We spoke with the Lady Aldora, my Lady."

"I thought you weren't going to speak with my parents?"

"We weren't going to speak with your father, my Lady. We know there are times he wishes to be uninformed.

But we do not serve you, my Lady. We serve the Lady Aldora and the Lord Yune."

I'm irritated by this, but also pleased. My mama has not asked me about this, which means she trusts that I'm up to something good. Instead, she just provided me with a dress.

"We need to do the same thing again," I tell them. It's only been a few hours, but I'm hoping the torture is finished, and we can speak with General Lirnal. We still don't know for sure where his cell is. I'm hoping it's one of the empty ones we passed.

"Yes, my Lady. The Lady Aldora has commanded us not to question you on what you are doing. We are to assist you in any way you demand. Would you like to collect a change of clothes for yourself?"

I nod and thank them, then close my door so I can have some privacy. I change into some traveling clothes, which will allow me to move more freely and for Rulf to climb down the ladder first as I won't be wearing a dress. Over that, I pull a thin dress that will cover my traveling clothes and collect another thin dress that I can change into when I return. I shove it in a bag, and I'm ready to go.

When I step out, Rulf is still waiting there. I know I can't tell him the secret code any more than I can tell anyone else, but we'll still go together. He's loyal, he's strong, and he's a good friend—despite his grumpiness.

I hand the bag to Denner, and he accepts it without a word. We then leave for the prison area.

When we get there, the soldiers keep an eye out while Rulf opens the passage, and we slip inside. When it shuts, I listen for a moment, half expecting Frindor to show up again, but he doesn't. I wonder if my papa has given a message to the soldiers to pass along. I wonder what kind of message he might give.

Rulf grunts, and it pulls me back to the moment. He heads off down the passageway as I pull off the thin dress. He growls and turns away, but I whisper, "It's okay. I just wore this overtop of my traveling clothes. I can move a little freer wearing this outfit."

We scooch down the hallway until we reach the crossroads. Rulf offers to let me go first, but I tell him that with my traveling clothes, it's okay if I go after him. He gets to the top of the ladder, climbs down, and I follow quickly after him.

When we get to the bottom, I'm reminded of the terrible smell. We move along, skipping all the cells that had people in them before. I would never remember this myself, but Rulf never forgets anything.

When we find one of the cells that had previously been empty, Rulf peers in. He slides over to another crack, and I look through the one he just peered through. Nothing. I can't see anyone.

Rulf moves on, so I figure he couldn't see anyone through the second hole, and in another minute, we reach the second previously empty cell. When we do, he stops and lets out a little grunt.

I come up beside him and find a small hole. I peer through and just see someone's shoulder. Whoever it is, sits on his bed or cot, staring at the door. What I see of his shoulder is from the back, so I can't make out the man's identity.

Rulf leans down to me. "Not sure. I think that's him."

I move over to another crack between two blocks. It's no better, so I move back to the one I looked through at first. Rulf can see through a crack that's a bit higher. Maybe he can get a better view.

I put my mouth up to the crack and whisper, "Lirnal!"

I look through and see he's shifted somewhat. I catch a glimpse of the side of his face. It's bloodied and bruised, despite the fact that Tilbur is not trying to hurt him. I guess they have to make it look somewhat realistic.

I whisper through again, "Lirnal! General Lirnal!"

I peer through, and he's turned. He stares at the wall. The look on his face is one of worry. I'm not sure why, at first, but then I understand. I think if I were in his spot, and I heard someone whispering my name, I would think I'd just gone insane.

"General Lirnal!" I whisper again. "You're not crazy. I'm just on the other side of the wall!"

He slouches back, so his right ear is next to the crack. I gather from the other doorway, it'll look like he's just trying to lean back against the wall.

"General Lirnal, this is Marleet. Lord Yune's daughter. I need some information from you."

He turns to the side and whispers, "I have nothing to say. I have no information to give."

My heart fills with despair. After all we've done. And I even have the secret code! Oh… the code.

I put my mouth up to the crack and whisper, "Hartor wears yellow underpants."

I look through again, and the General hasn't moved. In a quiet voice, he asks, "What would you like to know, Lady Marleet?"

"It is said that there is an artifact that you know about which can cancel an enchantment. I need to know where it is."

I see him give the slightest nod. "I had meant to use it on the Prince if he did not draw his sword the moment he was declared King." He sits there silently for a moment, then says, "But we never got that chance."

"Maybe we can do it now," I say.

"Maybe," the General replies. "But if the enchantment is broken, and Prince Roran lays claim to the throne, Parthun will claim that the Prince is wavering—that he is unsure and therefore incapable of ruling the Kingdom."

"Can we not prove that he was under an enchantment?"

I see a slight shake of the head.

"But," I say, "either way, the Prince must be freed."

He nods at that. "It is…" but stops.

The door to his cell swings open and two men come in. They drop some bread on the floor and pour out a single glass of water into the corner of the cell. The men laugh, turn around, leave, and lock the door behind them.

"Dinner is served," Lirnal says and gives a weak laugh.

I feel disgusted by what I just saw. "I'll try to get you out of here."

"No!" he hisses back. "You'll do nothing of the sort! Leave me here! I'm the King's focus right now. That leaves your parents free to work and leaves you free to find the artifact."

I don't like the sound of that, but there's nothing I can do about it. He's probably right. And if he and Tilbur actually planned for this, then I'd be working against them. I find my respect for General Lirnal grows. If he, third in line for the throne, can choose to stay in prison and endure torture for the kingdom… then he is a good and loyal man. If Caric doesn't take the throne, I know Lirnal will be a good king.

But Parthun holds the throne at the moment, and Roran is under an enchantment. I have to act.

"Tell me where the artifact is."

Lirnal takes a quick, short breath. I think, at the moment, that's all he can take. Even his breathing sounds painful. "It's in the last place you want to look for it."

My heart races. There is one place I've never wanted to go. There is one place I've dreaded—the thought of which makes me want to cry. "It's in the sewers."

Lirnal twists his head to the side. "What? No! Why would it be in the...? No! It's in the throne room. That's the last place you want to go! It's one of the most secure rooms in the palace! If you're caught in there without permission, you'll be hung, and your father will not likely be able to save you. You thought the sewers? What?"

"Oh," I say. "Well, maybe you should be a little less dramatic. That doesn't seem like the last place I'd want to go. I mean, really, the throne room?"

Lirnal grumbles to himself, but then continues. "Once you start trying to figure out a way past the guards, you'll quickly find out it's the last place you want to sneak into."

I decide not to tell him that I already know of a secret way in, but instead I ask, "Where in the throne room?"

"Statues line the hall on either side of the throne. On the King's right..." he pauses. "That's the left side of the throne room as you face the throne. Look to the third statue from the throne. He's wearing a silver helm. It's meant to remain on the statue—it represents that king's wealth and military might—but it has been adjusted to slide up just enough. Underneath sits the artifact. I'm not even sure what it is, but it must be small to fit in there."

"Thank you," I whisper.

"Lady Marleet?"

"Yes, General?"

"This is a great quest you undertake. To get the artifact and to get the Prince to hold it in his hand—you risk much."

"It's worth it."

He nods. "I'm glad it's you, then, who is undertaking this work. That artifact has been left there for such a time as this and for such a one as you. Fulfill your task and serve the kingdom, my Lady."

"I will, General."

The General leans forward again to the position he was in when we arrived. I gather that means our conversation is finished.

I stand up straight and motion to Rulf. He comes in close, and I whisper, "I know where it is. Let's go."

We move back up the tiny hallway. When we reach the stairs, I climb the ladder first. My mind is so focused on what General Lirnal said to me, that when I reach the top, I just keep going, not waiting for Rulf. I can't get it out of my mind—not only the matter of where the artifact is, but also how important this is to the throne and to the entire kingdom. I don't know what part Roran has to play in the future, but I know he cannot remain enchanted.

I stop short, and Rulf almost bumps into me.

He grunts, but I don't answer. A wave of fear just passed over me. If Roran is freed from his enchantment, he'll likely want the throne. But if because he abdicated, he can't have it, then Caric will still have to take the throne.

That means the rightful heir will not sit on the throne. And if Roran is resentful, he will be a constant threat to Caric.

Maybe I'm doing the wrong thing. Maybe it's best to leave Roran enchanted. At least right now he's happy.

I turn my head and face Rulf. It's squishy in here. Well, it's not bad for me, but I know Rulf must be struggling. I can't see him very well, but when he moves, I can hear his belly scrape along the sides.

"Rulf?"

I hear a grunt.

"I have a problem."

"I know."

"You know?"

"You always have a problem."

I frown at him, but I don't know if he can see it. "I mean, I have a new problem that we need to talk about."

He grunts.

"General Lirnal says that now that Roran has abdicated, he likely won't be able to put forward a claim for the throne—even if the enchantment is cancelled. The Regent will use his abdication to discredit him. My parents think the same thing."

Rulf doesn't say anything at first. He just stands there. I can see a bit of the shape of his head as there's a small amount of light coming through behind him. "I was afraid of that."

My eyes begin to well up with tears. It hadn't hit me like this when I spoke with the General, but now, in this moment, I feel like everything's falling apart.

"What do we do?"

Rulf grunts. "What do you mean?"

"I mean, should we just not find the artifact? If Roran is happy now, should we just leave him? If we release him, he'll be upset and angry."

"But if he's released, we might find a way to put him on the throne. In fact, if we can remove Parthun, Roran will be able to claim the throne. It's only Parthun who will discredit him. No one else will matter."

"But if we can't, then Caric will need to take the throne. And Roran will always resent Caric for that."

"Doesn't matter."

"Rulf, of course it matters! Caric can't lead well if Roran is against him!"

Rulf leans forward a bit. He lets out a big breath, and I think he's upset. "No, I mean none of this matters. Roran is still enchanted. We have to free him. If that means Caric has to suffer, then so be it. We can try to stop Roran from being difficult, but the right thing to do at this moment is free Roran."

I think Rulf's right. I'm not comfortable with any of it, but… I think he's right. We can't leave Roran like this— even if he seems happy. But it still worries me.

I scooch along until I kick my dress on the floor. We've reached the area where we came in. I grab the dress and pull it over my head. Once it's on, I whisper, "Okay, open it."

Rulf listens at a small crack, then pulls open the door. We step out, and he closes it behind us. My guard stands just down the hallway a bit. As they approach, Denner and Billot look at me a little funny, but neither man says anything. Denner just points at the same room I used before to change my dress.

I slip inside and find my clean dress. When I go to pull off the old one, I find out why the soldiers looked at me funny. My dress is on backwards. I pull it off and throw the clean dress on over my traveling clothes.

When I emerge from the room, both soldiers look relieved. I gather they didn't want me walking through the castle with a dirty dress on backwards.

As we walk, I whisper to Rulf, "When do you think we should go for the artifact?"

"Where is it?"

I lean in close enough to be careful, and Rulf brings his head down. I know Rulf's hearing is really good, so I speak so quietly I can barely hear myself. "Throne room."

He stands up and nods. After a moment, he says, "Now?"

23

The Helm

I nod. Now is the best time.

I wave my soldiers forward. "We have to make another stop." I look around and then add, "What we're doing is extremely important for the future of the kingdom. Your secrecy with this is a matter of life and death."

Denner leans in, smiles, and whispers, "Lady Marleet, your father and mother have my complete loyalty. It wouldn't matter if this was a life and death issue, if this is about the kingdom, or if this is a matter of what you will have for lunch, the loyalty we offer is the same. There will be no betrayal from either of us—ever."

I smile back at him. I hope that's true. Both a trustworthy man and a liar can say the same thing. But I have to trust. I choose to trust my parent's choice in these men.

"Then we need to slip inside another secret passageway."

The man nods and the two soldiers return to their position a short distance behind.

"I'll need to change into my dirty dress again, Rulf."

Rulf grunts, and we turn down a hallway. He leads me toward the throne room, although I expect we won't be going directly there. I know the castle hallways as well as Rulf does, but I don't know where most of the secret passageways are. In fact, before Rulf showed me the first one we went into, I didn't know of any—other than one room we occasionally used for spying.

We turn down passage after passage. I want to tell Rulf he's heading in the wrong direction, but he knows where he's going.

When we get there, he looks in a room and then backs out. He simply says, "Change."

I slip in. It's a small room used for occasional meetings. I used to help Hemot and the others clean rooms occasionally, but I don't think I've ever cleaned this one.

I pull off my clean dress and throw on my dirty one. When I poke my head out, the soldiers take my clean dress, and Rulf comes in. I assume that means the entrance to the room is in here. I ask my guard to come back in one hour. They give me a small bow and move on.

Once the door closes, I turn around to find Rulf sliding a painting off to the side. The wall behind the painting looks normal, but he gives a shove on one of the bricks, and a small doorway swings in.

I rush over to him, unsure how long we'll have privacy. Anyone could come in at any moment. The doorway is up around the height of my shoulders, but Rulf helps me up and then he climbs in after, sliding the picture back in place, then swinging the stone door closed.

"Ugh, I shouldn't have put on the dirty dress. Now I'm all tangled up in it!"

Rulf gives a little grunt as I struggle with it. I've been in one of these types of passageways before. It's small, and you have to crawl on your hands and knees. When I get the dress off and am in my traveling clothes, I whisper, "Ready. Let's go."

Rulf leads us through the dark. I'm still amazed at how Rulf can remember all this. His memory is perfect, so even though he hasn't explored these passages since he was around five, he still remembers every detail.

We crawl along until I hear Rulf slow down. It's hard to see past his bulk, but I think there's a bit of light ahead. A moment later, I see more of it as he steps out into a large area and moves aside. When I reach the edge, he helps me down.

We're in a larger tunnel. By larger, I mean it's wide enough for two small people to walk side-by-side, and the ceiling is as high as an average room. Holes poke through all along the walls—peep holes for spying—so that gives us plenty of light.

I wonder how such tunnels came to be. Certainly all the builders would have known about such a thing, and certainly they would have told people all about them. That means that the general population once knew about these tunnels… or all the builders were killed to hide the secret.

I hope the second possibility didn't happen.

What's also strange is that no one in the castle seems to know of the tunnels. Or… maybe they do; we just don't know they're using them.

That's a scary thought. It means we're not safe in here. At any moment, King Parthun or General Corter could come around the corner.

Whispering, I ask, "How far?" I gave Denner and Billot an hour. I hope that's enough time.

Rulf grunts.

"That's not an answer, Rulf!"

"Oh. Sorry. It's not far. If we move fast."

We move along at a good speed, careful to step lightly. I don't bother looking through any holes in the walls. For one thing, we don't have time. For another, I don't really want to spy on anyone. I detest that kind of thing.

We rush down passageway after passageway. It's not long before I've completely lost track of where we are and where we've come from. I don't think I could find my way back if my life depended on it.

When Rulf finally slows down, we come to a small tunnel. This area is a little different from any of the areas I've been in before. The ceiling is low, but Rulf can still stand at his full height. The walls are old, but are of dressed stone. But not just dressed stone—these stones are just about perfect. I think we're close.

It's also fairly bright, as the holes in this area let in more light. I think we're near some windows. Ahead, about chest height, is another small passageway—one of the ones you have to crawl through.

I wonder why Rulf isn't moving on. He waits for me to catch my breath before he leans in and says, "Tell me where it is."

"I'm going in there too!" I won't let him leave me out of this.

Rulf frowns at me. "What do you mean? Of course you're going too!"

"Well, then, why do you want to know where it is?"

"So you don't have to explain it to me in the throne room. We might not have much time. We have to move fast."

"Oh, sorry Rulf." I smile at him. I shouldn't doubt his intentions. He's always been good to me. I think I struggle to trust people sometimes.

I whisper to him all the details. He listens closely and then pauses for just a moment. "We're going to be coming out just behind the throne. The passage we're about to enter goes right near the King's quarters, so we have to be extra quiet. If he's in there and hears us, we're in trouble."

"Does he know about the passages?"

Rulf shakes his head. "Don't think so. But if he hears us, he might order the castle searched from top to bottom, and we might not get away."

Then he grabs me and tosses me into the dark hole.

I know I can trust Rulf, but I wish he were just a little more gentle. I don't bother saying anything, though. Rulf doesn't learn that kind of thing well. I crawl ahead and hear him quietly scrambling up behind me.

It's still a lot farther than I would have thought, but when I finally reach the end, I see light here and there. Although, it's still quite dark.

Rulf comes up beside me. I feel tiny anytime he's beside me, and seeing his shoulders in the dim light so far above my own as we crouch here on hands and knees makes me feel like a little child.

"I'll go check."

Without another word, Rulf moves off to the right and stands up. In another moment, he disappears.

When I follow him, I see he's gone up. A ladder sits secured to the wall right in front of me, and when I look straight up, I see him disappear off to the left.

I grab the rungs and climb. In a few seconds, I come in next to him, and he slides over. It's easy to see here— plenty of light. I peek through a hole and look out over the throne room.

I can't see the face of the King, but he sits on his throne. Down below him is Captain Granel, Ellcia's brother. He's bowing to the King and now he's moving off.

Captain Granel is loyal and good, but the King has kept him outside the city, for the most part, along with the bulk of the army. My papa believes it's strong evidence that he doesn't trust either Granel or the returned armies.

The King's scheme with arresting General Lirnal is likely causing Parthun a lot of fear—and rightly so. I haven't seen the army since everything with the General and the Prince happened, but I expect they're all angry.

It's hard to hear much of what's said in the throne room. Granel's gone now, and it's just a few people left. We wait, because there's not much we can do while the king is still there. I get an image of trying to sneak in there and climb the statue while the King's chatting with a few of his advisers.

I expect that would not go well.

We sit for a long time. Another person comes in—someone I don't recognize. He says something—can't hear. Then someone else comes in. Then someone else.

It's been a while. I'm not sure how long, but I think we're probably close to the hour mark. If we can't get that artifact soon, we should probably come back later.

I'm about to tell Rulf that, when I see someone else leave—one of my papa's friends, actually—and the King stands up. I could barely hear anything said in all the conversations, certainly not enough to know what they were talking about, but now I hear.

"What a waste of time!"

I'm irritated that the King of Sevord thinks dealing with soldiers and people is a waste of time, but then again, that's what we're up against. That's part of why we're trying to put the right person on the throne.

General Corter steps into view and declares with a laugh, "It's what you wanted, Parthun! I can always make a rule that no one is allowed to approach you."

The King laughs and waves his hand. "If only it were that simple, Corter."

The two turn around and walk back toward us. We're behind the throne, and the King's quarters are back here—just not in our tunnel. As I wait, Rulf quietly scrambles down the ladder. For a big guy, he sure can move quietly when he wants to.

I follow after him. When I get to the bottom, he whispers, "I heard the door close. The room should be empty."

I hear a slight scraping noise, and some new light pours into the area. He's moved a section of the wall back. It's small, only big enough for me to crawl through. Rulf will have to go down on his belly, but we'll manage.

It's incredible that whoever designed this could create hinges that could not only last this long, but could also work with stone walls. Amazing!

On the other side, I see a tapestry. I can make out a bit of the pattern. It looks like the part we're seeing is someone's foot. From the size of the foot, the tapestry must be huge!

Rulf listens for a moment with his ear up to the opening, then slowly pulls the tapestry aside. He looks left and right, then slides out.

When I crawl out after him, I take a look back and see the tapestry is actually quite small. It's just a picture of a man's leg. Part of me never wants to know the story behind that. Some things are better left unsaid.

We move around as quietly as we can. I'm not sure when everyone will return. It could be minutes; it could be hours.

When we come around to the front of the throne, we stop in our tracks. I dare not breathe for fear of being caught.

Standing at the far end of the throne room is a soldier. His back is to us, but he's watching a man work in the corner, cleaning something up. At any moment, either man could turn around.

Rulf grabs me and pulls me behind one of the statues on the King's right. We move along until we get behind the second one, check and make sure the two men aren't looking, then move along to the third.

The statues are up on platforms, then the statues themselves stand about six feet. I gather it's a proper height for the actual King it represents. On top of this statue's head is the silver helm.

"That's a long ways up!" I speak in a barely audible whisper.

Rulf just nods, but I can see he doesn't see it as a problem. From the way he keeps glancing at the men in the room, he sees them as the big issue.

Without explaining anything, which I don't particularly appreciate, Rulf grabs me by my legs—one leg in each hand. I hold my breath to stop myself from crying out in shock as he lifts me right up into the air.

When I stop moving, I'm within reach of the helm. I grab the back of the silver helmet with my hands, but then find myself twisted around, and I lean in close to the statue.

"Where next?" the soldier barks.

"Over there. King's left. That's where I found that rat's nest. Gotta check for droppings."

"Can you pick up the pace?" The soldier sounds angry. "I don't have all day."

I can't help but think the soldier does, in fact, have all day. When we're not at war, the soldiers don't actually do much. Guard duty is often thought of as a punishment. I expect what he's doing right now is far more interesting than standing outside the door. And… he wouldn't get to yell at the servant.

"Moving along, sir." The servant doesn't sound afraid or respectful, just annoyed.

I continue to hug the back of the statue. I hope they can't see me. I know some people often wish they were taller or bigger, but I've always been happy with my size. It's times like this that leaves me grateful that I'm as small as I am.

I feel Rulf shift somewhat, and my body slowly moves out. My legs hurt where he's gripping me, but not enough to worry about it. I do expect I'll have bruises.

I lift up the back of the helm, keeping my eye on the two men. There's not much room underneath, but I slide my hand inside. My heart goes cold as I feel around.

It's not there.

I feel each corner of the area, hoping it's just slipped to the side, but I quickly realize that there's nowhere for it to hide. The area is just empty.

I have a moment when I wonder if it's the actual helm, but I can see it moves up and down on a bolt driven directly into the head of the statue.

I wave at Rulf, and he brings me down. I mouth the words, "Not there!" to him, and he frowns. He does a quick look around—so do I. None of the other statues have a helm on it—at least one that's separate from the statue like this one.

"We leave!" he whispers.

We move back to statue number two, then to statue number one. I glance over at the two men, and the servant is in the process of packing up. He grabs his supplies, throws them in a sack, and walks ahead of the soldier to the front doors.

Once their backs are to us, we rush toward the throne and the door behind it, but then skid to a halt as the door to the King's chambers, just beside our exit, opens.

Rulf grabs me and pulls me to the right of the throne—King's left. I'm assuming that means the King comes around the other side. I don't know how Rulf knows these things.

We reach the front of the throne, but Rulf just peers around. I look back behind us. The soldier and servant are almost at the door. If they open it, we'll be seen by the soldiers on the other side. But if we move too fast, we'll be seen by whoever's coming through from the King's quarters.

After a moment, Rulf shoves me ahead of him toward our exit. I'm almost there when I hear it.

"Halt!"

It's the soldier who watched the servant clean the rat's nest! He's seen us! I glance back, but I'm now behind the throne and can't see anyone, except Rulf, who's still in the open.

I run for the exit and climb inside. I twist around and hold the tapestry back, hoping Rulf will make it through, but he hasn't moved. I nearly call out for him, but then I'll give myself away.

I can't imagine why he isn't running. He'd be inside the passageway by now…

The secret passageway… oh, that's it… he can't give our passageway up.

If he moves, they'll follow him and find the passageway, and not only will I be caught, but we'll lose our access to these tunnels. If he stays, he'll be caught, but I won't be, and the passageway will remain secure.

And… I can still try to free Roran.

I drop the tapestry back as my eyes fill with tears. I have to keep hidden. And I have to keep going to find that artifact.

Instead of swinging the stone door closed, I listen.

"What are you doing here?" That's the King's voice. "How dare you enter the throne room without permission!" A moment later, he orders, "Arrest him!"

"Yes sir!" the soldier says, but I hear the fear in his voice. I'm guessing he knows Rulf.

"You realize," the King says, "the penalty for entering the throne room without permission is death?"

Rulf grunts.

"You think your parents will protect you, Giant-spawn?"

I've never heard that term before, but I'm guessing it's not a compliment.

Rulf grunts again.

"Bind him. Tilbur will have some fun with him."

I quietly swing the stone door closed.

I feel alone. Like I was in the Shaloomd nest, but this time, my friend is arrested. The only hope I have is that they can't figure out a way to kill a boy descended from giants.

24

The Throne Room

I rush through the secret passageways. I don't have any idea where I'm going. It was all too dark and too unfamiliar when I came through with Rulf. I can't remember any turns or anything.

After a few minutes, I'm pretty sure I made a wrong turn. Nothing looks familiar. In fact, I'm seeing parts of the tunnel system which I'm sure I've never seen before. I turn down another way and then another.

My eyes are filled with tears, and they're starting to burn. I think I probably have a lot of dust in my eyes. It's probably pretty caked up with gunk.

I have to get my bearings, so I peer through one of the holes in the wall. I'm looking into someone's quarters. They're having tea. I've been in a lot of the rooms in the castle, but this one, from this angle, looks no different from any other.

I push on, take another look, find an empty, dark room. The next room I peer into is a small board room. I recognize this one, but I can't remember where it is. It's too much of a risk to just jump out here.

I peer through again and stop. It's a corridor. I recognize it.

It's one of the third floor corridors. I hadn't realized I was this far up in the castle. I remember climbing a few ladders and descending others, but I guess I've come up more than I've gone down.

My mind flashes back to a month or so before. It was near this corridor that I ran into Hemot on the way to listen to the Regent, or now King, talk about the Prince.

This might actually be a good spot to slip out, if there's a door.

I feel along the wall, doing my best to find anything that seems out of the ordinary. A few steps down from where the hole is, I find a little indent. I reach in, give it a hard tug, and the wall begins to roll back on a few hinges.

On the other side is a tapestry. I push it out of the way just enough to look. I can't see anyone down the one direction. I take the risk and step out. No one's within sight.

I reach back and pull the door closed behind me. It's amazing how hard it is to see once it's closed.

Down the hallway to my right, I hear voices. They don't sound happy. I expect there are a lot of angry people in the castle right now. I don't know what to do about Rulf, but…

My eyes well up again as I think of my friend, but I stop myself. I have to focus on getting back to my family's quarters.

I rush along, ducking into rooms when I see soldiers. I can't let myself be caught. A Lord or Lady never moves through the castle without a guard. Add to that the fact that I'm covered in dirt... well... it's best not to be caught.

I turn a corner, and two men grab me, roughly pulling me back into a side room. I feel a hand go over my mouth, and I struggle in vain.

When we get into the room, the hand comes off, and I recognize both the soldiers as my personal guards. Before I can say anything, Denner says, "Listen closely. Do as we say, no questions."

He pulls out my clean dress, tosses it to me, tells me to put it on fast, then both men spin around with their backs to me. Once I have it on, I tell them I'm ready, but before I can ask any questions, Billot grabs a vase with flowers, tosses the flowers onto the floor, pulls out a handkerchief, soaks it in the water, and uses it to aggressively scrub my face clean.

He's scrubbing so hard it actually hurts, and I feel like a little child, having my face scrubbed like this, but I know I need to put up with it. When he's about half-way through, Denner explains, "Rulfor has been caught in the throne room. He's there now, under guard. The Lord Yune and the Lady Aldora have been summoned as the soldier who saw Rulfor believes he saw you as well. We must hurry so you can join your parents before they reach the throne room."

I'm about to ask why we have to join them, but Billot seems satisfied that my face is washed well enough. Both men grab me and pull me out of the room.

"Follow us quickly, my Lady."

We rush down the hall in this awkward run-but-not-run, walk-but-not-walk, movement. We pass a few servants, and the soldiers slow down enough to try to hide that we're in a rush, but no one is fooled.

We come around a corner to find a dozen people. Most are soldiers, except for my parents in the middle.

My two guards push me into the center, and I join the procession.

At first, I had thought my parents were under arrest, but I see now that all the other soldiers are part of their guard. We've never gone anywhere with this many soldiers. I wonder what my papa's up to.

My parents don't appear to have noticed me yet. I move along behind them, walking the way they taught me to walk as a Lady, all the while trying my best to calm my breathing.

We reach the throne room, and the doors open immediately. The King must be expecting us. A man on the inside calls out, "The Lord Yune, the Lady Aldora, and the Lady Marleet here to see the King!"

I see my mama turn her head slightly at the mention of my name, but my papa merely pats her hand on his arm.

The throne room is filled with soldiers and Nobles. In the center, on his knees, bound and gagged, is Rulf. His head hangs low as if he's been beaten, but I can't imagine they could hurt him.

My heart races. I don't know what they can do to Rulf, but even if they can't harm him, they can still throw him in a prison cell. He could end up spending the rest of his life in the dungeons.

I watch my papa. My mama seems to think this is his battleground—this is the place where he shines. I don't have any other option but to trust him here. But despite how much I love my parents, I still struggle to trust them to take care of me. I've never really had that kind of thing before. Other than with Caric and Ellcia.

"Lord Yune!" The King speaks to my father, but his eyes are on me. I'm not sure I've ever seen anyone look at me with such hatred. "How nice of you to visit!" The sarcasm in his voice is entirely unhidden, and I hear the Nobles grumble. I don't think they're grumbling at my papa.

"My dearrrr King Parthunnnn. You neverrrr have to worryyyy that I might not commmme at the request of my Kingggg."

I focus on what he just said. My papa did not commit to coming whenever Parthun called, but whenever the King called. That's a minor difference, but that allows him to speak the truth without committing himself to Parthun.

"Yes, well, if you had not come, I would have sent soldiers to arrest you!"

Oh my… the Nobles are not pleased. They're not pleased at all. Not only do they put no effort into hiding their grumbles, but they shift on their feet.

The King glances their way for a second, and I can see him reconsider. A smile breaks out on his face, and he declares. "But let us not jest with one another! This moment is serious, my dear friend. Lord… oh my dear friend. Let us dispense with the formalities. Please, call me Parthun. May I call you Yune?"

"Noooo, Parthunnnn. Please call me by my titlllle, but thank youuuu for the invitationnnn to call youuuu by your given nammmmme."

I force down my smile. My papa is good at what he does, but he plays a dangerous game.

The King is irritated, but doesn't say anything. I begin to wonder how far my papa can push Parthun before the King turns on him. Perhaps… perhaps that's my papa's goal.

The King clears his throat and leans back. "As you might have heard, Lord Yune, the giant-spawn, son of Traltor and Nareesa, was caught in the throne room without permission. He was caught just as I was returning to the throne, which raises the question if he were trying to assassinate me."

My papa merely bows in return.

I don't know why he's not coming to Rulf's defense, but I do my best to remain quiet. As much as this is my papa's battleground, it's certainly not mine.

"It is also suspected that he did not act alone, my dear friend, Lord Yune."

My papa bows again.

"Do you know anything about this?"

"I knoooow about Rulforrrr."

"What do you know, Lord Yune?"

"I knooooow he is the sonnnn of Tralllltor and Nareeeesa."

"Well, yes… yes, we… know that already!" The King leans forward and rings his hands. My papa sure knows how to irritate the King.

My heart leaps for joy. If he's irritating the King like this, I suspect that means one of two things. One, he might be trying to push the King to act. Or two, the King might be just about to be removed. Either way, I think this will turn out well. If only Rulf can last long enough.

"Yessss, of coursssse, Parthunnnn."

The King clenches his fists for a moment, then forces them open. "Do you know anything about why he might have been in the throne room?"

Ah, now I know for certain why my papa did not want to know anything about my plans.

"Noooo, my dear Parthunnnn, I know nothingggg of why he was herrrre."

The King is getting more and more frustrated. He keeps opening his mouth but then glances to the Nobles standing along the side of the hall and closes it again. While I don't understand it all, I can see there's a huge play for power going on at the moment.

"The soldier who caught sight of Rulfor believes he saw someone else as well."

"Thennnn, we must catch the other mannnn."

"He does not believe it was a man."

"Thennnn, we must catch the other giannnnt."

"NO! Lord Yune…" The King is on the edge of his seat. He looks like he's about to run down the steps and strangle my papa. "No! He believes the accomplice was a girl."

"Ahhhh, yessss, Parthunnnn, that makes much more sensssse."

The King stands up. His fists balled and his face red. "HE BELIEVES THE ACCOMPLICE WAS YOUR DAUGHTER!"

My papa doesn't say anything at all. Instead. He just slowly—very, very, slowly—turns his head enough to look at me, then turns back to look at the King. He then turns slowly back to look at me again, then back to the King.

"Iiii, my dear Pathunnnn, am not familiarrrr with the abilityyyy to be in twoooo places at oncccce. Althoooough, I must claim ignorancccce on this matterrrr as I did not raise my daugherrrr, but she wassss, in fact, raaaaised in the castlllle. It is possiblllle that whilllle she lived heeeere that sheeee learnnnnned such a skilllll."

The King takes another step forward but stops before the top step. By this point, his voice cracks as he yells. "THEN HOW DID THE SOLDIER SEE YOUR DAUGHTER IN THE THRONE ROOM?"

"Iiii am not awaaaare that I have the abilityyyy to know allll that is possiblllle, Parthunnnn. Wherrrre is this soldierrrr?"

The King waves at the soldier who had been watching the servant clean the throne room. The man steps forward and points at me. "That's her, your Highness. She was running back behind the throne, wearing a pair of slacks and a thin shirt."

My papa, yet again, slowly turns back to me. It is amazing to me how slow that man can move when he wants to. I've seen him move fast, but everything he does is for a purpose. When his eyes land on me, he slowly lowers his eyes and scans my entire outfit from top to bottom, then bottom to top again, then winks at me, giving me the barest hint of a smile, before slowly turning back. He merely stares at the soldier until the man blushes.

The man purses his lips for a moment, then says, "Well, she could have changed."

"Absoluuuutely, she could haaaave."

The soldier frowns. "Maybe she's still wearing the other clothes underneath the dress!"

My papa slowly raises his hands, palms out, toward the man. In a voice that sounds not only horrified, but also faster than I've ever heard my papa speak, he says, "Are you suggestinggggg that my daughterrrr undreeeess in the throne roooom to show youuuu what lies beneeeeath?"

My papa then slowly draws a knife and holds it, point forward, at the man. Although I know my papa can handle himself with a blade, he holds it so awkwardly that it looks absolutely comical.

My papa is likely no physical threat to the soldier, but the message is clear. The soldier drops to his knees.

"Forgive me, Lord Yune. I would never suggest such a thing. I was wrong. I clearly did not see your daughter in the throne room. Please forgive me."

The Nobles in the room grumble again, but I can tell they are not upset with my papa. My papa then slowly puts his knife away and adds, "All is forgivennnn, my friennnnd, but I request that youuuu stay away from my daughterrrr from henceforth."

I've never really known what the word "hence" means, but it sure sounds good. I'll have to look that up at some point.

The soldier turns to the King and bows. When he straightens, Parthun gives him a dismissive wave, and the soldier leaves, walking along the outside of the room as if he's trying to stay as far away from me as possible, while my dad and each of our soldiers watch him closely. I notice that all our guards have their hands on the hilts of their swords as the man makes his exit.

This certainly is my papa's battleground!

25

The Danger

The King drops back into the throne and just glares at my papa. My parents simply remain where they are. After a moment, my mama steps closer and takes my papa's arm again. That action seems to irritate the King even more.

When I begin to think that no one is ever planning on speaking again, the King growls and says, "And what do you suggest we do with the giant-spawn?"

My shoulders tense, and my breathing quickens. I hadn't forgotten about Rulf. I just hoped the King would let him go.

"Wellll, my dear Parthunnnn. I think there are twoooo optionnnns."

The King waits, but my papa says no more. After nearly a full minute, the King growls, "And what two options do you see, Yune?"

My papa remains still—no response.

The King growls again and asks, "And what two options do you see, *Lord* Yune?"

"Eitherrrr punish him accordingggg to his crime or release himmmm."

"Well, we can't release him, now can we, Lord Yune?" The King isn't shouting, but there's a lot more volume to his voice than is necessary. His knuckles, gripping the armrests of the throne, are white.

"Noooo, I do not thinnnnk that is the casssse. Unnnnfortunatelyyyy, the punishment for his crimmmme is deathhhh, is it not?"

"You know it is, Lord Yune!"

"Thennnn, you must kill himmmm."

I begin to shake. I don't know why my papa would suggest such a thing.

The King scowls. "Well, we have some challenges to overcome with that, now don't we, Lord Yune? There is the obvious one, of course, of his parents. They would not be pleased. And while they don't have any official position as land-owners or even as minor Nobles, they certainly are dangerous. Word has reached me that Nareesa killed four men in a matter of seconds shortly before you left the caves."

Now, that's an interesting statement. I wonder what all the King is trying to say. Obviously, he's telling us he's well informed. He's also reminding my papa that he has not been in Sevord for many years. But I think the King is up to even more.

"Iiii have heard the sammmme thingggg, Parthunnnn. I suspect weeee would lose half our armiiiies before you could find a waaaay to stop themmmm."

"Do you know of no way to kill a giant?"

I am pretty sure my papa does know of ways. I hope he does not tell the King any of them.

I clench my teeth to keep myself from shouting as my papa says, "I know of twoooo such waaaays of which I can tell youuuu."

"And they are?"

"Onnnne, of course, is Gennnneral Gerannnn's sword."

"Yes, but that sword was lost years ago! Stolen from this very room!"

I don't want to mention that Caric has it. I wonder if my papa knows.

Caric! That's what the King was saying! When he mentioned about Nareesa in the caves, he's telling my papa that he knows all about Caric! I don't know if that means Caric is in more danger, but I don't think it's good.

"Thennnn, there is only onnnne other sword."

"Yes," the King says.

"But, my dear Parthunnnn, only the Kingggg knows how to uuuuse that sword to killll a giannnnt."

The King frowns. I think that means… oh… oh wow! The King has no idea how to use his own sword! The sword is enchanted, but not in just one way. I suspect there are multiple ways the sword is enchanted, none of which are easy to figure out! The King can't even use his own sword!

But he stands up anyway and draws his blade. "Should I then kill the giant-spawn?"

Ah, I get it. He's asking my papa to make the decision. He's asking my papa to anger Traltor and Nareesa.

"I thinnnnk that thoooough you are a valiant warriorrrrr, Parthunnnn…" At that statement, I see some of the soldiers fight down smiles. "… youuuuu, as Kingggg, cannot act as executionerrrr."

"And if I do?"

"Then the people'ssss trusssst will have been losssst."

The King hesitates for a moment, but then slides his sword back into its sheath. He drops onto his throne and then declares, "Take the giant-spawn away. Throw him in one of the pits!"

I don't know what this pit is, but I don't expect it's good. I know Tilbur's pit. Everyone knows that, but this must be something different. I try to catch Rulf's eye, but he doesn't look at me. I guess that's best. Good idea to keep our connection hidden, although it's likely well known.

My mama and papa give a bow and turn to leave, but the King waves his hand. "One more thing, Lord Yune. I do not wish to tarry on this matter of the wedding of Prince Roran. I wish for him to be married soon. Please reconsider your position on your daughter's marriage."

My papa bows yet again, then turns to leave. I follow a short distance behind.

Now, I not only have to find the artifact, but somehow I have to rescue Rulf from that pit while avoiding a marriage that I never want!

I sit in my room alone. I'm not sure who to turn to. I have plenty of allies, but Rulf was the only one I could talk to about it all.

I can't go to my parents, because then they would be aware of what was going on and could not honestly deny knowledge.

I can't go to Captain Granel as he's out of the city.

I can't turn to Ellcia, Hemot, or Caric, because they're who-knows-where!

There has to be another option.

I go through the list of people I think I can turn to, but no one stands out. Most people are either out of reach, or turning to them would put them at greater risk than I think they can afford.

I wish I could just try to do it on my own, but that's not possible. I might figure out some stuff, but I can't move around the castle alone, and I have no idea where to start to look for the artifact.

Just this morning, I had three requests from Prince Roran to visit him. Deep inside, I wonder if I can turn to him for help. I know that's a bad idea, though. I've been warned to stay away from him while he's enchanted. I think they're right. Besides, I also think he'll tell the King anything Parthun wants to hear.

There will be no secrecy with Roran.

I can trust my guards, I believe. I'm pretty sure I can. But their job is to guard me. I'm not sure I can work with them to figure out where to look for the artifact.

That only leaves one person. He's a risk, indeed, but maybe I can make it work. I'll go with my guard to see him, so then I hopefully won't have to worry about him harming me. It's not that I think he's dangerous, I just don't know if he isn't.

I get up and rush out of the room. "Mama, I need to go for a walk."

She examines me for a moment before nodding. She can see that I'm up to something, but at the same time, that's exactly what my parents want me to be doing. We're all fighting for the kingdom in our own way. We all play our part.

I head with my guard to the door, but Denner stops me. In a quiet voice, he asks, "My Lady, do you need a change of clothes this time?"

I shake my head.

"Are we doing something secretive?"

I nod.

He steps back to Billot, taking up a position behind me. I wave goodbye to my mama, and we head out.

Moving through the castle, I do my best to avoid popular areas. I don't really want anyone to know I've met with Hob. It's not that I'm embarrassed or anything, even though he's so odd, it's just that I don't want to draw attention to him.

I move down to the lower levels and walk along near the servants' quarters. This area is rarely patrolled, so I hope to go unnoticed, but it's also an odd place for a Noblewoman to walk. I'm not sure it's a good idea.

I turn a corner and come to a halt as I see someone. My face breaks out in a large smile. I haven't spoken to Tereese since I've come back. As a kitchen worker, I served under her for years.

I'm about to run forward and wrap my arms around her when she steps to the side of the corridor and bows her head in the traditional manner of servants before Nobles. My mouth drops open. I know I'm a Noble now… or I guess I always was… but… this feels odd.

I step up to her, and I'm about to say something when she hisses, "My Lady Marleet, it is wonderful to see you again, but if you speak with me, you will draw attention to me. We all must play our part. And my part is not to be seen with you."

I'm hurt, but then again, I know she's right. We're on a mission here. Each of us. We have to save the Prince. We have to save the kingdom.

I nod and move on without another word. I hope my interaction with her doesn't cause her any trouble.

I climb a set of stairs, move down a hallway, then up another set of stairs. The Forgotten Armory, as it's often called, is the only armory which is not on the bottom floor of the castle.

We're just about there when my guard behind me picks up speed. I hear Denner whisper, "My Lady, we are being followed."

I reach the Forgotten Armory and keep going. I try to think of where I could go that would look normal based on where I've walked so far. It hits me. There's a corridor not far from here with some statues of the King's family.

I turn right, then left, and come to a stop. Ahead of me is the hallway I'm looking for—or the one I'm looking for now that I'm being followed.

On my right is a bust. I step up to it as if I had intended to look at it all along. At the bottom is a small plaque which reads, "King Hartor, Son of Trevolay the Great."

I remember learning about King Trevolay, but I can't recall any details. I know there were quite a few battles, some of them quite impressive. It was a time when the giants were restless and caused quite a lot of trouble.

Now, King Hartor, of course, I remember a little more. I think it was because I could also remember meeting him once. Growing up, I thought I had just happened to meet him as a servant, but now I know I'd likely spent a lot of time with him and his family. My papa and the King were close.

Glancing back, I see only Denner. I'm not sure why that is, but he does not appear concerned, so I leave it with him. I'm learning more and more that they are honorable men.

I move to the next bust. The plaque reads, "General Geran, Hero of Reber's Gate."

Under my breath, I find myself whispering, "Caric's dad."

I examine the man's face. I don't know if I can see the resemblance, but statues are rarely accurate. I doubt General Geran truly looked like this.

My eyes well up with tears, and I find myself putting my hand on the cheek of the bust. I miss Caric so much. It brings back all the emotion of missing him and Ellcia. And Hemot. I miss them all. I can't believe we've been apart for so long. They've always been around—ever since I can remember.

I wipe my eyes and prepare to move on to the next one—General Lirnal—but I spin around as a struggle takes place behind me.

Both Denner and Billot are here now, but between them is a small man. He's dressed as a servant, but I know he's only recently become a servant. I knew everyone who worked in the castle up until a few months ago, at least by sight.

My two soldiers bring the man to me, and Billot kicks the back of his knees, dropping him to the floor. Denner pulls out a knife and places it at the man's throat.

"My Lady, we found this man following you. We don't know what his intention was, but I doubt it was good. Shall we dispose of him for you?"

The man's face fills with panic. He begins to mumble an apology, but Billot drives his fist into the side of the man's head.

As I stare at them, I realize with horror that at my word, my soldier would actually kill the man. At first, I'm not sure how legal that is, but then I remember that to threaten a Noble, especially a young Noble, is to invite death. The guard may kill the threat without any fear of reprisal.

I'm about to shout, "No! Don't hurt him!" when I catch myself. My parents are masters at this. I have to learn as well. If I'm to continue to live this life, I need to know how to navigate this world. I must find out what the man is after, but I can't be gentle.

I'm aware that my eyes might still be teary, but there's not much I can do about that. To my right is a window. The windows in this hallway open. I remember airing out this section once when Hemot spilled a large jar of pickles on the carpet.

I take a step to the window, unlatch it, and swing it out. I take a deep breath of the fresh air, doing my best to appear unconcerned. I lean out a little, just enough to see down below, then step back.

"Denner, I would like some answers to my questions. If this man hesitates for even a second to give me any answer I wish, or if you suspect that what he says is a lie," I turn my eyes to the man and say harshly, "throw him out the window without confirming with me first. I have no time for this."

"Yes, my Lady."

The panic on the man's face is quickly replaced with terror. He shakes, his eyes dart back and forth, and he struggles for just a second, but the knife at his throat is brought in tighter, and the man stops moving.

I hate to torture the man like this. I don't want to kill him, and I would certainly stop Denner from tossing him out the window, but we have to learn.

In a harsh voice, I order, "Your name. Tell it to me."

"Hillonot!" Tears stream down his cheeks, and he slowly wipes his hands on his shirt.

"Were you following me?"

There is the slightest hesitation, and Denner grabs him, pulling him toward the window.

"Please! Please, my Lady. Forgive me!"

"Give him another chance, Denner."

A very loud sound comes from Denner's throat. He sounds like he's very disappointed. I nod at him and say, "Don't worry, Denner. You'll likely get your chance. He's certainly not as cooperative as I'd like him to be."

"No, my Lady!" Hillonot's eyes are wild with terror. "I am very cooperative. Anything you want!"

"Were you following me?"

"Yes, my Lady." His words come out almost too fast to understand.

"Why?"

"I was sent by Captain Tilbur, my Lady."

I find that hard to believe at first, then not so hard. I want to get angry at Captain Tilbur, but I know he reports to General Corter and the King—neither of whom are honorable men. He has to play his part just as the rest of us do.

"And what are your intentions?"

"Nothing, my Lady! I was just told to follow you and let Captain Tilbur know everything you do."

"I don't want you to do this again."

The man shakes his head quickly. "I don't want to do this again either! But please, I have to follow orders."

"So… you want me just to allow you to follow me?"

"Yes! And I won't report back to him everything you do. Just a few things."

I purse my lips for a moment, then ask, "Does that sound as strange to you as it does to me?"

The man's face turns a deep shade of red. "I'll return to him right away. I'll tell him I was caught and that your soldiers are too wary to be fooled."

I don't really know what else to do, but that sounds good to me. "Do that! And if we find you following us again, my soldiers might find a window and throw you out before they even bring you to me."

The man nods, and as soon as Denner releases him, he bolts down the hallway. I feel a little mean for being so harsh with him, but I actually think I did a good job. I wish I could tell my parents about it, but that will have to wait until all this is over.

I step close to Denner. "Are we safe to return to the Forgotten Armory? I don't want Hob to get in trouble."

"I believe so, my Lady, but we will keep an eye out."

I feel the emotion of what just happened come over me, and tears stream down my cheeks. Denner and Billot step close. At first, I don't know what they're doing, but then I see it. They're shielding me in case someone enters the hallway, allowing me to cry without being seen. I think this is the moment when I know for sure these are good men.

"Do not worry, my Lady. That was an extremely stressful situation. You handled yourself far better than a Noble of years and years of experience."

Despite the tears, I find myself smiling. That was kind of Denner to say.

When I've composed myself, we move back through the corridors, reaching our destination in a few minutes. When we left here the last time, Hob was not only quite insane, but also asleep. I'm kind of expecting that he'll still be asleep.

When I step into the armory, I'm not disappointed. His chair, in the center of the room, is a hard, wooden, uncomfortable chair, yet his legs stretch out in front of him, his arms hang limply down at his sides, and his neck is twisted back at an unnatural angle. If I didn't hear the snoring, I'd think he was dead.

26

The Madman

I don't want to scare him, so I keep my voice to a whisper. "Hob." There's no response. I try a little louder. "Hob!" Still nothing. "HOB!"

He jumps up and lands on his feet in a fighting pose, but then loses balance and tips over onto his butt, rolling onto his back, then back onto his feet. I think he would have done well as an acrobat or even a clown.

When he sees me, his face breaks out in a large grin. "My dear Lady Marleet! It is so good to see you again."

He speaks so formally and so well that if it weren't for the crazy look in his eye, and the recent backwards roll, I'd think he was sane. But something about his entire demeanor lets me know he's only seconds away from doing something wild and maybe dangerous.

He grabs the chair and tosses it off to the side, then does a little spin.

That didn't take long.

"Thank you, Hob. It is good to see you again as well."

He gives a very deep bow—deeper than I thought people could manage and still remain on their feet—and then asks, "What might I do to help you today, my Lady."

I step closer and whisper, "I have important business, but it's of the utmost secrecy."

Hob slaps his cheek and then smiles at me. "Of course! But if you tell me anything that is against the throne, I will kill you."

That's not the kind of thing I like to hear. I also find it very disturbing that he says it while smiling.

"Come with me."

I follow Hob back through a doorway. It's actually the same doorway I used to find a small room to change in before I left the castle on the quest to find the Prince, but instead of turning right into the small change room, we turn left into a slightly larger room that appears to be a bit of an office for Hob. I take a seat across from him, while Denner stands on the inside of the door, and Billot stands on the outside.

I scan the walls to see if there are any holes or cracks that might indicate someone could be in a secret tunnel listening to us.

"Oh, there are no listening holes in this room. It is entirely private." He glances at Denner. "Can he be trusted?"

I nod. "Completely."

"What might I do for you, my Lady?"

"Before we left to find the Prince, I think you knew who all of us were, correct?"

He gives an overly dramatic nod.

"You even recognized the Prince?"

"That's why I gave him Agno. I didn't want him to be recognized."

"Is that what his armor is called?"

Hob gives a creepy giggle as his only response.

"Are you aware, Hob, of all that is going on in the castle right now?"

His face falls, and I see anguish in his eyes. "I know what Parthun did to Prince Roran."

My eyebrows shoot up. We all know he's enchanted, but we don't know much else. "What do you know?"

"I know."

"Will you tell me, Hob?"

Hob shakes his head vigorously. "I don't know if I can trust you. I trust Lord Yune, but his daughter might not be faithful to the throne. She has not proven herself yet."

At first, anger builds in my chest. I know in my heart that I'm nothing but honest and loyal, but I calm myself. He's right. He doesn't know if he can trust me.

I turn to Denner. "I haven't told you all my plans. You must keep what you hear to yourself, understand?"

"Of course, my Lady." From out in the hallway, I hear Billot give a similar response.

Turning back to Hob, I bite my lip for a moment, trying to piece together how I'll say it all.

"Prince Roran is enchanted. I was used as the one to pass along the enchantment, but it was against my wishes. I didn't know what I was doing. The Prince remains under the enchantment, and we must free him from it. While he had the King's Sword, he refused to draw it. But I have heard of another artifact that can cancel enchantments. I need to find it."

He nods and gives me a strange look. "What artifact is this, my Lady?"

"I don't know what it's called or even what it looks like, but I was told where to find it. It's supposed to cancel the enchantment, and the only thing I know is it's small."

"Who told you where it was?"

"I'd rather not say."

"Ahhhhh," Hob says, then adds, "tsk, tsk, tsk. My Lady wishes for me to trust her, but she will not trust me." He stands up and waves me away. "This meeting is over."

I remain seated. "No, Hob, this is important. I must know. I believe I can get it to the Prince and free him."

Hob stares at me and frowns. It feels like he's looking for something, but I don't know what. After a long time, he slowly sits down again. He grinds his teeth, and his face fills with rage. "I'm not worthy of being trusted, my Lady. I betrayed the King. It's my fault he's dead."

My mouth falls open. I'm about to run out of the room when I catch myself. "Why do you think that?"

"I could have done more. I could have fought harder. I could have found a way to save His Majesty. I could have helped him escape. I am a traitor to the throne. You should leave me here to rot before I betray you as well."

I decide to do what he's doing to me—stare at him. I examine his eyes. I'm looking for something. I'm looking for hope.

After a long while, I give up. There is no hope there. But that doesn't mean there can't be.

"I wonder, Hob, what King Hartor would say if he knew that Hob gave the Armor of Agno to his son to protect him on his way out of Sevord."

Hob's eyes brighten for a moment, then he gives up. He shakes his head but doesn't say anything.

"I wonder as well what King Hartor would say if he knew Hob gave enchanted armor to his nephew, the second in line for the throne. I wonder what King Hartor would say if he knew that Hob also gave an enchanted sword to his nephew—one that would help to keep him alive."

I lean forward. "I wonder what King Hartor would say if he knew that the armor Hob gave his son and his nephew helped those two make it to the mountains to find the loyal Free Armies of Sevord. I wonder what King Hartor would say if he knew of Hob's loyalty to him even years after his death."

Hob's face screws up as if he's about to scream. For a moment, he shifts in his seat and twists back and forth. I'm starting to get a little scared, but then he breaks down in tears. Not a few light snifffles, but giant, ugly sobs.

I reach over and rub his shoulder. "You, Hob, are a loyal, faithful servant of the King. The fact that somehow you managed to collect those enchanted items and give them to the right people is a sign of how loyal, faithful, committed, and ready you are." I grab his shoulder and add, "Would King Hartor not want you to do all you can to free his son?"

Hob continues to cry, and I remember something else. This might not help convince him to trust me, but Hob should know. "Hob, before I forget, outside the city, I ran into a man named Berin."

Hob's head jerks up, and his wide eyes stare into mine. "Berin? He's alive?"

I nod. "He helped me. He gave me food and encouragement when I needed it badly."

"Is he living in his cottage?"

I shake my head. "I don't know where he's living. I ran into him northeast of the city."

Hob laughs, still with the tears on his cheeks. "Well, that's good news, isn't it?" He looks intently at me and adds, "I'll tell you what you want to know."

I'm surprised. I feel like that was a little too easy, because I still haven't proven to him that I can be trusted. But perhaps that's not important.

Before I can ask again, he adds, "But you will tell me who it was who told you about the artifact and where it was."

My shoulders slump. I feel like crying. I can't do that. "Hob, I'm sorry. I can't tell you that. It's not a matter of trust toward you, it's a matter of trust for him."

Hob leans back in his chair and asks in a sharp voice, "What do you mean?"

"The person who told me trusts me not to tell anyone. If I tell you, I will betray his trust." My head drops, and I hold my face in my hands. I can't believe I'm losing it all here. "I cannot betray his trust."

"But it might cost you your Prince, my dear," Hob says with a wicked smile on his face. "Loyalty to the throne or loyalty to your friend."

My shoulders shake. That's no choice. I cannot betray someone and still be the woman I want to be. But I can't leave the Prince in his enchantment. I clench my fists, shake my head, and stand. "Then I will find another way."

Hob laughs. "And if there is no other way?"

I screw up my face and grind my teeth. I thought I could trust this man. I thought he would help us. "Then I will die an old woman, still searching for a way to free Prince Roran from his enchantment."

I turn and storm out of the room to the sound of Hob's laughter. My face feels hot, and I'm still shaking. I can't believe I trusted him. I've now told him that there's an artifact and that I'm looking for it. He could just as easily go to the King and betray us all.

I'm lost again. I don't know what to do, where to go, or how to move on from here. I want to turn to my parents, but I know I can't. What I saw in the throne room is proof that the best way I can honor them right now is to leave them in the dark.

I reach our apartments and head inside. I give a nice smile to Rint and ask him to inform my mama that I'm back, all the while trying to act cheerful. They all know I'm doing my best here, but they don't need to know I'm failing.

I thank Denner and Billot, dismiss them, and head into my chambers. I drop down on the bed and just weep. I thought I had such a good idea. I thought I might be able to figure it all out.

I weep until I fall asleep.

"Marleet?"

I take in a deep breath and try to figure out where I am. I'm in a nice bed. It's comfortable. I'm still in my regular clothes. My face feels tight, like I was crying.

"Mama?"

My mama rubs my back as I lay there, face down in my pillow. It's all coming back to me. The disappointment. The failure. Hob's laughter. Roran still enchanted. Rulf still in prison.

"Are you okay?"

I shake my head.

"Is this something we can talk about?"

I shake my head again. I just wish I was six years old again, and my mama could wrap her arms around me and hold me, telling me it'll be all right.

I feel her arms come around me, and she pulls me into an embrace. Even if I'm not six years old, it feels good just to be held, especially by my mama.

"Did I ever tell you what it was that made me fall in love with your father?"

Now, that's something I'd never even wondered about. But now, I'm curious. I shake my head.

"It might seem silly, actually. I had men who were interested in me. Some would come speak eloquently to me, others would petition my father for a chance to be married, others would try to speak to me, but would stumble through. One man demanded that I be given to him, as I would be considered lucky to be married to him. One man asked me for a walk through the gardens and spent the entire time telling me how wonderful and beautiful I was, comparing me to the newest horse he'd just purchased."

Soaking in my mama's voice, story, and history, I smile to myself. I want to know her, and this is exactly the kind of thing I'm after.

"I knew of your father. We'd met many times. He was from a well-respected Noble family. His father had been an Earl. My father was a minor Lord. We owned some small property in the north of the Talic Region—not too far from the Milterite family, actually. Your friend, Hemot, is a Milterite."

My heart leaps at hearing Hemot's name. There must have been an obvious reaction because my mama gives me an extra hug.

"Don't worry about your friend Hemot. He's a strong young man from a strong family. He's also with two very strong young people. Trust them to survive."

I squeeze my mama back. She knows the right things to say.

"So, back to your father. I knew him, and we'd spoken before. I could tell he was interested in me, but he was far too focused on political matters. I didn't like politics and the movements of the court, but your father… he was well known as an exceptional man. People would tease him for the way he spoke, but everyone respected him—even as a young man. His parents had died young and left him everything, and most expected him to rise to become one of the greatest Nobles in the land. Which, I might add, he did before he reached his mid-twenties."

I pull back so I can see my mama's face as she speaks. Her eyes are unfocused as she stares off at nothing.

"Well, a certain young Nobleman approached me about having my hand in marriage. He was… arrogant. A handsome man, but arrogant. He thought the world belonged to him, and he seemed to believe that everyone else also believed that." She shook her head. "The problem was, I was at an age when a Nobleman's daughter should be married, and that man was a powerful man from a powerful family. It made sense for me to marry him."

"Did you love him?"

My mama laughs. "My dear Marleet, do you think I could fall in love with an arrogant man?" She shakes her head again. "No, I did not love him. But the pressure was on."

"One day, your father approached me. I had never considered him as a marriage prospect, though I knew he had his eye on me. I thought perhaps he was coming to ask for the chance to court me, but instead, he spoke about something else."

My mama begins to stroke my hair. In one sense, it makes me feel like a little girl again. I feel awkward with that, but then again, it's exactly what I want. I want a bit of time not being the warrior.

"He told me about a young couple he knew who were in debt to… well… to the Noble who wished to marry me—the arrogant one. He spoke about how they could not pay, but if they did not, they would lose their home and their livelihood. And… you might not know this, growing up in the castle, but to lose all you have leaves you in a terrible situation. For that couple, there would be no safety, no hope, nothing—especially since they would continue to be indebted to the arrogant man."

My mama takes a deep breath. "Your father could not merely give the young couple money to free them of their debt, as it would be seen as an act against the arrogant Noble. Your father had tried many ways to rescue them from their situation, but had failed every single time. So, he concocted this ingenious plan that would force the sale of a portion of the Noble's lands, which would shift the couple's debt to your father, and he needed my help to do so. I agreed, and as we worked together, I learned that he did this kind of thing all the time for people. Once the debt was shifted to him, he found a way to release the people and help them. When it came to this particular couple, he didn't even actually know them until he heard of their situation."

She looks down at me with pride in her eyes. "There is a reason why your father is so loved not only by the Nobility, but also by much of the common folk of Sevord. It is not because of his fame or his odd way of speaking. It is because so many have been cared for by him. But not only did his kindness shine forth, but I learned he was also a man of deep character. He refused to lie; he refused to cheat; he refused to use his power for himself. That is a rare thing among Nobles."

"What happened to the other Noble?"

"A lot happened, actually. He never married, but he grew more and more powerful until…" My mama looks down. I can see she is not sure she wants to say the next part. "He did many bad things, Marleet. You know that, because he is the man sitting on the throne today." My mama closes her eyes and then says, "He cannot stand your father because he is a man of honor and integrity, because he has more influence and power than the throne, and because your father has only ever stolen one thing."

"What's that?"

My mama laughs again. I love her laugh. "When I saw the kind of man your father was, he stole my heart."

It feels good to smile. I take a deep breath and sit up straight, but my mama's not finished.

"I told you that story for a few reasons, my dear. First, why we do things is important. If you are doing things for the right reason—to care for others or to be honorable—then you are doing the right thing. Second, when we do the right thing and we fail, then we can be confident, even in our failure. In fact, when we fail, we can even wear our failure with pride, because we acted with honor. And third, if it is truly the right thing to do and truly important, we can sometimes find another way to accomplish it, while still maintaining our honor."

She's right. I know she's right. And… and I'm glad. It doesn't matter that I've had another door slammed in my face. My part is to free the Prince. I'm going to do that, and I'll do it in a way that I can be proud of.

"Thanks, mama."

"You have no idea, Marleet, how proud your father and I are of you. Just be safe, okay?"

"I will do my best. Oh, and Denner and Billot have been very helpful."

My mama nods. "I know. They have served us faithfully for years. They've been your father's personal guard, but he felt you would need them more."

I climb out of my bed, and my mama calls Mildren to bring in a bowl of water for me to wash up. Once cleaned, my mama gets me a new dress—something simple and easy to move in, but also quite pretty.

I step out into our family's private sitting room. The main sitting room is down a short hallway, and I see Denner standing there. He signals to me, and I go to him.

"My Lady, I received this note."

I open it and read:

Come
H in the FA

At first, I have no idea what I'm reading, but then it hits me. Hob wants to speak with me.

"We have to go for another walk."

"Yes, my Lady."

Denner waves to Billot, and we leave after I inform my mama we are heading out. I keep my eye out for someone following us, but I didn't notice the other man before. I'm not sure how my guard did, but they're good at what they do.

When we're nearly at the Forgotten Armory, I slow down. "Denner, is anyone following us?"

"Not that we have noticed, my Lady."

The Forgotten Armory comes into view, and we enter. Hob isn't sleeping this time. Instead, he's about ten feet off the ground, climbing on shelves. From the way he moves as he scales up and down, he does this all the time.

"Ahem."

Hob's head whips around, and he stares at me as if he's trying to figure out who I am. A moment later, he rushes down and then waves for me to follow him.

Back in his small meeting room, I take my seat with Denner just behind me, and Billot once again outside the room.

"I thought you weren't going to help me, Hob."

"I needed to know if you would give up someone's trust in you. I needed to know if you had your parent's integrity."

"So, it was a test? You refused to help me to test me?"

Hob giggles and nods his head vigorously. "I know! Wasn't it ingenious?"

"It was irritating."

"What did I say?"

"You said it was ingenious."

"Same thing."

I grumble at that, but Hob just giggles again.

He leans forward, and instantly the smiles are gone and his face fills with rage. "When the traitor killed my King and my General, I set out to protect the royal enchanted items. I knew if I didn't, they would be used to further the traitor's plans. I gathered them up, all the while keeping my eye on the four of you in the castle and Rulf and Prince Roran's ghost in the city. All six of you were well cared for, but I was ready. I know who told you about the artifact. There were only three who knew, and one of those three, my General, is dead."

"Three who knew?" I ask, trying to ignore that weird comment about Roran's ghost. "I thought there were only two."

Hob giggles. "I found out by accident. General Geran swore me to secrecy. Perhaps I should have left it where it was, but Parthun searched the throne room for enchanted items. I feared he would take the helm off the statue."

My heart leaps for joy. "You have it?"

He reaches under his shirt and pulls out a small chain. On the bottom, hangs a tiny pouch which he carefully opens. Grabbing my hand, he upends the pouch into my palm, and something falls out.

I stare at the object for a moment with my mouth open. "It's a ring!" I hadn't expected that, although I didn't really know what to expect. It's too big for me, but maybe the right size for Roran, and it's clear, as if it were made of glass. It's... perfect! I can give it to the Prince, and he can wear it the rest of his life without anyone knowing.

"Thank you, Hob."

"You're welcome, my Lady." He stares at me with that odd way of his for a moment and then adds, "You just make sure you always do what's right."

I nod. "I'll do my best, Hob." I'm about to stand up when I ask, "Do you have more enchanted items?"

Hob giggles. "When you need something, come see me. But I won't just give you everything now in case you don't need it." He stands up, puffs out his chest, and begins to sing.

I take that as a sign that it's time to leave, and we slip out.

27

The Prince

"Papa, I need to speak with you. May we speak in my chambers?"

My papa gives a slight bow and smiles. "Yessss, my dear Marleeeeteeee."

We move into my chambers, the only place I know for certain that I can speak freely without fear of being overheard. I sit down in one of my chairs, and my papa takes the other one.

"Papa, is it still your rule that I never meet with the Prince?"

"It issss, my dearrrr. It would not be saaaafe for you to see himmmm. His enchantmennnnt is too powerfullll. It seems to grow daaaaily."

I can't tell my papa what I'm up to, but I have to see the Prince. "Papa, I wish to speak with the Prince." I don't think that's enough, but I'm not sure how to word this.

He stares at me for a bit. I can see he's quite worried. "Is it a neeeecessary visiiiit?"

"It is, Papa."

My papa sits there, just staring at me. It's like he's trying to figure me out. Finally, he says, "Thennnn, visit him tomorroooow, at the first hour of the afternoooon. Annnnd you must keep your guard withhhh you at allll times. Buuuut, you may only visiiiit him this onnnne timmmme."

"Yes, Papa."

He stares intently at me again, then slowly nods. "Beeee saffffe, my daughterrrr."

As my papa leaves the room, I lean back in my chair. Now, I just have to figure out a way to get the ring onto the Prince's finger.

Try as I might, I can't come up with anything good. The best I can think of is to say something like, "Hey Roran! It's been a while. I have a gift for you. Please put it on."

I can't imagine that's a good way to approach the situation, but it's a start. Denner and Billot are aware of the situation. They know they are not allowed to leave me under any circumstances. They also know that we have to get the Prince to put on the ring. Now, it's possible it just needs to touch his skin. If that's the case, it'll all be a lot easier. But even then, I don't think I'll be able just to walk up to him and say, "Here! Feel this!"

My papa's instructions were clear. I have to go at the first hour of the afternoon. I think I'm timing it right. I had Billot go for a walk last night to try to time it just right. I want to get to his room just a minute before I'm supposed to get there.

Of course, if he resists the ring, and if he is well guarded, then I expect this will go terribly. I don't want to be a pessimist. I'm trying to be a realist. But my papa says a realist is just a pessimist in denial. The more I think about that, the more I think he's right.

On the way to Roran's room, we pass Captain Frindor. It's an awkward interaction. For one, he's a traitor to the throne and a traitor to the Prince, and he tried to have Caric killed—the second in line to the throne. He's a wicked man.

For another, it's a little difficult to know who should give way to the other.

When I was a servant, if a Noble came by, I would stand at the side of the hallway with my head bowed while they passed. But it's different among the Nobility. If two Nobles meet, one will give way to the other, based on who is of a higher status. If my papa met Captain Frindor in the corridor, the Captain would naturally step aside.

I, however, am not my papa or my mama.

Captain Frindor stands in front of me, refusing to step aside.

I normally would just step aside myself. I'm not so arrogant that I can't let someone else go first, but to step aside now would suggest that I am either afraid of him or that he is great. I'm not afraid of him, nor do I think he's anything but a Shaloomd dropping.

I smile at that insult. I just made it up. It was a good one.

My smile, however, also works to my advantage. It shows Frindor that I'm not intimidated by him.

"Captain," I begin, "I'm unaware as to why you are not giving way to me to allow me to continue down the hallway unimpeded. Are you suggesting that a man of your rank is greater than Lord Yune and Lady Aldora's daughter?"

I know I'm playing with fire here, but I want to put him in his place. I will see that he is punished for his crimes against the throne.

The conflict raging inside is obvious on his face. He knows he does not want to step aside, but he also knows that to insult my parents by treating me with disrespect would be a difficult matter to recover from. I may be playing with fire, but he's the one about to be burned.

He clenches his fists but calms himself and smiles. A moment later, he steps off to the side, along with the four soldiers with him. He does not, however, bow his head as I pass. I wasn't actually expecting that of him, but I use the opportunity to glare at him as I walk.

I will see that he is arrested when all this is done.

We continue on our way, but I'm conscious of the fact that he was likely coming from Roran's apartment. This is a real problem. It means he will figure out that I'm heading there, and he might return. If he's there, we will not free the Prince.

When we reach the Prince's quarters, his personal guards stand outside the door. Each man eyes me warily.

Before I speak, I evaluate the men. They look solid. If my guard has to hold them off… well… it doesn't matter if Denner and Billot can overpower these men. If we're in that kind of situation, there's no way I could physically overpower Roran. My only hope would be if the ring just has to touch his skin. I can likely manage that.

Something about their expressions, though, aren't quite what I expected. The King seems to want me to end up with the Prince, but the soldiers do not look as happy as I would think they would be at my arrival. That is… if they are working for the King. I had assumed Frindor or the King appointed the guard, but what if my papa influenced that decision? Or what if Tilbur appointed them? What if he appointed two men who are loyal to the throne?

"I am here to see the Prince," I announce.

One of the soldiers bows to me, just slightly. "He is available to meet with you. Captain Frindor was just called away to a short meeting with the King and Lord Yune."

Interesting... so my papa chose the time so he could remove Frindor. To add to this, the soldier told me that information when he had no reason to. He's telling me something. A short meeting... I don't have much time.

"Thank you. May I enter?"

He gives another bow and opens the door, stepping inside for a moment. I hear his muffled voice, following by an enthusiastic, excited voice. A moment later, the door opens for me to enter, but I hear the guard whisper to Denner, "Protect the Lady well."

I step inside but give a yell as I see Roran charging toward me. My soldiers jump into action and stand between him and me, and Roran comes to a halt.

"I'm not seeking to harm the beautiful Lady Marleet. I'm coming to embrace her and tell her how much I love her. To tell her that this time away from her has been agony to my very soul. My feet are itchy with desire for her."

Again, with the weirdness. The other stuff was kind of sweet, but that itchy feet thing... it's like the pimple analogy. That enchantment has to go.

My soldiers part just a little, but not entirely. I give a curtsy to Roran and say, "Your Majesty."

"Please, my sweet Lady Marleet. You never need curtsy to me. I am in love not only with you, but also with your eyebrows."

A small laugh escapes Denner's throat, but he catches himself. I find this all very awkward.

"Thank you, Roran."

I glance back. One of his soldiers has come into the room and closed the door behind him. That's proper, I guess. To leave the Prince alone with us would be wrong.

"Prince Roran, I have a gift for you."

Roran bounces on his feet. "Is it your heart? Is it your hand in marriage? Is it your undying love to match my own? Is it a pair of cufflinks?"

This boy throws me off in just about everything I try to say. "No, Roran, it's none of those things. It's a ring."

"You're ready to marry me now?"

"Oh, no, Roran… oh… I… I mean, not a wedding ring or anything like that. I'm not proposing to you. We're… I'm… Uggghhh!" I close my eyes and take a breath. This is hard. "It's just a gift. It's something I'd like you to wear. Will you wear it for me?"

"I will do anything for you, my dear Lady Marleet, even if I must count all the toes of each Noble in the land."

I squeeze my lips together, hoping I can maintain a serious expression. It's not easy when you have a vivid imagination that pictures everything everyone says. I pull out the ring and hand it to him. "Here, please put this on."

Roran steps up with a greedy, hungry look on his face as he reaches for the ring in my hand. But at the last second, he pulls back with a horrified expression. "What is that thing?" he screams. "What have you brought to me?"

I hear a sword come out of its sheath. I look back to see Roran's soldier standing ready to attack as Roran's second soldier rushes into the room. My soldiers have drawn their weapons as well, and I fear this is about to turn bloody.

"Wait!" I say. "There's no need to fight. It's just a gift."

I turn back to Roran. He's crouched in a corner, shaking and weeping. Over and over, he's mumbling, "don't touch… don't touch…"

"If it's just a gift, why is the Prince terrified?" the taller of Roran's two soldiers demands. He's big enough that I wonder if he alone could overpower both Denner and Billot.

"… don't touch… don't touch…"

I decide to take a risk. If I can't convince these two men to help us, then I'll just have to jump on Roran and touch him with the ring, hoping it'll do the job. "You know the Prince is under an enchantment," I say. "This ring will free him from it. If you are loyal to the throne, you will help us."

"… don't touch… don't touch…"

The soldiers glance at one another. Their expressions tell it all. They know about the enchantment. They want to free him from it, but they don't know if they can trust us.

The taller one, the one who has been the only one to speak to us so far, asks, "May I see the ring?"

I look down at it. I can't risk losing it to these men. I slip it on my finger, hopefully allowing me to hold on to it better, and hold out my hand.

The soldier touches it, spinning it around on my finger. "It'll remove any enchantment?"

"… don't touch… don't touch…"

"That's what I've been told. I have heard this from a reliable source, a man who is loyal to the throne and loyal to Prince Roran."

The soldier glances at the other one, and they nod. Both men put away their swords and nod to me. "We will help."

"… don't touch… don't touch…"

The five of us approach Prince Roran, but the closer we get, the more desperate he becomes. He tries to climb the wall to get away from us, and screams louder and louder, "… DON'T TOUCH… DON'T TOUCH…"

His own soldiers grab him, and my soldiers jump on him, pinning him to the ground. Although Roran's much larger than I am, he's not a big guy, but the four soldiers struggle with him, each one holding a limb, while one of the men uses his hand to cover Roran's mouth.

He thrashes around on the floor, knocking furniture out of the way, and nearly throwing the four men aside. The enchantment does not want to give him up.

I come in close, and Roran snarls at me. I try to put the ring up against his forehead, but he pulls his mouth away from the soldier's hand and nearly bites my own.

"… DON'T TOUCH… DON'T TOUCH…"

I push it down on Roran's arm, and he begins to convulse. He's no longer screaming, but instead, he's looking at me with desperation in his eyes. In a quiet, halting voice, he says, "No, Marleet. Not on my arm. It has to be on my finger. It won't release me until I wear it."

When I pull away, he screams out again, "… DON'T TOUCH… DON'T TOUCH…"

The large guard drops onto his belly, holding Roran's arm with the weight of his own body. With his free hands, he grabs hold of Roran's fingers and begins to pry them open. He tries with the index finger but gets nowhere. Then with the middle finger, but it's still too tight and strong. He manages to get the third finger pulled back, and I slip it over the tip. The moment it touches him, Roran calms a little, and I can slide it fully on his finger.

His body relaxes.

Roran begins to weep. He's no longer struggling, but instead, between sobs, he's whispering, "I'm free… I'm finally free…"

The soldiers warily climb off him, and Roran curls up in a ball on the floor, clutching the hand with the ring. He just lays there, weeping.

His two soldiers crouch next to him. The one puts his hand on Roran's shoulder and asks, "Your Majesty, are you truly free?"

Roran, in the midst of his sobs, nods his head.

I begin to cry myself. I can't believe it's over.

"Your Majesty," the soldier continues. "I know you must be overwhelmed, but Captain Frindor will be back in a matter of minutes. You must compose yourself."

Roran just continues to weep and does not straighten at all. "Let him come! I'll order his death!"

The soldier's shoulders slump. "I'm sorry, Your Majesty, but you do not have that kind of authority. The King, your uncle, cannot know that you are free from the enchantment. The moment he finds out, he will kill you. You must continue to pretend to be under the enchantment until we can find a way to remove the traitor. Please, compose yourself!"

I kneel down next to Roran and put my hand on his shoulder. "Roran, he's right. You have to do this. You must pull yourself together. There is more at stake here than any of this. The whole kingdom will be lost."

Roran clenches his fists, and I think he's about to scream, but he calms himself. He sits up with a look of determination on his face and grits his teeth. A moment later he's on his feet and at a washbasin, cleaning his face, then straightening his clothes in the mirror. He turns back to me and in a shaky voice says, "Marleet…" he pauses, looking unsure. "It… it wasn't all the enchantment."

"Pardon? I don't understand."

He shakes his head. "Never mind. Before Frindor returns, I must know something. I must know if I'm free or if the ring is merely keeping the enchantment away." Turning to his soldiers, he says, "Hold me, and the Lady Marleet will take the Ring off. We'll see if the enchantment returns."

I don't like that idea, but he's right. We need to know.

The four soldiers grab hold of him, one of them holding out his arm toward me. Roran's fingers are extended, so I gently begin to pull the ring off. At first, there is only a slight reaction, but when it passes the middle knuckle, he convulses in their arms and hisses, "Put it back on! NOW!"

I slide it back, and he relaxes. He's breathing heavily, and he whispers, "So, now we know. It does not free me from the enchantment, it only keeps it away." He examines the ring on his finger. "I gather that's why it's clear. So it's hard to see you're wearing it."

"Your Majesty?" The taller of his two soldiers glances at us and back at Roran.

"Right! Yes, you three must leave immediately. Do not let Captain Frindor know you've been here. We will have to maintain the illusion until we can figure out what to do—how to remove that usurper. We must all continue to act as we have in the past, but I will wear the ring from now on." He looks directly at me. "You can trust these two soldiers. They are loyal to the throne and loyal to me. If I need to send you a message, I will do so by one of these two men."

I give a small curtsy, and we rush to the door. As we leave, the two soldiers rush around, putting the furniture we knocked around back in place.

We head the opposite direction down the hallway from which we had arrived. As we turn the corner, I hear the sound of soldiers behind us. I think we got out of there just in time.

28

The Threat

I feel like I was born for this kind of life.

I don't mean the wealth and the comfort.

To be honest, I was happier in that sense when I was living out in the Talic Region with nothing but my clothes, sword, armor, and pack. The constant danger and threat and running was all very exciting.

But what I love about my life now is the excitement of learning how to move this kingdom in such a way that protects it from Parthun's control. That traitor will fall. I don't know when, but he will.

And I will do my part.

I've been in the castle for over two months now. It's been a dangerous life, but it's been good. Very good.

I'm still not allowed to see Roran. He plays his part well, sending me notes and requests for my presence almost on a daily basis. He does it well enough that I almost believe he's taken off the ring. But his soldiers bring me secret messages now and then, and that convinces me he's held true.

Tilbur left the castle days ago, along with many of King Parthun's loyal soldiers. Every citizen of Sevord and the Talic has been ordered to give an oath of allegiance to King Parthun, and the soldiers are going to ensure it is done. Captain Tilbur and the soldiers with him have gone north, up the coast. I have come to suspect that Hemot and the others are up that way, but my papa tells me not to worry.

Rulf, sadly, is still in prison. I haven't been able to see him, although I've gone down into the secret passageways of the prison a few times in the hopes of speaking to him. He's in one of the pits. Not Tilbur's Pit, which is a dangerous place, but one of the regular pits. Captain Tilbur assures me Rulf is fine—something about his giant blood keeping him safe—but I still worry about him and wish I could rescue him.

Traltor and Nareesa have nearly torn the castle apart to free their son, but somehow my papa holds them back. I think they want to start breaking necks. No, that's not true. I don't just think they want to start breaking necks.

That's exactly what they said they want to do.

It's a good thing Rulf's parents trust my parents.

I've now also survived over two months without seeing or hearing anything from Hemot. In one sense, it seems like an eternity. I can't believe it's been so long. In another sense, I console myself with the knowledge that this is only for a time.

I can manage.

"Arrrre you readyyyy, my dear Marleeeeteeee?"

I nod. "Yes, papa."

Neither he, nor my mom, nor I know why the King has summoned us. My papa continues to call him "Parthun" in public, which continues to irritate the King, but it's the King's own fault.

I'm actually excited about today. I look forward to figuring out how we can continue to undo and undermine what the false King is up to.

We reach the doors to the throne room, and they open for us. We walk in, my papa in the center, my mama on his left, and me on his right.

Along the right side of the room stand the Nobles. There are always those who are away from the palace, staying on their lands—in fact, there are many more out in the Talic Regions than at the castle—but there are often still at least thirty or forty here at any time. At the moment, it looks to be almost fifty. And just behind them are rows of tables filled with food and drinks. A celebration must be in the plans.

To add to this, Roran is present. He's to the left of the throne, down below, standing on the floor. He's by himself, separated from the Nobles.

When we reach the appropriate place near the throne, my papa bows while my mama and I curtsy. The King is, unfortunately, wearing a smile. When he smiles, it often means he has some secret agenda that's underway.

"Welcome, Lord Yune, Lady Aldora, and Lady Marleet!"

Now, that's odd. He doesn't normally address me. That means I'm important to this conversation.

That's not good.

"Thank youuuu, my dear Parthunnnn. To whaaaat do we oooowe the honorrrr of this summonnnns?"

"Ah, what a glorious day," the King declares. "A day of joy! A day of wonderful announcements."

My papa merely gives another bow.

King Parthun rubs his hands together, and his smile grows. "I wish to announce to you the wonderful news.

Prince Roran and I have agreed that he and your daughter will be wed in thirty days. All the Nobles have been informed and received a personal invitation—the messengers have already gone out. The date is set, and I wish to rejoice with you over such a wonderful occasion!"

My heart races. The King has pressured us to get married on many occasions, but it's always just been pressure. Now, the date is set? What am I supposed to do with that? I don't want to marry Roran!

I await my papa's response, hoping he can find a way out. The invitations have already been sent, however. This might be a difficult one to undo.

My papa steps forward and bows again to the King. "Thank you, my dear Kingggg, for allowingggg me to take parrrrt in this joyous occasionnnn!" He then turns to the Nobles, and bows in their direction, then finally, he turns to Roran, and bows in his direction.

The Nobles clap. They're smiling, but I can see that they're displeased. I begin to shake, but I do my best to calm myself. I don't mind taking on a challenge like finding a hidden artifact, or even crossing the Talic Region to reach the mountains, but this is out of my control.

"So, my dear Lord Yune," the King says with a wicked smile, "do you have a blessing to offer on this future wedding?"

I tense up. If my papa gives his blessing, then no one will question the marriage. They will assume the King and my papa planned this out—presumably with my knowledge and consent.

My papa bows again to the King, then to the Nobles, then to the Prince. He smiles at me in a tender way and then announces, "It is difffficult, my dear Parthunnnn, to give a properrrr blessingggg as this is the firsssst I've hearrrrd of these plannnns."

"Well, then," the King says, still with a smile, but I can see he is displeased, "we will have to communicate better in the future, since your daughter will be marrying my only nephew."

I almost holler out, "What about Caric?" but I know it's not the time. The King knows about him, he just doesn't want to acknowledge his existence.

"In the meantime, my dear Lord Yune, I invite you, your lovely wife, and your betrothed daughter to have some refreshments with us."

My papa bows, and the Nobles begin to move around, picking up food, eating, drinking, speaking with one another. Many come to congratulate my parents and me. We all just smile in return.

When the lineup has finished, Roran approaches me, and the others step back, giving the betrothed couple time to speak alone.

His face is filled with his goofy grin. He's still doing his best to pretend he's enchanted.

"How are we going to get out of this, Roran?"

I'm surprised to see his face fall just a little. He pauses for a moment, then says, "I know this is not what we had planned. I know we barely know each other. I know I'm young, and because of the enchantment, I'll never be King, but… Marleet… would it really be so bad?"

"So bad?" I don't understand at first, but then I do. I now know what he meant when he said it wasn't all the enchantment. He had feelings for me before the enchantment was placed upon him. He still does.

"Roran… I… I'm in love with Hemot."

Roran frowns briefly, but then pulls his face back into the goofy grin of the enchantment. "But would you not even consider me? We might not have a choice."

"There is always a choice, Roran," I whisper. "And I will not be married in thirty days."

The grin is still there, but the eyes suggest he is not only disappointed, but angry. I'm not sure what else to say to him, but my papa rescues me.

"My dearrrr, it is time to leeeeave."

I step away and take my papa's arm, and my mama takes my other arm. We move toward the door without another word. On the way out, my mama whispers to me, "Leaving so soon, without a word, and with you between us, sends a clear message. Walk slowly, my dear. Let them see us leave."

Out in the hallway, our guards take up position on either side. I have learned that you can sometimes have a private conversation in the hallway if you are moving and whispering.

I take a deep breath. In a quiet, shaky voice, I ask, "Is this really going to happen?"

My papa and my mama casually look around at each of their soldiers. When they seem satisfied, my papa whispers, "Thissss, I did not expect. The false Kingggg is taking a rissssk here in disappointing the Nobllllles. They will aaaall plan to attennnnd the weddingggg, but not onnnne will be pleeeeased."

"So, I am to be married?" I want to cry. I'll flee the castle before I allow that to happen.

"Noooo, my dearrrr. It will not commmme to that. You seeeee, if you are wed, the Noblessss will slowlyyyy reject the false Kingggg. It will send a messaaaage to the Noblessss that their children could be marriiiied at the whimmmm of the thronnnne. If the weddingggg takes place, it will cost the Kingggg his thronnnne. Marriaaaage is not the dangerrrr."

"What is the danger, papa?"

"The Kingggg knoooows you cannot be wed. Howeverrrr, he is not lookingggg for a marriage. He is lookingggg for a tragedy. A tragedy willll secure his thronnnne. He will thennnn be able to unite the nationnnn under the desirrrre to right the wrongggg."

"What tragedy? What wrong will take place?"

"Iffff, my dearrrr, we do not get you out of the castlllle, then youuuu, my dearrrr, and your mother and Iiiii, and the Prinnnnce, will be dead within twenty-ninnnne dayssss."

Continued in The Last Hope
Book Four of the Sevordine Chronicles.

Pronunciation Guide

Now, you might think that I have tried to create a proper pronunciation guide, but I don't know how to do that. I could look it up, but not only do I not understand diacritical markings, but I think most people don't. So… I made a pronunciation guide that makes sense to me with the capital letters pointing out the emphasis.
And here it is.

Berin	BARE-rinn
Caric	CARE-ick
Corter	CORE-ter
Draydon	DRAY-dunn
Ellcia	ell-CEE-ah
Farnum	FAR-num
Frindor	FRIN-door
Frippolee	FRIPP-oh-lee
Granel	GRA-nell
Gratter	GRA-terr
Haner	HAY-ner
Hartor	HAR-terr
Hella	HELL-ah
Hemot	HEM-mot
Hillbin	HILL-binn
Leito	LAY-toh
Lirnal	LIR-nall
Marleet	mar-LEET
Morgin	MOR-ginn
Nordin	NOR-dinn
Parthun	PAR-thunn

Rainer	RAY-nerr
Reber	REE-berr
Relin	RELL-linn
Shaloomd	sha-LOOM-d
Shalsee	SHALL-see
Shawn	AWE-some
Talic	TAL-ick
Tallia	TAL-lee-ah
Tilbur	TILL-burr
Trevolay	TREV-oh-lay

CHECK OUT THESE BOOKS BY
Shawn P. B. Robinson

Adult Fiction (Sci-fi & Fantasy)

The Ridge Series (3 books)
ADA: An Anthology of Short Stories

YA Fiction (Fantasy)

The Sevordine Chronicles (5 Books)

Books for Younger Readers

Annalynn the Canadian Spy Series (6 Books)
Jerry the Squirrel (4 Books)
Arestana Series (3 Books)
Activity Books (2 Books)

www.shawnpbrobinson.com/books